DATE DUE

(

[

A NOTE FROM THE EDITORS

It is with a mix of pride and sorrow that Hyperion presents *Bad Twin*, the last novel by a wonderful author who was taken from us in the very prime of his writing life. As many readers are already aware, Gary Troup has been missing since September 2004, when the jetliner that was carrying him from Sydney to Los Angeles crashed somewhere over the South Pacific. While nothing is more human than to hope for miracles, reason tells us that the author and his fellow travelers cannot have survived this disaster.

As his books so vividly attest, Gary Troup was a master of quiet irony; perhaps he would have savored the cruel but undeniable irony of his own demise en route from Sydney. In recent years, Australia had become an increasingly important part of his life; he loved the land Down Under, and the land Down Under seemed to love him back. A new readership was discovering him in the Antipodes; he seemed reenergized by the acceptance he found there, as evidenced by the letters that follow—correspondence that Troup shared with us when submitting his manuscript, just days before departing on his fateful journey.

But it wasn't business alone that accounted for the author's increasingly frequent trans-Pacific travels. Somewhere in the skies above the ocean, he seemed to have found a great romance—and this, to those of us who knew him well, came as a delightful surprise. Gary Troup was a confirmed bachelor. Long on charm but short on commitment, he'd kept his affections in check—until he met Cindy Chandler, a flight attendant on Oceanic Airlines. All indications are that he was completely smitten with her: It is to Cindy that he dedicated this book; with characteristic slyness, he even gave her a cameo role to play . . . If death can ever be kind, perhaps it was a kindness that the new lovers were lost in the same catastrophe, neither having to mourn the other.

Walkabout
PUBLISHING

Christine DeVries, Senior Editor

August 16, 2004

Mr. Gary Troup
481 West 68th Street
NY NY 10023
USA

Dear Mr. Troup,

I wanted to drop a line to tell you how delighted I am with the draft of *Bad Twin*. I think it's the cleverest and at the same time the spookiest thing you've done. Good move setting some scenes in Sydney and at the Reef, not to mention including such an appealing if not necessarily trustworthy Aussie woman as a love interest. Your growing audience in our hemisphere will no doubt appreciate the local references.

I am happy to tell you that we are planning a major promotional push for this book, and I am wondering if we could lure you down here sometime soon, to meet with our marketing people and to work out some details of your publicity tour. We would insist, of course, on arranging your accommodations and covering your expenses, as well as trying our very best to show you a damn good time while you are with us! Please let me know if you are willing to make the journey.

Warm regards,
Christine

GARY TROUP

Ms. Christine DeVries
Walkabout Publishing
4200 Queen Street
Sydney NSW 2316
Australia

August 23, 2004

Dear Christine—

Thanks so much for your kind note. Like every other sort
of salesman, I rub my hands with glee at the thought of
expanding my territory—and Australia is a *big* territory.

Regarding my willingness to come to Sydney, you should know
that I *never* miss a chance to visit your beautiful city—and
if the trip is on the publisher's dime, so much the better.
I trust that entertaining me will not be too difficult for
you and your colleagues; just have a few bottles of your
excellent shiraz on hand at all times.

Which reminds me, please don't call me Mr. Troup anymore. I
write private-eye books, not literary novels, and I am not
to be taken too seriously.

Let me know when it would be convenient to have me visit.
Early September would work for me.

Cheers,
Gary

BAD TWIN

GARY

TROUP

BAD

TWIN

HYPERION

New York

ISBN: 1-4013-0276-9

Note to Reader:
This is a work of fiction, and all names, characters, and incidents
are used fictitiously; the author himself is a fictional character.

Hyperion books are available for special promotions and premiums.
For details contact Michael Rentas, Assistant Director, Inventory Operations,
Hyperion, 77 West 66th Street, 12th floor, New York, New York 10023,
or call 212-456-0133.

Designed by Fritz Metsch

FIRST EDITION

1 3 5 7 9 8 6 4 2

For Cindy, my highest-flying angel

BAD TWIN

I

Paul Artisan did not expect to need his gun that day, but you never knew. Sometimes things got very personal very quickly.

People reacted strangely when they were caught in squalid little lies. Sometimes their posture drooped and their faces slackened, and they seemed almost relieved to be found out, to have their cheesy deceptions discovered and ended. Other times people seemed almost proud of themselves for being recognized as liars, cheats, adulterers, and frauds; confronted with their sins, they couldn't quite squeeze back sick and twisted hints of smiles, nasty twinkles in narrowed eyes. *Look at me. I'm hell-bait!*

But sometimes people did get violent. Like cornered animals, they soon ran out of subtle options. If they couldn't slink away and hide, they saw no other possibility but to stand and fight, to the death if necessary. It was better to take the gun.

The problem was how. This was an incognito job. A country-club job. The disguise was tennis clothes. There was no room to stick a 9 mm pistol in a pair of tennis shorts; there was no place to hide a holster underneath a natty, cabled tennis vest. Artisan decided to stash the gun in the zippered bag that held his racquets. This was not ideal—it would take time and a bizarre ruse to free the weapon from a tennis bag—but it would have to do. He called down to the garage to liberate his car, took his cell phone off the charger and stuck it in his pocket, and locked up his tiny office.

It was August, and an excellent day to get out of Manhattan. The air had an unwholesome brownish-orange tinge; a deep breath felt grainy in the nose. The softened asphalt of Tenth Avenue seemed to suck at the tires of Artisan's old Volvo. Heading uptown toward the George Washington Bridge, he used red lights as opportunities to review the small folder that held a photo and some background information on his intended target.

Her name was Sally Handler. Age forty-eight. Occupation: Housewife and investor. Divorced from a midlevel executive in the telecom business. Two grown children. She did not look like a criminal, a would-be perpetrator of a multi-million-dollar fraud. She looked like a lady from Teaneck. Hair a fraudulent blonde, though if that were a crime, the jails would be as crowded as Calcutta. Friendly seeming eyes with some moderate wrinkling at the corners. A bit of thickening beneath the chin. A woman you might meet in any supermarket in America, especially in the aisle where they sold the low-carb crap. Not a crook. Artisan gave his head a small involuntary shake. With human beings you just never knew.

On the Jersey side of the river, he found his way past shopping malls and town-home developments to the Palisade Pines Golf and Tennis Club. The club was miles from the Palisades and Artisan did not see any pines. Then again, there hadn't been any towns where the town-homes were. What there were, on this weekday morning in the parking lot of this midlevel suburban club, were a lot of Acura and Lexus SUVs, the usual sprinkling of BMWs and Benzes. Retired men in unforgivable trousers bent painfully to retrieve their golf clubs from their trunks. Knots of chattering ladies adjusted their visors so as not to squash their beauty parlor hairdos. Artisan slung his unnaturally heavy tennis bag over his shoulder and headed for the door.

Inside, a chipper desk clerk wished him a good morning, tentatively reached a towel in his direction, then asked if he was a member.

The simple question allowed Artisan to do one of the things he was very good at, namely, gain admission to places where technically speaking he did not belong. The scary part was how easy this usually was. In recent years, people had gotten crazy about security, but security tended to be yet another fraud, at best a comforting illusion. Put a bouncer at the door. Give him a stun gun and a walkie-talkie. So what? Even locked doors had to open now and then. There were plenty of ways to get past the velvet rope. Bribes still worked, though they were crass and seldom necessary. Usually all it took were a few magic words suited to the particular occasion and said in a calm, unthreatening manner.

For example, Artisan now confessed that he was not a member. Then he said, "I'm new to the area. Still seeing what's available. I've booked an eleven o'clock lesson with Ryan."

New to the area was a magic phrase. It conjured images of initiation fees, a nice commission for the membership rep, a few bucks for the clerk who'd made first contact. *Booked a lesson* was a magic phrase. It meant some poor bastard of a teaching pro would make seventy-five bucks on a Tuesday morning when things were generally dead.

"Ah. Welcome!" said the clerk, and extended the towel. "If you don't mind, there's this liability form—"

"No problem." Artisan knew from liability. He filled out the form, even signed his real name.

The clerk stuck the paper in a drawer and looked at a clock behind him. "It's only ten thirty. Would you like to have someone from Member Services show you—"

"Maybe later. I'd really like to hit some serves. Little rusty."

"Sure, sure. Have a good hit."

With that, the clerk gestured beyond the little pro shop to the tennis courts. And Paul Artisan, whom no one knew from Adam, and who had a 9 mm pistol nestled in his tennis bag, went out to find his quarry.

He had no doubt she'd be there. The papers from her own lawsuit confirmed she was a member of this club; one of her lies was that she could no longer use the facilities for which she'd already paid. She had a doubles game at 10 a.m. Ryan the teaching pro had in all innocence confirmed that when Artisan told him he wanted to schedule his lesson so he could say hello to her, as she was a friend of a friend. Didn't people realize how easy they were to find, how readily they could get nailed?

The tennis courts were arranged in a double row, with low wooden bleachers in between. Artisan strolled down the middle aisle, glancing left and right. There was a fair bit of suburban tennis going on; it wasn't pretty. Bandy old men with giant racquets, slicing and dicing and making bad calls. Matronly foursomes sending lob after lob into the humid Jersey sky. As at every club, a macho guy in too-tight shorts, trying to play like he'd seen on television.

Sally Handler's court was the last one on the left. Very casually, Artisan sat down on the bleachers that faced it. The women briefly looked up at him. Idle curiosity: a new man at the club. Then they went back to their game. Artisan put his tennis bag on the bench beside him; he partly opened the zipper to the compartment that held the gun.

For a couple minutes he watched them play, and he felt almost bad about what he was about to do. They seemed like nice ladies. They made little jokes between points. There was something sweet and heartbreaking about the little pleated skirts encircling tummies that were no longer flat; about the pastel bloomers stretching around soft thighs struggling to run; about the wristbands on plump arms trying so hard to be strong. They were just regular people of a certain age wanting to enjoy their lives. How had one of them turned out to be a would-be criminal? Was her ex-husband a total deadbeat? Was one of her kids in trouble or sick? Had she just messed up with her own investments, put herself in jeopardy of losing the modest privileges and comforts she'd forgotten how to live without? It was sad, but sympathy was a different thing from justice.

Finally it was Sally Handler's turn to serve. Artisan took his cell phone from his pocket.

She moved to the service line. He gently snapped open the phone. She bounced the ball in front of her, once, twice, three times. With a practiced lack of hurry, Artisan raised the phone toward his ear but then subtly shifted it in front of his face and focused it on Sally Handler.

With her left hand she tossed the ball a few feet above her head. Her right arm lifted, dropped into a backswing, then came up high above her visor and her hairdo to strike the yellow ball. Artisan snapped the picture at the moment of contact.

And that was it. That was the end of Artisan's workday and it was the end of Sally Handler's fraudulent five-million-dollar suit against her orthopedic surgeon. She'd had her rotator cuff 'scoped just under a year ago. Her suit alleged that the doctor had screwed up and she could no longer raise her arm beyond the level of her shoulder. Did she really expect not to be found out? Artisan would now send the photo to the orthopedist's insurance company. The company, most likely, would forward the image to Sally Handler's lawyer with a terse note saying they were not inclined to settle and would gladly meet her in court. Sally Handler would drop her case and Artisan would receive his day rate of five hundred bucks from the insurance company.

The detective slid the phone back into his pocket and secured the zipper of his tennis bag. He hoped to slip away without a confrontation, and he more or less succeeded. As he rose from the bleachers, Sally Handler's gaze locked onto him and irresistibly drew his glance in return. Their eyes locked only for an instant of mutually abashed communication. Sally Handler's eyes told him she knew that she'd been photographed; that she didn't want her tennis-lady friends to know what she had done. Artisan's eyes sent back the lame message that it was nothing personal.

Then he walked away. It was just after ten thirty when he got back to the front desk. He actually had time to take the lesson he had booked. But he didn't feel like it. He felt bad for Sally Handler. He felt bad, also, for himself. He paid for the lesson and he left the club.

2

Driving back to the city, with the Empire State Building seeming to pinwheel in front of him with each bend in the highway, Artisan reflected for the thousandth time that this was not why he'd become a private eye. He took no pleasure in saving millions of dollars for the insurance companies; like everyone else, he hated the insurance companies. For that matter, he wasn't crazy about doctors either. But that was where the work was, that was mostly how he paid the rent.

Besides, if the malpractice gigs were dreary, the matrimonial cases were downright sordid. Catching investment bankers soliciting blow jobs underneath the remnants of the West Side Highway or sneaking out of cheap hotels with buff young men in sleeveless shirts; enduring endless stakeouts to see if their wives back in Greenwich were consorting with the gardener or some other swarthy fellow whose low social status only enhanced his forbidden allure. No, this was not why he'd become a private eye.

He'd become a private eye because he was a certain type of hopeless and incurable romantic.

He would never have said it aloud, and would have been embarrassed even to let the words take firm shape in his thoughts, but the fact was that Paul Artisan saw himself as a new version of a very old breed—a righter of wrongs, a champion of those who needed help. He believed—or desperately wanted to believe, which is nearly the same thing—that things made sense, that effects had causes, that locks had keys, that if you truly got to the bottom of something, logic would be satisfied and justice would be done; logic and justice would converge, in fact, and that would be the definition of a kind of earthly paradise.

As some people are fools for love and others are even bigger fools for money, Paul Artisan was a fool for truth. He was addicted to it and was miserable without it. And if—as lots of hip and cynical people proposed—there was no such thing as truth, if it was all subjective and dependent on the situation, then Artisan would be not just obsolete but ridiculous.

He'd become a private eye to prove the cynics wrong. And to protect himself against becoming one of them.

So it was no small irony that Paul Artisan, friend of the underdog, crusader for the real, spent the great bulk of his working hours doing the bidding of powerful interests that used their size and their resources so that the fields they played on were never quite level; so that truth itself ceased to be the smooth and lovely and simple thing it was meant to be, and became warped, the way space and time are warped by the presence of very massive objects. This affronted Artisan every working day—but what could he do? He was part of an old breed that was not much in demand these days.

Still, each morning when he went to work, the detective rekindled the ever-fainter hope that a very different sort of case might fall his way. A case that mattered. A case that would sweep his ideals off the shelf of fine sentiments and into the realm of action, that would blow the dust off his largely untested courage, and would show what he was made of.

Driving east on the George Washington Bridge back toward the grainy sepia air of New York, Artisan had no way of knowing that a case like that was waiting for him on the other side. Or that, before it was concluded, he'd have ample reason to recall the Chinese proverb that counsels caution in what one wishes for, just in case the wish comes true.

3

"Good game?" said a voice behind him, just as Paul Artisan was sliding the key into his office door in the third-rate building that was too far west on Fifty-seventh Street.

He turned to see a man in a beautiful suit. The suit was the first thing that registered. It was pearl gray, made of some mysterious mix of linen and silk that draped with boundless confidence and somehow managed to look crisp and cool even through the urban miseries of August. Beneath the suit was an immaculate shirt of slate blue with a businessman's contrasting collar of perfect white, set off by a silk tie festooned with tiny paisleys the size of teardrops.

"Actually," the detective said, "I've been working. Can I help you?"

The man in the splendid suit seemed unconvinced about the working part. But he nodded toward the door and said, "May I come in?"

Artisan unlocked it, then held out a hand and introduced himself. The visitor answered with a firm though not overly emphatic handshake. He didn't offer his name, which came as no surprise. Prospective clients often withheld their names or started out with fake ones. Artisan preferred the former. That truth thing again. He gestured the visitor past the office door, with its archaic pebbled window.

The detective seldom met with clients at his office—most of his gigs came in by phone or e-mail—and if he had, they would not have been impressed. The space was small and badly lit, and appeared dustier than it really was because of the dinginess of the stale paint on the walls. There was a tiny anteroom where a secretary might have sat, but there was no secretary, just a ghostly desk and an old-fashioned appointment book that Artisan seldom bothered writing in. Beyond a narrow doorway, the detective's inner office was maybe twelve feet square, graced by a single window that faced out on what was fancifully called a courtyard but was in fact an airshaft. Artisan slid around his dinged-up wooden desk and directed his guest toward one of two plain chairs on the far side of it. "So," he said, "how can I help you?"

The visitor paused a few seconds before he answered. It seemed he needed to get more familiar with his surroundings before he spoke. This did not take long. His surroundings consisted of a couple of deeply unattractive file cabinets, one of which had a closed laptop computer perched on top. On one wall was an immensely detailed map of the borough of Manhattan. On the opposite wall was a grade-school sort of map of the entire world. That was it for furnishings, but the visitor seemed satisfied. "I want to know," he said, "if you can find someone for me."

Artisan leaned back in his chair and tried to appear confident and businesslike. This was not so easy, as he was still wearing tennis shorts and sneakers in the middle of a working day. Also, he had to labor just a bit to avoid feeling cowed by the splendor of his prospective client's suit. "Finding people is what I do," he said. "Who is it you're looking for?"

The visitor let out a quick exhalation that stopped short of being a sigh; it was the first small sign that what was he doing was difficult for him. "Someone I care about."

He left it at that, and Artisan took a moment to study him. He was, all in all, about as perfect as his clothes. Thirty-five or so, with a face saved from mere prettiness by some weathering at the corners of his eyes and a slight thickening at the bridge of his straight nose. Great haircut, the short brown hair arcing just slightly down above his forehead in a hint of something boyish. Dark blue eyes set far back and shuttered by lashes that many women would envy.

After a silence that was starting to become uneasy, Artisan said, "Your wife, perhaps?"

"Not my wife. My wife is dead," the visitor said.

It seemed to the detective that he said it not without emotion, but with what was left of emotion after all the juice had been squeezed out of it. "I'm sorry," he said.

The man in the beautiful suit did not acknowledge the condolence. "I couldn't save my wife. This is someone that maybe I can save. Maybe. To tell the truth, I'm not that optimistic."

Artisan put his palms together and bounced the index fingers against his chin. "This person—he, she?—"

"He."

"Okay. You say he needs saving. Saving from what? Is it your impression he's in danger? Do you know of someone who wants to hurt him?"

At that the visitor gave a strange and quickly swallowed laugh. There was something bitter in the laugh but also something rueful and something darkly amused. "Anyone who's known him for more than twenty minutes wants to hurt him."

The detective opened up his mouth to speak, then realized he did not know exactly what to say.

"He *dares* people to want to hurt him. He invites it."

"Invites it how?"

The visitor paused, as if he were gauging the distance from one side of a crevasse to the other and wondering if he could make the leap. Then his voice took on a tone of long exasperation tempered by bewilderment and maybe a kind of battered affection. "Invites it by doing bad things to people. By sucking people in with charm and promises and then making them feel foolish. He lies for no reason. He steals money he doesn't need. He betrays friends just for the sake of letting them down. He fucks women he shouldn't fuck, not because he wants them but because he shouldn't. He's just bad. Always has been."

Artisan struggled to keep his face neutral, worldly, free of judgment. He was a detective. He'd made a choice to spend his working days on the seamy side of life, the side where people were creepy and perverse and sometimes violent. But that didn't mean he'd ever quite gotten used to the idea of people being awful to each other and destructive toward themselves. It still distressed him; sometimes it disgusted him. But in an odd way it seemed he needed his distress; his distress was what he had to give. In his work, he made brief visits to other people's hells. So far he'd always managed to emerge intact. Now and then he had the satisfaction of believing that he'd helped someone ascend with him back into the light and air. That didn't make it a whole lot easier to venture into hell again.

"This person," the detective said. "You say he's always been like this. What makes you think he's in danger now?"

"I haven't heard from him in about four months."

"And that's unusual? That lapse of time?"

The visitor looked down at his lap, where he was rubbing one hand against the other. "Until lately, no. He was always disappearing. Four months. Eight months. I'd get a call from a bar in Key West, or a casino in Monaco, or a whorehouse in Sydney. *Hey, how ya doin'?* Like no time had passed, like there was nothing weird in how he ran his life. Sometimes he needed money. Sometimes he needed detox. Sometimes he needed strings pulled to get out of trouble. Never a thank-you. Never an apology. Just onward to the next disaster."

The prospective client paused. His suit was still as crisp as ever but he himself no longer was. The crinkles at the corners of his eyes got deeper; his full lips flattened as his jaw grew taut. Artisan kept quiet.

"The bitch of it?" the visitor went on. "The bitch of it is that lately it seemed like he was turning things around. Getting a grip. Finally growing up. Spent a lot of time in New York this past year. Actually worked. Actually *talked.* Seemed like he was trying really hard . . . then he disappeared. And that's why I think it's different this time. Like he tried and now he's giving up."

Paul Artisan leaned back and rubbed his chin. In the last five minutes something strange but not unprecedented had occurred between himself and the man in the gorgeous suit. Confidence and poise had somehow flowed out of the client and into the detective; with it, for better and for worse, had come responsibility.

Slowly, gently, Artisan said, "This person. I can't find him unless you tell me who he is."

The visitor gave a little twitch of genuine surprise. "Ah, I haven't told you, have I?"

He exhaled, inhaled, then fixed the detective with a glance whose candor seemed to hold more than a hint of a dare. "He's my brother. My twin. My identical twin."

4

Guess I won't need a photo to work from, thought Artisan.

Behind him, the midday light was growing viscous as it slanted toward afternoon. The detective's thoughts also grew somewhat sticky as he tried to process what he'd just been told. "How identical?" he said.

"Excuse me?"

"Dumb question, I guess," Artisan admitted. "But I'm asking . . . you, your brother . . . there must be *some* differences in how you look."

The visitor gave that rueful and bewildered little laugh again, as if having a twin, and a bad one, was some sort of nasty cosmic joke that had been played on his family, or maybe on him alone. "He's a lefty."

"That's the only difference?"

The visitor nodded. "We're what's known as mirror twins." Another and perhaps more bitter laugh. "Two halves of the same cracked egg. A lefty and a righty, and otherwise identical. Same eyes, same lips, same hair. Same DNA."

Without quite meaning to speak aloud, the detective said, "Must be strange."

"It truly is."

There was a pause. Artisan leaned forward and tapped his fingers on his desk. It seemed he did that a lot; there were places on the desktop where the wood had darkened from the oils in his skin. "You have any idea where he is right now?"

"Not really," said the visitor. "But I'm guessing he's not on *that* map." He gestured toward the street-by-street picture of Manhattan. "Pretty confident he's on *that* one."

Artisan's eyes followed his visitor's gesture toward the schoolroom map of the world. The world looked really big. Artisan felt rather little. "Look," he said, "I'd like to help, but I'm just not sure—"

The guest raised a hand and cut him off in the midst of his disclaimer. "Mr. Artisan, are you discreet?"

"Completely. Absolutely. But a job like this—"

"Are you thorough?"

"As thorough as the client wants me to be. I work by the day. Five hundred plus expenses. The thoroughness usually ends up coming down to money."

"I want you to be very thorough. I want you to find my brother. Money is not an object."

The detective clenched his molars to prevent himself from smiling. *Money is not an object.* It had been a long time since he'd heard those words. It was odd—everyone said times were good, everything was fine, but clients seemed to get cheaper and cheaper and it got harder and harder to make a living. Still, the money aside, it made no sense to take a job he couldn't do, a job that he would fail at.

"Listen, Mr.—"

"Widmore. Cliff Widmore."

Artisan leaned back and let the name roll around inside his ears a moment. Then he said, "As in the Widmore Building?"

The visitor nodded.

It seemed to the detective that he also puffed up just the tiniest bit inside his gorgeous suit, a probably unconscious reflex of family pride. Artisan didn't know a great deal about the Widmore family, but he knew they'd been around awhile and he knew that they were very rich. The Widmore Building was a beautiful old warhorse of an office tower—lots of gilt, splendid old clocks above the banks of elevators—a crucial few blocks east on Fifty-seventh Street. The building was the flagship of an empire that had begun with midtown real estate, then expanded to the financial district, Florida, California, the Caribbean, and God only knew where else. But aside from these transparent holdings, there were other aspects to the Widmore businesses—aspects not widely understood or often talked about: arcane construction and engineering projects, investments in a wide range of scientific enterprises, both mainstream and fringe. At times there had been murmurs of Widmore involvement in offshore ventures that would have been illegal on U.S. soil; other rumors hinted at classified defense contracting or private security work of questionable ethics. But this much was for certain: The Widmores weren't prosperous and they weren't wealthy. They were rich.

Paul Artisan frowned down at his fingers. "Listen, Mr. Widmore—"

"Cliff."

"Okay. Cliff. Understand. I work alone. I'm one guy with a cell phone, a couple cameras, and a laptop. With your resources—"

Once again his guest cut short his protestations. "I know, I know. I could hire anyone. A big firm with a thousand detectives spread out on five continents. The kind of company that gets security gigs in Baghdad . . . I don't want that."

"But—"

"Mr. Artisan—"

"Paul."

"Thank you. Paul. My family hates publicity. We've had way too much of it, generally for lousy reasons. Ugly reasons. We don't want any more. You understand?"

Artisan said nothing, just silently drummed his fingers on the darker part of his desk.

"My father is now in failing health," the Widmore heir went on. "Failing physically and mentally. He's got a heart condition—there've been some scary episodes. I think he's getting senile. He imagines he's stronger and sharper than he is. It's a very fragile situation. My stepmother—*this* stepmother—is a loose cannon and a bit of a hysteric . . . I'm trying to protect everyone. Their peace of mind, their privacy. I don't want a big firm to know our business. I don't want my brother's name spreading out through databases and I don't want journalists snooping around. I want to deal with one person I can talk to and can trust."

Sounding a little bit surprised, Artisan said, "And you've decided I'm that person?"

"I operate on instinct, Paul. Always have, and it's served me pretty well. You strike me as a solid guy." He paused, and then, for the first time since he'd come into the office, he smiled. It was a smile of remarkable charm that revealed a set of smallish but perfect teeth and gave rise to concentric creases at the mouth corners, which stopped just short of being dimples. "Besides," he said, "I admire a person who works in tennis clothes."

The detective smiled in turn, but only for a moment. "Cliff, what you're asking me to take on—it's a big decision. For both of us. Why not sleep on it and talk tomorrow?"

Widmore waved off the suggestion. "My mind's made up. Is ten thousand enough to get you started?"

In an average work week, Paul Artisan notched one or two paid days. Some weeks he made zilch. Ten grand guaranteed was a lot of money to him.

He said, "Listen, I'd really like to do this. But I need to think it over. I've got responsibilities at home. Domestic things. The prospect of a lot of time out of town . . . I'm sure you understand."

Widmore's charming smile curdled into a rueful one. "Ah, family obligations."

"Something like that," said Artisan. "Can I call you tomorrow?"

"I'll call you," Cliff Widmore said.

5

The domestic responsibilities that Paul Artisan alluded to came down to this: He had a dog.

More precisely, he had half a dog.

He shared the dog, fifty-fifty custody, with his closest friend, who lived around the corner from him on the Upper West Side. Half the time the dog stayed in Artisan's fourth-floor walk-up in an Eighty-fourth Street brownstone. The other half he got to luxuriate in a relatively fancy doorman building on Riverside Drive. Whoever had the dog took responsibility for giving him his morning walk. But when it came to the evening walk, the two friends had a ritual that was very important to them both, not to mention heaven for the dog. Most days, at 6:15 p.m., they met at a certain bench that faced out toward the Hudson and the three of them strolled in the park together.

From Paul Artisan's perspective, there was just one drawback to this arrangement. Both the dog and his best friend had gotten to be quite old gents—the friend was seventy-six, the dog was fourteen, which worked out to ninety-eight in people years—and this fact freighted the detective with a constant weight of worry. It was a burden he did not resent, but it was a burden nonetheless.

He accepted it as the payback for years of companionship and caring, for the many things he'd learned both from the friend and from the dog.

On this particular August evening, the weather had stayed hot and muggy, and Artisan hadn't bothered changing out of the tennis clothes he'd worn since morning. Still, as he walked toward Riverside, he saw that his friend was sitting on his bench in baggy corduroy pants, a cardigan sweater neatly folded on his lap. His friend always wore long pants; they'd known each other eighteen years, and Artisan couldn't remember ever seeing his best friend's legs. The cardigan was a constant as well. The friend had a horror of real or imagined drafts.

His name was Manny Weissman. He'd been a professor of Artisan's when he was at Columbia. Taught classics.

Which is why the dog was named Argos. The original Argos was Odysseus's dog, the most loyal hound who ever lived. For twenty years, while his master was off, first at the Trojan War, then wandering lost through all the islands of the ancient world, Argos lingered in the doorway back at Ithaca, never doubting that his master would come home. When the wanderer returned at last, gray-haired and in the disguise of a beggar, Argos alone saw past the masquerade and the diminishments of age. He knew his master as surely as he knew the scrap of rug he lay on. Tail struggling to wag, legs twitching to rise and run, Argos gave a single joyful whimper of welcome, and died. What a dog!

Not that Artisan's dog Argos was anything quite that heroic. He was a chocolate Lab with a gentle face but without the square and massive head that defined a champion. His legs were a little short and his spine had grown a bit concave. In the past year he'd developed diabetes, and the disease was making him go blind. His eyes were getting milky; his gaze seemed faraway or nowhere at all, which created the illusion of a philosophic bent. He was

starting to bump into things—tree trunks, table legs, fences. He
never seemed to mind.

The dog lumbered to his four feet as Artisan approached. He
slowly chased himself in a small tight circle then trembled all over
with happiness.

Manny Weissman labored to his feet as well, and the two friends
shook hands. They shook hands every day. It was part of the ritual.
Then they walked into the park through the same entrance that
they always used.

"So Manny, what's new?" said Artisan.

The old professor gave the same shrug he always did in answer
to the question. "Mets choked again," he said. "Al Leiter gave 'em
seven scoreless and the bull pen pissed it away. And Leo—the real
old deli guy at Zabar's?—he cut his finger slicing whitefish. I hate
to say it, but he really should retire. When it's time, it's time. And
you? How was your day?"

They were halfway down the slope that led on to the river.
Argos was sniffing around, trying to decide which side of a
sycamore tree to pee on. The old dog could hardly lift his leg anymore, and when he tried to do so he usually wobbled and his urine
squirted in a faltering and random stream. Sometimes he didn't
bother and just squatted like a female, looking vaguely abashed.

"Really pretty good," said the detective. "Snagged a malpractice fraud before lunch. Then a possible missing person case came
in this afternoon. Don't know if I'll take it but it could be pretty
interesting."

"Tell me," Manny Weissman said.

"I really shouldn't talk about it."

"You always say that and you always do."

It was true. Everyone needed someone he could talk to, and
Artisan, for all his insistence on discretion, talked to Manny. He
could not have picked a better confidant, because not only was

Manny the most honorable and trustworthy person he'd ever known, but Manny hardly spoke to anyone but Paul. Who else did he talk to? The guy from whom he bought the *New York Times* each morning? The dry cleaner who once a year did the moth-proofing on his cardigans?

Besides, when Artisan talked about his cases with his former teacher, it generally constituted a wonderful though usually unconscious exchange of gifts.

What Manny Weissman got was a snapshot of a much bigger world than the one he lived in day to day. For all his fascination with Odysseus the great wanderer, the fact was that Manny Weissman hardly ever left his neighborhood. He was that kind of classic Westsider who seldom ventured south of Lincoln Center or north of the Columbia campus, for whom a bus ride to the East Side was an outing that required thought and planning. His urologist was on West End Avenue, his cardiologist was on Eighty-sixth and Columbus. He had season tickets to the Philharmonic and full privileges at the Columbia library. Where else did he need to go?

But if the old professor's body lived within a tiny orbit, in his mind he'd traveled everywhere. A constant and voracious reader, he'd visited every century and every continent and nearly every culture. He'd toured Iron Age Babylonia through the epic of *Gilgamesh,* literature's first great buddy-story; through *Beowulf* he'd seen the England of the Druids and felt the hero's courage in confronting the monster on whom people projected their deepest fears. Plato had been his guide to classic Athens; with the help of Herman Melville he'd visited the Encantadas—the enchanted isles—and learned the special magic of outposts far offshore.

By the breadth of his armchair travel, he had learned to recognize the things that were true in all times and all places. The basic things that did not change. What he could give back to his young friend, then, was the gift of context and broad reference. Daily life came at a person in the form of flurrying details; Manny Weissman saw the patterns in the flurries.

So, as he knew he would, Paul Artisan opened up to Manny.

"Basically it's this," he said. "Guy comes into my office—rich, successful, seems to have it all together—and he wants me to find his brother, who's just the opposite. Troublemaker, self-destructive, a total mess."

"Hm," said Manny Weissman, as the two friends veered off the paved path to where Argos was feebly digging for something underneath a lilac bush. "Did you ever read a book called *A River Runs Through It?*"

"Sounds familiar," said Paul Artisan. "Trout fishing? Big scenery? I think I saw the movie."

Weissman shook his head sorrowfully. "Saw the movie. There it is: the great divide. Anyway, it's the story of your case. Dutiful brother tries to rescue screw-up brother."

"Lots of drinking and brawling, right?" said Artisan. "But I can't remember how it ended."

With infinite calm, the professor said, "Badly, of course. The bad brother destroys himself, because it's his destiny to do so. The dutiful brother lives on, wracked by guilt, because he feels that no matter how much he did, he didn't do enough. Moral of the story: Loving isn't saving. In the end, no one can save another person."

"That's cheery," said Paul Artisan.

"True stories usually don't have cheery endings," said Weissman. "A cheery ending usually means the story has been tampered with, the game has been rigged. That's why tragedies ring true, and comedies are more like vacations from the true."

Artisan didn't really accept that—that the truth of life was essentially tragic. Young people seldom did accept it. But he knew better than to try to out-debate his teacher. He said instead, "These two. They aren't just brothers. They're twins."

"Oy," said Weissman. "Even worse."

"Worse than what? Worse how?"

The old professor said, "Do you remember what a *doppelganger* is?"

"Doppel—where?"

"*Doppelganger*. Literally means double-goer. It's a notion that came out of the German romantics. The generation right before Freud, when people started looking inward and finding all sorts of creepy and unsavory things. The idea is that everyone has a double somewhere, and there's a universal yearning to find that double. But if you *do* find him, you will be destroyed. Because all the things you struggle to keep down in yourself—sexual weirdnesses, the impulse to violence—are right there in your doppelganger. The doppelganger throws them in your face. No one can survive the confrontation."

"So the idea," said Paul Artisan, "is that the double, the twin, is really just the dark side of yourself?"

"If you insist on taking all the drama and poetry out of it, yes."

The detective thought that over as the two friends followed the meanderings of their half-blind dog. Argos followed a highway of smell apparent only to himself. It crisscrossed sidewalks and circled trees and continued under shrubbery.

After a moment, Manny said, "Identical, these twins?"

"Mirror images. One's a lefty."

"Sinister."

"Maybe he's sinister. I don't really—"

"No," said the professor. "What I'm saying is that *sinister* is the Latin word for left. Strange, isn't it, how long the bias against lefties has been around?"

They walked. The low sun seemed stuck in haze as it hovered just above the Palisades. The river had taken on a coppery sheen unbroken by a single ripple. Argos found a stick and started playing with it as though he were a puppy; or rather, as though he were a puppy with arthritis, and crabbed hips, and breath that soon grew wheezy with exertion; a puppy that needed two shots of insulin a day to stay alive. Still, there was a giddy and unbridled joy in the old Lab's gnawing and twisting and pained attempts at jumping, as if this stick were some great treasure, the finest stick in all the world.

Paul Artisan watched the dog and, apropos of nothing, said, "Yeah, well I don't think I'm going to take the job."

"Of course you're going to take the job. Why not?"

"It really should go to a major agency. It's way too big for me."

"Don't think like that," said Manny. "In fact, it's just the opposite. The big jobs are always handled best by one determined person. Look at the labors of Hercules. Were they done by Hercules, or by five hundred little pissants that reported to Hercules?"

"Okay," said Artisan. "But *he* was Hercules."

"Everyone is Hercules," said Weissman. "It's just a matter of finding the task that brings it out."

Artisan kept looking at the dog. It took Argos about thirty seconds to lose all interest in the stick.

"I don't know," said the detective. "It might involve a lot of travel, a lot of time away."

"So?"

"That's not our deal. With the dog, I mean."

"Am I complaining?" Manny Weissman asked.

Paul Artisan braced himself and sighed. To spare his old friend's pride, he gestured toward the failing chocolate Lab. "Manny, I worry when I'm away."

"You're too young to worry," said his teacher. "And if you don't mind my saying so, you're too young to piss away your time on these boring jobs you're always complaining about, these trivial cases that waste your smarts and have no meaning for you. I think you need to do this job."

Artisan looked out toward the river. The coppery sheen instantly turned leaden as the sun set over Jersey. "I'll think about it."

The moment that the sun went down, Manny Weissman slipped into his cardigan.

6

The next morning, Paul Artisan dressed in what was, for him, more normal business attire—crisp khaki slacks and a presentable shirt. He carried but did not put on an old linen blazer with a tie rolled up in the pocket. He wanted the jacket and tie just in case he decided to take on the Widmore job.

He didn't know that he had already made the decision, but he had. It was a mysterious process; somehow, overnight, the case of the missing twin had gone from being something that he feared to something that he wanted. In truth, he feared it still. But in spite of that or more likely because of it, he felt that it would be a disappointment, a small hole in his life, if the job did not go forward.

He strolled up to Broadway, headed for the subway, then decided he would walk to work. It was another muggy morning, not at all pleasant for walking. The sidewalks had barely cooled overnight; there was a vague smell of mildew and overripe fruit in the air. The dregs of yesterday's sodas had turned sticky in the wire trash cans at the street corners; hordes of flies buzzed all around them.

But Artisan walked, because he didn't want to get to work too soon. He didn't want to fret about whether Cliff Widmore would in fact call. He didn't want to spend the morning thinking about his life in the absence of this new possibility that frightened him and seemed somehow to be testing him before it had even begun. Say this didn't happen; what might the next malpractice gig be? A hip replacement that allegedly crumpled? A boob job that purportedly sagged? Better not to think about it.

He reached his office at a quarter till ten. He had a few e-mails but no telephone messages. He tried not to admit that he was nervous. He wished his office afforded more ways of wasting time. But there were no plants to water, nothing worth dusting. For a few minutes he read the online version of the *Times*. Then he decided to Google the Widmore Corporation.

Something over ninety-seven thousand references came up. There were sites about the sale of eleven-million-dollar co-ops on Park Avenue, and articles about the construction of office towers in Singapore. There were references to joint ventures with something called the Hanso Foundation, and links to engineering journals about new techniques for reinforcing concrete. There were society-page mentions of benefit galas, and investigative pieces about alleged environmental violations in obscure corners of the world. The sheer bulk of information was dizzying, and Artisan was relieved when the phone rang.

It was Cliff Widmore.

"Paul," he said, "have you decided?"

Why was it so hard for human beings to know what they wanted, to commit to something and stay with it? Until the heartbeat that the job was offered, Paul Artisan had wanted it badly. Now that it was his, he wavered once again. These recurring qualms—were they guilt about spending time away from Manny and Argos? Or were they just part of an embarrassing urge to shirk what might be difficult? The detective licked his lips and said, "If you're really sure you want a one-man show, I'll give it my best shot."

"Excellent," said Widmore. There seemed to be real relief but also something automatic in the way he said it. It was probably the word he used anytime he closed a deal. "We should talk. You'll need more information. Are you free this morning?"

"I am."

"Can you come down to my office? Say in half an hour? The building's at—"

"Everybody knows where the building is."

"Forty-seventh floor."

Wearing the tie he wasn't sure he'd need, the detective made his way east on Fifty-seventh Street. It was a brief but fascinating journey. If Manhattan was a tiny universe unto itself, then Fifty-seventh Street was a world within a world, seething with ambition, baroque in social strata. In shabby buildings like Artisan's, over near Ninth Avenue, small-timers of every stripe struggled for a toehold— theatrical agents whose acts seldom worked; young graphic designers with hip portfolios but no commissions; ancient squint-eyed accountants whose garment-district clients kept going belly-up or dying. Moving east also meant moving up. On Eighth Avenue were publishers of glossy magazines; trust-fund girls from Bryn Mawr wore five-hundred-dollar shoes to jobs that paid them almost nothing but prestige. Then came Carnegie Hall, monument both to life's more refined pleasures and to the launching of highly lucrative international careers.

But the real dough was still farther east, in the art galleries that trafficked in million-dollar reputations, and the many enterprises that saw an edge in glomming on to the ambience of culture. Haberdashers where you needed an appointment to buy socks. Jewelers whose baubles showed up at the Oscars. And of course the law firms and brokerages and real-estate concerns for whom a Fifty-seventh Street address was money in the bank.

That was the part of the boulevard where the Widmore Building was. It wasn't the tallest structure on its block, maybe not even the most expensive on a square-foot basis, but it was the most elegant and the best-known. It was the kind of building where Paul Artisan always felt he might be required to explain that he was in fact a professional person rather than a messenger.

Now he went up to the security desk, a handsome rosewood hexagon in front of the soaring travertine slabs that framed the elevator banks. He gave his name. To his surprise, they were expecting him; they even had a name tag ready. The guard asked Artisan if he knew where he was going, and the detective confidently said he did.

Then, once inside the elevator, he was no longer quite so certain. In his nervousness and his preoccupation, he hadn't listened hard enough when Cliff Widmore told him where his office was. He was pretty sure he'd said the forty-second floor. He pushed the button.

The car ascended swiftly and then when the doors opened the detective stepped out. Almost at once he realized something was wrong. In the hallway and in the cubicles behind a glass partition, there were some dozens of busy people milling, but they weren't wearing business suits; they were wearing lab coats. Some of the lab coats were white, some were mint green. Men and women both had neat short hair.

Artisan approached a receptionist who sat behind a chrome desk so bare and clean that it might have been a dissecting table. "Excuse me," he said. "Is this the Widmore Corporation?"

She gave him a smile that was entirely pleasant yet somewhat robotic. "No. This is the Hanso Foundation. Widmore's on forty-seven."

"Ah," said Artisan. "Sorry to bother you." He turned back toward the elevator, then his curiosity got the better of him. Gesturing toward the people in the white and mint-green lab coats, he said to the receptionist, "What is it you *do* here?"

She flashed that pert, mechanical smile again and pointed to the plaque mounted to the wall. The plaque read:

> The Hanso Foundation stands at the vanguard of social and scientific research for the advancement of the human race. For forty years, the foundation has offered grants to worthy experiments designed to further the evolution of the human race and provide technological solutions to the most pressing problems of our time. The Hanso Foundation: a commitment to encouraging excellence in science and technology and furthering the cause of human development.

He got back into the elevator.

On forty-seven he was relieved to find a more normal-seeming office, where men wore ties and women wore skirts and people had faces that actually moved. He was met by a winsome brunette who showed him into a handsomely appointed waiting room and brought him a glass of Pellegrino. With hardly any delay, he was ushered in to see Cliff Widmore.

The mogul's office was L-shaped; the detective's entire premises would have fit into the entry alcove that formed the short leg of the L. The main part of the office was smaller than a basketball court, but not by a whole lot. An enormous Persian carpet overlay a parquet floor. Walls were lined with shelves that held a miscellany of the emblems of privilege and accomplishment. There were half-hulls of racing sailboats, photographs with mayors and governors; Cliff was pictured on safari with a herd of Kenyan elephants, shown stalking polar bears somewhere in the Yukon. Squash trophies nestled alongside testimonials for acts of philanthropy. There was a large sepia photo of the laying of the cornerstone for this very building; Cliff Widmore's great-grandfather, the founder of the dynasty, was pictured in a top hat, holding a shovel, about to scoop the first historic crumbs of earth.

The Widmore heir now came around his king-size desk, hand extended. He wore another magnificent shirt, lavender this time, but no tie and no suit jacket. His hair was as effortlessly perfect as before; his soft shoes whispered on the rug. If class is the ability to blend the regal with the perfectly informal, Paul Artisan thought, then Cliff Widmore was the embodiment of class. He shook Artisan's hand and motioned him toward a cluster of settees.

The detective took a moment to select his seat. He picked one that faced north and had a view across the tops of other buildings to the entire vast rectangle of Central Park. Artisan didn't get a lot of chances to look at Central Park from a sufficient height to see it whole.

Widmore put his back to the view. "Paul," he said, "I really appreciate your doing this. I can't tell you how much it means to my family."

For this Paul Artisan had no answer. He hadn't yet done anything, and he couldn't help feeling that maybe Widmore was a shade facile in his gratitude.

A moment passed, and the detective's new client gave a slightly nervous sigh. "So," he said, "where do we begin?"

Artisan produced a small spiral notebook and a twenty-nine-cent pen from an inside pocket of his jacket. "For starters, why don't you tell me your brother's name?"

7

"**Z**ander," said Cliff Widmore.

"Excuse me?"

"Zander as in Alexander. But he never liked the name Alexander, and for some weird reason he wouldn't go by Alex. He decided on Zander as a little kid, and it's been Zander ever since."

Widmore gave the same rueful laugh that Artisan had noticed the first time they'd met. The laugh had no pleasure in it but seemed to sum up all the bemusement and irresolvable ambivalence that went with family feelings. Affection ground against regret; love was humbled by the inability to truly understand even those who in all the world were closest to us. "Typical of my poor brother," Widmore went on. "He was meant to be an A. He chose to be a Z. There you have it."

Paul Artisan nibbled on the butt-end of his cheap pen. "You say he disappeared four months ago?"

"About four months and a week. The last time I saw or heard from him was early April. The fifteenth, to be exact."

"I think you said that before he disappeared, he was doing better. What do you mean by that? Better how?"

"For one thing, he was wearing shoes," said Widmore. He shook his head and looked down at the carpet. "I shouldn't be flip. But Jesus, it's just so fucking complicated. I don't know where to start."

Artisan waited. He put his notebook down. It was a small thing but it seemed to help.

After a moment, Widmore said, "Paul, don't be offended, but I presume you don't come from a very wealthy background."

"Good guess," said the detective.

"You're lucky," said the heir.

Nestling against the creamy leather of the settee, looking out through spotless windows at the green expanse of the Park, Artisan tried to process that. His own settee at home was made of some crappy kind of fabric interlaced with dog hair; his small smudged windows faced across narrow spaces at other small smudged windows. He had no investments and a tenuous few grand in the bank. In restaurants, even funky ones, he looked at prices then pretended to decide what he really felt like eating. He couldn't afford to move out of the apartment that he'd rented cheap a decade ago and would never own, and he knew that if he got sick he was screwed.

As if answering these unspoken thoughts, Cliff Widmore said, "Your life is your own. You make your own choices. If you happen to accomplish something, you have the satisfaction of knowing it was you that did it. If you fuck up, it doesn't make the papers.

"Rich families—rich families like mine, at least—things are very different. Your path is laid out for you. You go to the schools your grandfather and your father went to. You play certain sports, join certain clubs. You meet a certain range of people. It's clear you don't fraternize with other sorts of people. And when the time is right, you join the family business."

"Some people would call that privilege and success," said Artisan.

"It is," acknowledged Widmore. "And some people play it to the

hilt. Some people never seem to notice that the privileged path
they're on is also a confinement. How can I put it? It's almost like,
instead of really living life, you're stuck inside a nice comfy insu-
lated tube that runs through life. That make sense, Artisan?"

"I see what you're saying."

"My brother chafed at that for as long as I can remember.
Kindergarten, there was a certain day school we were supposed to
go to out in Locust Valley. Zander didn't want to go there. He cried
and kicked and screamed. When it came time for boarding school
at Exeter, his protest was basically the same, but now it took the
form of doing drugs and sleeping all day long and spending nights
with the bad kids from the town. He got kicked out, of course, and
ended up in one of those private schools of last resort, the kind
where you can knife the headmaster and still graduate as long as
Daddy's checks keep coming.

"College," Cliff Widmore continued, "he got into Yale, which
was really a joke. But there's a law library that has our family name
at Yale, so they took him. Did he ever go to class? Not that I know
of. I think he read some books. Not the ones on the class lists, of
course. Weird books. Mystical crap. Guidebooks for the clueless.
After two years, Yale finally gave up on him."

"And your parents?" said Paul Artisan. "How did they deal with
all of this?"

"My mother died when we were three," said Widmore. "Solo
car crash after a party at the country club."

He paused, and locked his dark blue eyes on Artisan's.
Between his sets of beautiful lashes, there was a challenge that the
detective couldn't quite interpret. Was he being dared to judge?
Was he being bullied not to judge? "You're wondering if she was
drunk," the client said. "Yes. Very. Now you're wondering why she
was driving home alone. From things I heard later, she was in a snit
because my father had his face buried in the neck of the woman

who would soon become our stepmother. Not our *current* step-mother. The one before. The second Mrs. Widmore. An extremely jealous woman. Which meant that all pictures of my mother were banished from the house. I barely remember what she looked like."

"I'm sorry," said Paul Artisan.

"Not required," said Cliff Widmore, dismissing the sympathy almost savagely. "Besides, it was the relationship between Zander and my father where the voltage seemed to be."

The rich man paused. Paul Artisan could not help noticing that even in the enormous office with the privileged windows, the atmosphere was growing rather pinched and airless.

"That was and is a strange relationship," the client continued. "Frankly I wish I understood it better. My father suffered Zander's screw-ups. I don't just mean he was disappointed or angry. I mean he seemed to feel it personally, like Zander's failures were his own. But at the same time—how can I put this?—it was like in some twisted way he rooted for Zander to take it to the limit. They battled all the time and they both got something from the battling."

Artisan said, "Your father never had his own rebellion?"

"My father wanted to be an architect," said Widmore. "Had a passion for design. Which was fine, because he had an older brother who was going to step in and take over the business side. Commerce and art under the same roof—very tidy for a family that built buildings. Then the brother got killed at Okinawa. My father gave up architecture and studied law and business. In other words, he did what was expected of him." The client paused; his throat seemed to tighten down and his voice became not louder but more penetrating. "Which—excuse me for sounding so bour-geois—was also the grown-up thing, and the unselfish thing, and the decent thing."

The rise in emphasis took the detective by surprise. He stole an instant by shifting in his seat. "And it's what you've done," he said.

It was an offhand comment; if it bore any intention at all, it was intended as a compliment. Still, it seemed to have a completely unforeseen effect on Clifford Widmore. His eyes receded and vertical lines appeared between them, roiling the smooth sweep of his forehead. His voice dropped but took on a hint of command, almost of menace, the tone of someone who knew he was writing the checks and could have things as he wanted them.

"This isn't about me, Artisan," he said. "It's about my brother. If we're going to work together, you really need to remember that. Okay?"

8

The detective swallowed and held up his hands in a gesture of tentative surrender. "Okay," he said. "So let's come back to Zander. Kicked out of Yale, then what?"

"Just sort of bummed around a few years. Tended bar on Maui. Worked on dive boats in the Keys. Hung out in cafés in Paris, making like an artist. Then, just when he turned twenty-seven"—and here his brother could not hold back a brief derisive snort—"he decided he would be an entrepreneur. At least that's how he put it to our father. Very convenient. Twenty-seven was when we could start drawing dough from our trust funds, but only with approval from the trustees.

"Turns out Zander had met a couple of very sharp guys who were looking to start a hip-hop label. The music business, of course, was irresistible to him. Drugs, glitz, groupies. He threw in a quarter-million bucks and probably got to poke a couple really gorgeous black women. At the end of the adventure, there was a big stack of invoices for studio time and not a single CD that could be released.

"My impression," Cliff went on, "was that there were some mutual hard feelings, and Zander thought it prudent to leave town

for a while. Next thing we hear, he's in California, living in some
woo-woo community with a bunch of New Age nut-jobs. And what
do you know—he's got another great business idea and needs
another quarter-mil. This time it's importing Chinese herbs. I'm
still not sure if his partners were crooks or just flaky. They liked
their herbs, though, that's for sure.

"By this time the trustees were clamoring to shut off Zander's
funds or at least put in more oversight. My father overruled them.
'He's learning things,' my father said. 'He's making some mistakes.
So what?'

"*So what?*" echoed the brother who had done what was expected
of him. "Fair question, I guess. Compared to the total that was in
trust for Zander, the losses weren't terribly significant. But the pattern went on for years and years. The ideas were just plausible
enough to keep the money flowing. Eco-lodges in Alaska. Cheese-
making in Australia. But here's the thing: We never actually *knew* if
there was anything remotely real about any of this. We never saw
anything closer to a business plan than an excited e-mail or two
from Zander. We never met the supposed partners; conveniently,
they were always far away. We never saw a goddamn piece of company letterhead, let alone a product.

"I started thinking the whole thing was one ongoing scam—
stealing from his own inheritance. Was the money going up his
nose? Was he gambling it away? Was he funding something spooky?
My father never questioned anything. Never seemed to suspect. Or
never mentioned it, at least."

Paul Artisan said, "And this went on until when?"

"Until a year or so ago," Cliff Widmore said. "That's when
Zander came back home."

"And straightened out," said the detective.

"*Seemed* to straighten out. My brother is awfully hard to read.
Things don't show on him. He could be stoned off his gourd and

you wouldn't know it. He could be awake three days and his eyes would be as clear as yours or mine. And he's charming. Extremely charming. The scary part is that he's so damn charming he can even fool himself.

"He just showed up at the Locust Valley house one evening—showed up out of nowhere, unannounced, in a taxi from JFK—and he played our father like a violin. Apologized for how selfish he'd been, for all the worry he'd caused. Talked about the hard lessons he'd learned. Said that if my father would still have him, he'd love to come into the business, starting as a clerk, a rental agent, anything.

"To my father, this was like the Second Coming of Christ. He was beside himself with happiness. He threw banquets, cocktail parties—everybody had to come and say hello to Zander, celebrate the long lost son's return. Zander played it to the max. In conversation he struck a perfect balance between remorse for his youthful mistakes and tall tales of his big adventures. He got a haircut, put away the sandals and aloha shirts. He started borrowing clothes from me, the kind of clothes that put people we know at ease. Oxford button-downs, tassel loafers. We hadn't dressed alike since we were kids, and I don't mind telling you it was a little freaky now. People I worked with every day could barely tell us apart.

"My father wanted to start him at a quite high level in the company," Cliff went on, shaking his head incredulously. "Actually wanted to put him in charge of a big business deal we were making in South Korea, going into a partnership with Paik Heavy Industry. But old man Paik is tough as they come. He would have eaten Zander alive. Thank God the board insisted on having a more experienced person handle the deal. We started Zander on smaller things, closer to home—selling co-ops in residential buildings. And you know what? He did great. A natural salesman. Then there started to be trouble."

"Trouble how?" asked Artisan.

Cliff Widmore didn't answer right away. He leaned forward, elbows on knees, fingers interlaced. "Paul," he said, "yesterday we talked about discretion, about publicity. We very clear on that?"

The detective just nodded.

"Okay. It began to seem that money was being diverted. Not exactly stolen or embezzled—there were safeguards against that. But in this market, people were paying premiums over the asking price to buy apartments. There was bidding, but the bids were sealed. No one knew what the next guy offered. Since Zander was not a licensed broker, he had to work with someone who was. This person began to suspect that my brother was rigging bids. You know—slip me fifty grand and I'll make sure you get that three-bedroom with the park view. If the company doesn't get the best price, too bad."

"Was it ever proved?" asked Paul Artisan. "Was he ever confronted?"

"Confronted, yes. Proved, no. I confronted him. He denied everything. But denied it with a smirk. There was no proof. The kickbacks would have been in cash. The buyers were complicit—they wouldn't have admitted anything."

"The confrontation," said Artisan. "What was it like?"

"Look, things were strained between Zander and me, that's obvious. My father is still the nominal chairman and CEO of this company, but for all practical purposes, I've been running it for at least a couple years. I think Zander was jealous of that. He certainly didn't like me talking to him as a boss. On my side, frankly, I didn't trust him. I thought he was disruptive. Other employees sucked up to him because of his last name, but they didn't really respect him. It was bad for morale."

"Did you talk about this with your father?" the detective asked.

"No. Why would I have? The last thing my father needs is to get his blood pressure raised. Besides, his mind wanders, he gets his facts mixed up. He tends to remember things as it pleases him to think about them, not as how they were. He was thrilled to have his other son at home and working in the company. Why complicate that for him?"

"But the other son left anyway," said Artisan.

"Yeah," said the son who had stayed home. "After this business with the kickbacks, I felt I had to keep a closer eye on him. I didn't want something blowing up, getting in the papers—that would kill my father. And it seemed that Zander's behavior was getting increasingly erratic. Sometimes I thought he was hopped up on coke or even meth. Sometimes I thought he was drunk at ten a.m. But like I said, he's hard to read. He seemed mad at me. We hardly talked. Then one day he disappeared."

"You said that was April the fifteenth," said Artisan. "You're sure about the date?"

Cliff Widmore gave another version of that rueful sound that was midway between a mirthless laugh and an agonized sigh. "I'm sure," he said. "It was the day of my wife's funeral."

This was softly said but there was something seismic in the words. To Paul Artisan it seemed that the floor of the enormous office shifted, that the beautiful windows rattled in their frames. "Jesus, Cliff, I had no idea her passing was so recent."

For just a moment, Widmore looked away. His face grew shadowed but it was impossible to tell if this was grief or merely embarrassment that something in his tidy and appropriate life had turned out to be so messy. Turning back to the detective, he said, "Artisan, listen, I'm not a callous person, but don't expect me to fake things I don't feel. I'm sorry my wife is dead. I'm sorry that anybody's dead. But I'm not going to pretend it's some deep tragedy to me. We had a lousy marriage. We were headed for a lousy divorce. Shannon was a deeply troubled person, terribly unhappy, and after lots of therapy and lots of medication, I think we'd both stopped believing that that could ever be fixed. Maybe it's an awful thing to say, but in a way it's a mercy that she's gone."

Paul Artisan leaned forward and bounced an index finger against his lip. "The funeral," he said. "Your brother was there?"

Cliff Widmore nodded. "Stood at the back. Was with an old friend from the crazy high school he ended up at. And after the ceremony he was gone."

"The friend," said the detective, picking up his long-abandoned notebook. "You know his name? Where he lives?"

"Keith Baker. Last I knew he was living out on Peconiquot Island."

"And you think there's a connection between the funeral and Zander's disappearance?"

Bitterly, Cliff Widmore said, "Hell of a coincidence if there isn't." He paused, recrossed his ankles, suddenly seemed to have an itch at the back of his neck. "Listen, Artisan, I don't know this for sure, okay? I don't even know if want to know. But I think my brother might have been fucking my wife. And I think that might have been part of why she killed herself . . . Think you have enough to go on?"

Paul Artisan just nodded. He tried to keep his face neutral, worldly, unshockable. He was a private detective. It was his job to peek into the dark and fetid places, to get down with the grime and cobwebs where the demons lurked. But he found himself feeling very grateful that he was not, at least, the scion of a rich, accomplished family.

Cliff Widmore reached into the chest pocket of his beautiful mint-green shirt and came up with a check. He handed it to Artisan. It was for twenty thousand dollars.

"We agreed on ten," said the detective.

"Ten for your fee," the client said. "Ten as a draw against expenses. There's going to be expenses, Paul."

9

"It's the Prodigal Son all over again," said Manny Weissman, after his young friend had spoken to him about the events of the day. "Remember that story?"

"I know the phrase," said Artisan. The two friends were following their hobbling dog down through the sloping byways of Riverside Park. Familiar bums sat here and there on benches. Newcomers to the neighborhood, far more stylish than the old violinists and writers who were there before, pushed babies in designer strollers.

"New Testament," said the old professor. "Book of Luke, if I remember."

"You always remember," said Artisan.

Weissman let the compliment pass. "A prosperous man has two sons. The older one is dutiful. He stays on his father's land, tends the flocks, sows the fields, oversees the harvest. The younger son is restless and out for himself. He asks the father to give him his half of his eventual inheritance so he can go out into the world and make his fortune. Except it doesn't work out that way. He squanders his wealth on fast living and prostitutes, and finds himself hungry and friendless in a foreign land."

"Serves him right," said Artisan.

"Maybe," Weissman answered. "But that's reason speaking, and the story isn't about reason. It's about love."

There was a pause as Argos the half-blind Labrador blundered into an azalea bush. Twigs snapped; dirt flew as he labored to dig himself out. He shook himself weakly to rid his fur of bits of leaf and papery flowers.

"Anyway," Manny Weissman went on, "years pass. And finally the prodigal returns. He's desperate, broken. He finds the father, throws himself at his feet, pronounces himself unworthy to be his son, and begs to be taken into the household, only as a slave—"

"Or a realtor in this case," Artisan put in.

"Whatever. But the father embraces him, says that his return is the greatest thing that ever happened. He gives the prodigal his very finest robe. He kills the fatted calf in his honor and throws the best party that the land of Canaan had ever seen. And the older son, who's been loyal and hardworking all this time, and who never once has had such a fuss made over him, is furious."

"I don't blame him," said Paul Artisan. "I'd be furious too. It sucks. It isn't fair."

"No, it isn't fair," agreed the older man. "But that's the power of the story. It has a twist that goes beyond mere logic. Leave aside that the father stands for God, and that leaving the family home is a metaphor for falling away from faith. The bottom line is that love trumps justice. Or at least that's the lesson we're supposed to take away."

The detective, appearing unconvinced, frowned out toward the river. A change of weather was on the way. It could be read in the Hudson's silvery surface and shallow cat's-paw ripples. "And the dutiful brother?" he said. "The one that basically gets screwed. He buy this happy ending?"

Argos hunkered next to a young oak tree. He rounded his

back and dropped his quivering hindquarters, and Manny Weissman, deep in thought about one of the sublimest of the parables,
got the plastic bag ready for picking up the turds. It was incongru-
ous but that was life.

"We never quite find out," the old professor said. "Which is
another brilliant thing about the story. It ends with the father trying to smooth things over with the older son. But we don't quite
get the son's reaction. Is he reconciled? Is he angry? Does he
hold a grudge? Does he plot revenge? We have to decide that for
ourselves."

Weissman's gaze went out of focus, as if he were puzzling out
the question in that very moment. His younger friend took the
opportunity to snatch the refuse bag from his hand. Paul Artisan
didn't like to watch his friend bend down. The stiffness in his
back was all too obvious to see. The strain showed in his legs when
he tried to straighten up. Artisan retrieved the dog shit and
dropped it in a garbage can. "I just can't believe he wouldn't be
pissed," he said.

"Maybe. And that's what interests me about your case," the
older man replied. He had a gift for long parentheses. He was one
of those people who could resume a conversation after several
weeks had passed, picking up in midsentence if that was where the
last installment ended. "Your client. The dutiful son. How does he
feel? Presumably he loves his brother. But he doesn't seem to like
him. It doesn't sound like he was comfortable having him around.
I don't quite understand why he's so keen to have him found."

"I told you," the detective said. "He's concerned that he's in
danger."

"I know you told me that. But unless I'm missing something, I
haven't yet heard anything that sounds so dangerous. He's always
been a screw-up and a nomad. He's being a screw-up and a nomad
again. Why chase him down this time?"

The detective pondered that a moment. A scrap of breeze, the first hint of the fall-like weather that was on the way, rattled sycamore leaves that were already dry and mottled. "For the father's sake, I guess."

Decades of responding to students' endlessly inventive excuses had finely honed the old professor's knack for skepticism. He could convey doubt with hardly a change in inflection. "That would be extremely noble and unselfish of him," he said.

"So you don't think that's the reason?"

"I didn't say that. It's just that it seems to me that it's in the nature of siblings to want to be the favorite of the parent. So why would a brother who feels taken for granted try to bring home a brother who is fawned on?"

"You think Cliff Widmore has some other motive?"

"Did I say that?" said Manny Weissman. "Don't put words in my mouth. I said I find the shape of this extremely interesting. That's all I said. Now where did Argos get to? Argos? Argos?"

10

Next morning, Paul Artisan delivered the shared dog to his friend's apartment, then headed to Peconiquot Island, the home of the last person known to have seen Zander Widmore.

The weather had turned gorgeous overnight; crisp blue air had swept down from the northwest, banishing the haze, seeming to turn the whole city from a sickly ochre to a silver that was full of a simmering joy. The facades of buildings twinkled. People stood straighter as they walked to work. The detective drove through town with his windows open; good smells came out of bakeries and coffee shops.

Even the Long Island Expressway seemed benign on a morning such as this. The traffic was not so much smooth as animated; it seemed to have a pulse. Exits slipped by. Queens vanished, Nassau was quickly left behind. The driving seemed effortless, almost unconscious, as though, on such a rare and perfect August day, some invisible force were pulling Artisan and every other attentive creature toward open countryside and salt water.

Where the Expressway ended, a different world began. Potato fields and vineyards traced out the low mounds and shallow gullies of the North Fork. Old farmhouses with green shutters nestled sleepily in the shade of ancient trees. Roadside stands where you left your money in a cigar box offered fresh-picked corn and tomatoes and zucchinis with the flowers still attached. Just before the North Fork's easternmost village, there was a turn-off for the ferry to Peconiquot.

The detective snaked through narrow streets to join the ferry line, a half dozen cars already waiting in front of him. He could smell the salt tang of the bay, redolent of iodine and clams. Overhead, seagulls screeched; cormorants perched on top of pilings, cocked their wings at prehistoric angles to dry them in the sun. When the stubby ferryboat had churned into the slip, Artisan drove the old Volvo onto its clanking metal deck.

A mile or so across the water, Peconiquot Island rose up as a graceful cluster of sandy bluffs and patches of oak woods and rambling houses whose improbable lawns stretched right down to the beach. As with every island, there was something slippery and mysterious about Peconiquot. It was connected to the larger world, and then again it wasn't. It had a logic of its own, a highly local mythology that made perfect sense within its confines yet fitted uneasily with the mind-habits of the world beyond its boundaries. Like most New Yorkers, Paul Artisan had heard of the island but knew almost nothing about the place. The ferry kept it just slightly difficult to access, saved it from becoming one more overrun precinct of the Hamptons. It had a certain reputation for being counter-chic, the haunt of people who had achieved the higher hipness of just not needing to be cool. If you needed to impress, you didn't go to Peconiquot. Likewise if you were a working stiff who couldn't afford a couple extra hours of travel time on summer Fridays and Sundays. Peconiquot was for people who followed their whims and made their own schedules. This included rich people, of course, but also lazy people and artsy people and people who just didn't quite fit in, who by their deepest nature would be out of sync with any given program.

Being an island, and a small one at that, it was also a place where people were easy to find.

Halfway across the bay, as green water streamed past the ferry's hull and red buoys bobbed in the chop, Paul Artisan went up to one of the ferry crew, a husky young man with a denim shirt and a ponytail, and asked him if he knew a fellow named Keith Baker.

"You mean Moth?" the crewman said.

"If that's what he's called," said Artisan. "Guy about thirty-five?"

"Yeah. Moth."

"Why you call him that?"

" 'Cause everybody does. Guess because he's a little guy who usually comes out at night and sort of flits around. Good guy. Sort of jumpy though."

"Know where I can find him?"

The ferryman grew a little cautious. "You a cop or something?"

Artisan gestured toward his dinged-up and lusterless old Volvo and down at his dirty tennis shoes. "I look like a cop?"

"Off-island people, it's hard to tell."

"I'm a friend of a friend is all. I said I'd look him up."

The ferryman struck a tone of friendly warning. "We look out for our own here. Moth's a guy a lot of people like. And you still need to get off the island."

Artisan raised his hands in a gesture of surrender. "Duly noted."

The ferry guy glanced at his watch. "Two o'clock. He'll probably be at work by now. At the boatyard. Hap's." Then he squinted up at the flawless sky. "Sunny day, he'll probably be inside."

"Hap's," said Artisan. "Where is it?"

"Follow the shore out toward Goat Harbor. First left after the causeway. If you hit the water, you've gone too far."

Island humor. Very funny. The detective thanked the ferry guy and got back in his car.

"You Moth?" asked Paul Artisan.

The man he was speaking to didn't answer. He hadn't heard the question and apparently hadn't noticed the visitor standing three feet to his left. That was probably because he was wearing goggles and a face mask as he wielded a power sander to smooth out the bottom of someone else's sailboat. The sloop—a good size, maybe forty feet, a third of a million dollars' worth of fiberglass and teak with the name *Escape Hatch* etched into the transom—was lifted in a giant wooden cradle in the hangar-like shed of Hap's Marina; there was something rude and almost obscene about the sight of the boat's raised, bare bottom, its stiff keel stabbing downward like the penis of an excited whale.

The detective moved into the other man's line of vision and waved.

The sander was turned off. It wound down with an unpleasant whine. Keith Baker swept off his face mask and goggles to reveal features that were squeezed a little too close together under a tangle of thick brown hair flecked with bits of paint and fiberglass.

"You Moth?" Artisan said again.

"Yeah," Keith Baker said. He said it tentatively, like he was being accused of something.

"Got a minute? I'm trying to find a friend of yours."

"You a cop?"

"People keep asking me that. I guess cops aren't so welcome on this island."

"Or anywhere else," Moth said.

"Well, I'm not a cop. Name's Paul Artisan. I'm a private detective and I'm looking for Zander Widmore."

Moth tried to wipe some dust from his eyes, but his hands were just as dusty. "Oh, Christ. Who sicced you on Zander? The old man?"

"No. His brother. Cliff."

"Ah. God's gift."

"You don't like Cliff?"

Moth gave a noncommittal but basically dismissive shrug. "I barely know the fucking guy. He may be terrific. He may deserve a Nobel prize, okay? But I'm Zander's friend so I see it Zander's way."

"Cliff thinks Zander is in danger," said Artisan. "If you're his friend I think you ought to talk to me."

Moth considered that a moment, then put the sander down and jerked a thumb toward the naked sloop. "Okay. This asshole can wait a little longer for his boat."

Beyond the open doors at the water side of the shed, sunlight was glinting off of gently rocking masts. Out there the delicious air smelled of seashells and chlorophyll. Keith Baker took a couple steps in that direction, and Paul Artisan imagined they were going into the bright clean day to talk. But no. Sunshine and fresh air were not Moth's thing. He preferred the dim shed with its heady reek of bottom-paint and varnish. He sat down on a short three-legged stool next to an oil drum and motioned for the detective to sit down next to him. "S'okay," he said. "What can I tell you?"

"For starters," said Artisan, "you were with Zander at his sister-in-law's funeral—"

"Shannon, yeah. What a piece of work she was."

"Is that the last time you saw him?"

"Pretty much. Yeah."

"Pretty much?" said Artisan. "Did you see him afterward? Did he come back here with you?"

"No. I dropped him at the airport. Islip."

"You know where he was headed?"

"Not exactly. No."

"Not exactly?"

"Look," Moth said, "there's only so many places you can go from Islip. It isn't fucking JFK. I think he was going to Florida."

"But he didn't say he was?"

Moth shifted on his stool, gnawed an index finger for a moment, scratched behind his neck. "This is making me like edgy. Wanna smoke some reefer?"

The detective considered the offer but raised his hand no. Not without a hint of nostalgia, he said, "I don't think I've smoked pot in fifteen years."

Moth produced a joint from his shirt pocket. Before he lit up, he said, "Man, if you haven't smoked in fifteen years, you haven't smoked. Shit is different now." He struck a match, put it to the jay, and inhaled deeply. Without letting out much vapor, he went on. "Hybrids or some shit. Strong. Plus it's like they took the paranoia out. Sure you don't want some?"

"I'm high enough from the fumes in here," said Artisan. "So anyway, you think he went to Florida."

Leaking smoke, Moth said, "Probably Key West would be my guess. He spent time there off and on. Maybe he mentioned having something going on down there, something he needed to wrap up."

"Maybe?"

"I think so. Yeah."

"He say what it was?"

Moth just shook his head, a plume of pot smoke following his face around. "I had the feeling it was something maybe better not talked about too much."

"As in something illegal?" the detective ventured.

"I have no idea," said Moth. "Besides, how do you define illegal?"

"Call me conventional," said Artisan. "I define it as against the law."

"The laws are total bullshit," said the man with the joint in his fingers.

"I'm not taking a position on that. But there's a drawback to doing illegal things. It puts you in contact with criminals, and criminals tend to get nasty if the game doesn't go their way. No value judgment, okay? I'm trying to find out if your buddy is in trouble."

Moth drew on the jay again. The sucking motion pulled his features even closer together, gave him a furtive look. Paul Artisan wondered if maybe this was the story of the guy's life: Through no fault of his own, he'd been born with a wiry body and a furtive face, a face that made people not quite trust him; feeling untrusted, he became untrustworthy. Which came first?

With two tokes under his belt, he now veered off from the linear. "Zander and me, we've always had authority issues. That's what made us friends. Test the limits, piss off teachers, drive parents crazy, shit like that."

Since it didn't seem like he could lead the conversation, the detective now tried to follow it. "Cliff said you met way back in high school."

Moth gave a little laugh that had not a trace of fond remembrance in it. "High school. What a fucking joke that was. They called it a school for *gifted underachievers*. That's a good one! How about fucked-up rich kids?"

The dust-covered man saw, or imagined he saw, a hint of skepticism in the detective's face.

"Yeah," he went on. "My family's on the rich side. Not like the Widmores, but rich enough. Or too rich, I should say."

He gestured toward the sloop that he'd been working on. "You see that fucking boat? I was born to sail on boats like that, not work on 'em. But I don't want to. It's my choice. 'Cause here's the thing. I know that boat inside and out. I know how it rides the water, what happens underneath. People think that boats just float. That's bull-shit, man. They don't float, they *plow*. It's a beautiful and violent thing, and I get it because I understand the whole entire boat. I know every stay and shackle that ties the thing together. I know how the diesel works, and what holds the goddamn rudder on, and where the piss goes when you flush the head. These rich idiots who sail the boats, what do they know? Nothing. They take the helm on a summer Saturday with a gin and tonic in their hand and they skim across the surface. That's as deep as they go. You see what I'm saying?"

The detective gave a diplomatic nod. "Yeah, I see, I see. That's why I don't buy a million-dollar sailboat either. But coming back to Zander, the two of you have stayed in touch all these years?"

"Off and on. He went everywhere. I stayed here. He knew where to find me. Sometimes, if he was in this part of the world and didn't want to see his family, he'd come out here, I'd put him up."

Moth took a last quick pull on the joint, then stubbed it out against the edge of his stool and put the roach back in his pocket. "You see how pure the stuff is now? Three little whiffs, I'm good at least till dinner."

"This last time he was out here," said Paul Artisan, "he seem different to you at all?"

"Different," mused the stoned guy. "Not really. I mean, he sure dressed different. Preppy shirts, fucking Wall Street shoes. He looked like a goddamn clone of Cliff. First time I saw him, I did a double take, like why's this dickhead suddenly being nice to me? Once you got past the clothes, though, he was the same old Zander."

"Even though he was working in the family business?" the detective said.

"Which I never understood," said Moth, "even for a second. I guess he was sucking up to the old man, but why bother?"

It occurred to Artisan that the reason to bother was that Widmore senior was near the end of his life, and perhaps his wayward son would like in the late innings to make him happy. He didn't think that line of reasoning would make much sense to Moth, and so he changed the subject.

"Let's come back to Shannon for a minute. You said she was a piece of work?"

"Yeah, she is. Was."

"How so?" asked the detective.

"Wow," said Moth, and tugged an earlobe to help himself think. "You know how, some crazy people, it's immediately obvious they're crazy? They have weird tics. They talk to themselves. They get that white shit at the edges of their mouth. Shannon was just the opposite. Like Miss Totally Perfect. Went to Vassar, Wellesley, one of those. Had perfect teeth, perfect hair, those perfect little tits that well-bred WASP girls are supposed to have. Manners like the queen of England. But she happened to be loony."

"Loony covers a lot of ground," said Artisan. "Loony how?"

"Had a tough time telling truth from fantasy, for one thing. And she'd take any pill that she could get her hands on. Uppers, downers, didn't matter. Didn't matter if she was being the perfect hostess at a dinner for twenty. If there was a pill within her reach, she'd eat it."

"That how she killed herself?" asked Artisan. "With pills?"

"Pills plus Scotch plus car exhaust."

That seemed pretty definitive to Artisan. Pills alone might have been a cry for help; pills plus booze plus car exhaust seemed like a cry to have things over with.

After a moment, Moth went on. "According to Zander, though,

her attitude about pills was sort of different. She didn't take 'em for thrills or even recreation. She took 'em for relief."

"Relief from what?"

"Fuck if I know," said Moth, though not without a certain gruff compassion. "Depression? Anxiety? The strain of being so fucking perfect? Whatever it was, she didn't find the cure."

"Or she did," said the detective. "Zander was close to her?"

"This last visit, yeah, they seemed pretty close. Real close, in fact. Like they had a bond. He brought her out here a couple times. You know, just to take a drive. That's mainly how I got to know her."

Artisan could not keep down a note of surprise. "He brought her out here? Where was Cliff?"

"Who cares?"

"Were they having an affair?"

"An affair," echoed Moth, as if he'd never heard the word before or its formality was just too foreign to him. "You mean like sex?"

"Sex is usually a factor in affairs, yeah."

The stoned man pondered this and after a beat it struck him not exactly funny but uncomfortably, even creepily, amusing. "How weird would that be? Fucking your husband's identical twin? Like, hey, I've seen that little thing before. What if she got pregnant? You couldn't even do the DNA thing."

"Moth," said Artisan, the paint fumes giving him a headache and his patience wearing thin. "Do you think they were having an affair?"

The tone made Moth stop laughing. Feeling scolded, he went silent. Then his eyes wandered off, as if he were rethinking something that had passed him by. "I really have no idea," he said. "But Zander liked her. She liked Zander. He was all busted up at the funeral. Cried like a baby."

"You said they had a bond. What do you think it was?"

Zander's friend was gripping the edges of his low stool with both hands. He now looked up at Artisan from under dust-flecked eyebrows. "Seems obvious to me," he said. "They both couldn't stand Cliff. And they both felt like they were stuck with him for life."

The detective thought that over as he reached for his wallet and fumbled to find a business card. Handing one to Moth, he said, "If you hear from Zander, will you call me?"

The other man didn't answer right away. Instead, he glanced at the card and said, "Man, you don't give these out very often, do you? It's all smudged and wrinkled. Looks like the condom I carried in my wallet for half a year in high school."

"Moth, will you call me?"

"Not unless Zander wants me to," he said, and Artisan could not but admire the little guy's loyalty.

"Or if you really feel that he's in trouble?" the detective coaxed.

"Okay, fair enough. If I really think he's in trouble I'll give a call."

11

On the ferry ride that carried him away from Peconiquot, Paul Artisan sucked deep breaths of the salty air, trying to clear his head of marijuana smoke, varnish fumes, and the frustration that lingered from dealing with Keith Baker's chronic vagueness. Watching the bow wave as it spread away from the ferry's blunt and rusting hull, the detective chewed his lip and tried to figure what he had so far.

Very little, he admitted. Two brothers who didn't seem to like each other. One who did all the right things and seemed pretty clearly to resent it; one who did all the wrong things, who was AWOL and supposedly in danger because of the reckless way he ran his life. A dead sister-in-law who, according to one biased and stoned-out witness at least, was fonder of the one to whom she was not married.

Then there was the question of the family fortune, which seemed to warp everything and to cloud or even invalidate most of the usual motives. There was a strong suggestion that Zander Widmore did illegal things. But if he didn't need the money, why would he? For that matter, absent the need for dough, why did anyone do *anything*? For glory? Spite? Just to fill the hours? This

was one of those profoundly basic questions that people somehow overlooked: Why do anything at all? Why not just sit still in a
room? A question to discuss with Manny Weissman.

Artisan stared down at the swirling eddies, but there were no
answers in the water. Buoys leaned eastward on the outgoing tide.
Gulls cackled and, high above, an osprey circled, patient wings
making the most exquisite small adjustments to the shifting cur-
rents of air. By the time the ferry clunked and squeaked into its slip
on the Long Island side, the detective had figured out one small
thing at least: that whatever else the search for Zander Widmore
turned out to entail, it was first and foremost the story of a screwed-
up family.

He decided that, on the way back to the city, he would make a
stop at the estate in Locust Valley and try to have a chat with the
father of the twins.

Locust Valley was one of those ever-rarer enclaves that had been
able to insulate itself against the ravages of democracy and change
by the simple expedients of wealth and influence. Quite close in to
The City on the north shore of Long Island, the town was largely
surrounded by hideous suburbs full of tract houses and strip malls
and Wal-Marts and Home Depots. Yet all these offensive sights
somehow fell away before reaching the town line, giving place to
an ambience that was all graciousness and quiet.

Locust Valley was a town where the trees had never been bull-
dozed to divide the land into neat sixth-of-an-acre plots; huge
sycamores and maples made tunnels of the shady streets. It was
a town where greengrocers still wore clean white aprons and
selected pears and apples one by one; a town where people still had
store accounts written down in ledger books. There was a gas station landscaped in rosebushes, with a man who still pumped gas.

Paul Artisan parked his old Volvo in front a florist's shop with a window full of irises and lilies. Inside, a white-haired lady dressed all in pink gave him a polite but slightly dubious smile and asked if she could help him. He said he was making a delivery to the Widmore place but had lost the address. Did she happen to know the way?

The lady seemed relieved. As a deliveryman, this carelessly dressed young fellow was plausible. And of course she knew where the Widmores lived, having sent them three arrangements—a small one for the foyer, a large one for the living room, a medium-size one for the master bedroom—every Tuesday and Friday for many years. She directed him through the village and down Piping Rock Road toward the Long Island Sound.

Artisan drove past stone walls and iron gates and massive hedges, catching glimpses here and there of sprawling houses with ivy reaching to their chimneys. Finally, framed by some hundreds of yards of tall, dense privet, he found a gated driveway with a discreet sign that said ISLAY HOUSE—CLAN WIDMORE. The detective pulled up to the intercom and rang.

After a moment, a servant's voice said, "Yes, may I help you?"

The detective gave his name and said he was there to see Mr. Widmore.

"Is he expecting you?"

"Well, no."

"May I tell him what this is in reference to?"

Artisan began to speak, then checked himself. Quite suddenly he experienced a dilemma he'd never in his life had to confront before: How much did one tell the help? Corollary to this, he realized with fresh vividness that *he* was the help as well. Carefully, he said, "I'm an acquaintance of Cliff's. And I'm looking for Zander."

"Mr. Alexander isn't here."

"Yes, I know that. I'm hoping to find him. That's what I'd like to talk about with Mr. Widmore."

Somehow the servant managed to send a note of disapproval through the silence of the intercom. "Wait a moment, please. I'll tell him that you're here."

The detective waited, sniffing honeysuckle, watching tree-shadows stretch across spectacular lawns as the sun slipped toward the west. Then the gates silently swung open and he pulled through to where the driveway ended in a graceful arc.

The house was smaller than, say, the Supreme Court building, but not by a whole lot. Half-timbers of dark wood defined squares and triangles of weathered gray stone; the stone surrounded leaded windows. Flanked by lilacs and hydrangeas, a wide stoop led to an enormous front door in whose vacant frame a butler was standing. "Come with me, please," he commanded.

He led Artisan through a maze of hallways and sitting rooms. The detective dawdled as much as he dared, trying to take in his surroundings. On one wall was a gallery of portraits—Widmore ancestors, no doubt, some of whom were wearing kilts. Here and there, pillows of tartan plaids were strewn on leather sofas. An ancient map labeled CALEDONIA gleamed beneath a museum-style light. Finally, having passed a dining room of baronial size and a living room with a head-high fireplace, they came to the most surprising space of all: a sort of solarium with ancient curved glass windows, tinged just slightly greenish by the years, that fronted on the Sound. Past a swath of perfect grass and a narrow strip of private beach, light glinted off the water; in the distance, the shorelines of Westchester and Connecticut loomed low, green, and seemingly unspoiled.

An old man and a woman who was considerably younger, though not scandalously so, were sitting in angled armchairs facing out. At the sound of the approaching footsteps, the old man rose with something that might have almost passed for spryness.

"Welcome, welcome," he said, extending a hand. "Mr. Anderson, is it?"

"Artisan."

"Artisan. Yes, yes. Clifford's mentioned you to me. And I must say, if your detecting skills are as good as your timing, that's a hopeful sign. You're here just in time for sunset and for cocktails. Will you have a Scotch?"

The way he said it made it clear that no other beverage was thinkable. Which was fine with Artisan. He liked Scotch.

"With water, sir? Soda?" asked the servant.

"Neat, please."

"Ah," said Arthur Widmore. "You know how to drink your whisky. Another good sign. I'll hope you'll feel highly complimented that Clifford selected you for this troubling business. I asked him more than a month ago to get someone on it. I'm sure he researched the matter carefully."

Artisan said nothing, and Widmore senior gestured toward the woman who was still sitting in her armchair. "Allow me to introduce my wife, Vivian. The third Mrs. Widmore. Let's hope there'll be several more, at least."

Vivian Widmore extended a hand that was surprisingly warm and gave Artisan a clasp that was surprisingly lingering and friendly. "A comedian, my husband. Don't believe a word he says. He's completely devoted to me. And I'm even growing fond of him after five years of wedded bliss."

With a twinkle in his eye, the old man said, "And let's not forget the two glorious years of living in sin."

Vivian rolled her eyes, and Artisan had the impression that this was a routine that Mr. and Mrs. Widmore had trotted out before. "I was waiting to be legally declared a widow," she explained. "I hardly think that qualifies as living in sin."

"As you like," her husband said. "Still, there was definitely a frisson to it, a bracing whiff of scandal." To Artisan, he said, "Please, sit."

Waiting for his drink, the detective stole a moment to study the handsome couple. Arthur Widmore, probably in the second half of his seventies, was still a fine-looking man, although in a rather archaic way. He had one of those thin mustaches that went out of fashion decades ago and yet was perfect on him. His silver hair, which he brushed straight back, was burnished with some final hints of the brownish-blonde that used to be. He was trim if slightly stooped, and Artisan guessed he'd been a good athlete in his day; he guessed this because of the grace with which the old man pulled off his nearly perfect parody of spryness. Almost undetected, he'd used his arms to help his legs rise up from the chair; sitting, he hid the small shock as his buttock muscles failed and he fell the last inch back into his seat.

As for the third Mrs. Widmore, she was fifty-seven, fifty-eight, he guessed, a fading but not quite faded beauty of a certain type—a *Town and Country* portrait before the touch-up artists had gotten hold of the film. Her big dark eyes were wide-set, made up within the bounds of taste, and edged with very faint crow's feet which she hated but which were actually quite becoming. Her nose was small and straight, her lips full and with a certain sensual mobility. Her best feature was her hair, a thick mane of upswept black with just the occasional contrasting strand of gray. Was she letting the natural gray come through, or covering all but a fraction of it to create the impression that she had nothing at all to hide?

The servant brought a drink for Artisan and refreshers for the Widmores. They clinked glasses, and the detective took a sip of the strangest and best whisky he had ever sampled in his life. It tasted of smoke and moss and leather, and after the nutty flavor of grain came a completely unexpected finish that was something like toasted banana. "My God," the detective blurted. "What *is* this?"

Old man Widmore beamed at the reaction. "Rather good, eh? Twenty-one-year-old Laphroaig. From the Isle of Islay. Which happens to be where my family is originally from."

Vivian Widmore gave a slight but stagy groan. "Please, Arthur, the fellow's here to talk about Zander. Do we have to start with the Scottish thing again?"

"We'll get to business in due course," said her husband, holding his drink up in the dimming light and admiring its amber hue. "And why not talk about 'the Scottish thing?' What's wrong with honoring the place you're from and the people who came before? You see anything wrong with that, Artisan?"

Blandly, the younger man said, "Well, no."

Widmore turned to his wife. "There, you see?" Speaking again to his visitor, he said, "America, this whole melting pot idea, it's all well and good, but the problem is that no one is actually *from* here. I mean, we're not Indians, Artisan. We came from somewhere else. And my contention is that if you don't know where you came from, you don't know who you are. What were the old traditions? What gods did your ancestors believe in? What laws did they follow? . . . This country doesn't *have* traditions. What passes for tradition in America? The Super Bowl and a hot dog? I mean, is that the best—?"

His wife's face clearly showed that she had heard this line of argument many times before. When she could stand it no longer, she cut in. "Artisan," she said. "That sounds like what my husband would call a fine, strong Anglo-Saxon name."

The detective sipped his whisky. "Actually, it's a name that was screwed-up at Ellis Island. My family's Basque."

"Basque," said Vivian Widmore. "Aren't those the people who are always making trouble in Spain?"

"No, actually it's the Spanish who've been making trouble in Basqueland for the last thousand years or so."

"Well said, Artisan!" commended Arthur Widmore, and, rather absurdly, the detective was tickled to have scored a point with the old man. "You've got to be true to your blood. How's your drink, Artisan? Let's have another. We'll toast to your people, the Basques."

He gestured for the servant, and Vivian Widmore said, "So what happened with your name?"

"Well, the family name was actually Berasategui. But there was no way that the guy at Ellis Island could spell it or even sound it out. Now my great-grandfather spoke three languages—Basque, Spanish, and a little French—but no English. So a friend who'd been to America briefed him on what to say: first your name, then your occupation. So when the Ellis Island guy asked him to repeat the name, he thought he was being prompted to say his job. He said *artzain,* which is the Basque word for shepherd. The immigration guy got Artisan out of *artzain,* and here we are."

The servant brought more drinks. Outside, the sun had set and the breeze had quieted; the Sound had taken on the pale sheen of a moonlit lake. Old man Widmore raised his glass. "To the proud and ancient race of Basques!"

Artisan sipped the wonderful Scotch. The burn in his belly reminded him that he hadn't got around to eating lunch and he dimly noticed that the alcohol was going to his head. He fumbled for a way to get back to the business at hand. "Now about Zander," he said. "I'm sorry if this is difficult, but I'm trying to figure out where he might have gone after . . ."

"After Shannon's funeral," Vivian said softly.

"Yes," said the detective.

Something happened to Arthur Widmore's posture and for a moment, as he turned toward his guest, he showed the full weight of his years. "Troubling business," he muttered. "Troubling business. Fine girl, Shannon. You liked her, didn't you?"

"I never met her, Mr. Widmore."

"Of course. Of course. You *would have* liked her is what I meant to say." He sipped his whisky and then strove for a brighter tone. "You'll stay for dinner, Artisan?"

It was a question, but just barely. "That's very kind," said the detective. "But I dropped in unannounced, I don't want to impose—"

"Please," said the older man. "It won't be any trouble. Just some simple lamb chops and Bordeaux, eh? We can talk at leisure over dinner."

Paul Artisan groped for the right thing to say, and it dawned on him that the invitation was not an entirely unselfish one. It was at least entirely possible that Mr. and Mrs. Arthur Widmore were bored to tears in their magnificent and empty house and badly wanted another person they could talk to. The detective said, "All right. Thank you. I would love to stay."

12

They used the smaller dining room, which was painted a beautiful dark red. Tall candles were arrayed in the center of the table and in iron sconces on the walls. In the soft light, wearing a loose gray jacket against the evening chill, Arthur Widmore looked, in fact, like the Scottish aristocrat he pictured himself as. His wife had changed into a simple black dress that showed off her graceful neck and collarbones and perfectly set off her splendid head of hair. In forgiving candlelight she looked nothing short of regal.

A servant brought two slightly dusty bottles to the table. "The Haut-Brion eighty-two, sir?"

"Yes, yes. Good, good," said the host. Turning to his guest, he said, "It's actually still a little on the young side. But at my age, who's got time to wait? No sense in being outlived by one's wines, is there, Artisan?"

The wine was decanted and poured. It was preposterously good, tasting of black currants and cold stone and finishing with a slight suggestion of mint and violet.

"Ah," said Arthur Widmore. "With that in front of me, I think I can face anything. Shall we talk about this situation with my son?"

"Our son," the stepmother put in softly.

"That's sweet of you, darling."

Artisan couldn't tell if this last remark was meant to be sarcastic. He sipped some Bordeaux and carried on. "Okay. Cliff seems to think that Zander is in danger, but he doesn't know exactly why, or where, or what the danger is about. So I'm trying to figure out where he went when he left here, and what his frame of mind was at the time."

Vivian Widmore perched her pretty face on crisscrossed fingers. "His frame of mind was not good," she said. "It wasn't good at all."

Her husband seemed decidedly uncomfortable with her directness. "Now, darling, you have to remember what a trying time it was. A trying time for all of us."

"Agreed. Shannon's passing was a tragedy. But Zander seemed to take it harder than anyone. Harder than her own husband."

Arthur Widmore ran his napkin across his lips, and Paul Artisan could not help wondering if maybe he was secretly biting a corner of it. "That really isn't fair," he said. "They have different ways of showing things."

He sipped some wine and turned to the detective. "For some odd reason, I seem to spend a lot of time defending my son Clifford. He's a wonderful man, solid and reliable, and I'm extremely proud of him. But he's often misunderstood. He comes across as cold. But he isn't cold. He's holding his emotions in check so that he can carry on with the things that need doing. It's men like Clifford who hold the world together. He's very demanding—that I grant you. But he's no tougher on others than he is on himself."

"He was far too tough on Shannon."

"Darling, please."

A stare was exchanged and everybody drank some wine. Attempting to change the subject, Vivian Widmore said, "You have extraordinary eyelashes, Mr. Artisan. Do all Basque men have such long lashes?"

"Um. I really couldn't say."

Soup was served. Artisan was just about to spoon into his when a servant appeared at his elbow to add a splash of sherry.

"As to Zander's frame of mind," his father resumed, "if it was troubled, I'm afraid I bear some of the blame. The evening before he left, we quarreled. Rather bitterly, I'm sorry to say."

"Can you tell me what the quarrel was about?" asked the detective.

Arthur Widmore had had two spoonfuls of his soup. He pushed it away from him and went back to his wine. "Actually, I can't," he said. "Or won't. Family is family, Artisan. That's sacred to me. Some things just don't go beyond."

Paul Artisan sipped his wine. "Even if it has to do with Zander's safety?"

"It doesn't," said the father with finality.

The detective drank more wine. He was feeling somewhat tipsy, which seemed odd because the level of his glass had hardly changed. Belatedly, he realized that this was because every time he took a sip an unseen hand refilled it.

Somewhat to his guest's surprise, Arthur Widmore slightly reopened the door he'd just slammed shut. "Zander has always had some strange ideas. Extremely strange. I've sometimes thought he brought them up just to engage me, taunt me, so we'd have something new to argue about. We both have a zest for arguing, it seems . . . When poor Shannon died, he got all worked up about his craziest idea yet. And, predictably, when he brought it up, I took the bait. I attacked. We battled."

The soup was cleared and the lamb chops arrived. They were gorgeous lamb chops, lightly charred on the outside and rosy pink within. Paul Artisan could not quite shake the feeling that his hostess had given him a slightly lewd look as she raised the first meaty morsel to her lips.

Widmore senior was still wandering from car to car down the full length of his train of thought. After a while he resumed. "The thing is, after Zander left, I started feeling he was right."

"Right about—?" said Artisan.

"I've told you I can't say."

"No, of course not, darling," said his wife.

But nor could the old man let it go. "Zander took something completely fundamental to what I've always believed, and he stood it on its head. Turned it completely upside down. And the damnable thing is that I've been coming to feel that maybe he's right and I've been wrong. That's part of the reason I want him found. So I can tell him that. While there's still time."

The two bottles of Haut-Brion had mysteriously disappeared. The servant decanted a third. After the lamb chops there was peach tart, and after the peach tart there was cognac. Sipping from his oversize snifter, Paul Artisan noticed that something had changed either about the angle of the candlelight or about Vivian Widmore's posture. Earlier, the soft gleam had played about her neck and shoulders. Now it seemed to pour itself toward her cleavage and the gentle swellings that marked the tops of her breasts. Trying to pull his eyes away, the detective said, "I really should be going." His voice sounded thick inside his ears.

"Nonsense, Artisan," said his host. "Stay the night. It's late, no time to be driving. We've had a bit to drink. We keep a room made up. Please."

"Yes," said Vivian Widmore, her shoulders bunching, candle-flames playing in her wide-set eyes. "We'd love to have you. Really."

The room that Artisan was shown to had everything an impromptu guest might require. There was a thick terry-cloth bathrobe and a new toothbrush wrapped in plastic. There were soaps and shampoos and even an assortment of magazines and books next to the bed. But the visitor was far too tired to read. He took a warm shower, dried himself on towels soft as clouds, and slipped in between the sheets.

Even half asleep he was somehow not surprised when there was a soft knock on his door. "Mr. Artisan?"

"Yes?"

The door fell open and Vivian Widmore stood there like a portrait in the frame. She wore a thin white cotton gown. The hall light that was behind her traced out her silhouette. Artisan saw the fullness of her breasts, heavier than they'd seemed in clothing, and the taut peaks of her nipples. He saw the slight and sensuous roundness of her tummy, saw the way the smooth line of her torso was blurred at last by the vague nest of her pubic hair. He saw the curved flesh at the tops of her thighs, and the light that passed between them.

"Are you quite comfortable, Mr. Artisan?" she said.

"Yes. Very. Thank you."

"Is there anything else you'd like? Anything else at all?"

"Uh. No. No. Everything is great."

"Are you quite sure, Mr. Artisan?"

"Um. Yeah. Yes. Thanks."

"Good night, then, Mr. Artisan."

She closed the door, and the detective, who had been so close to sleep, spent a long time wondering how it would have been if she had come into his bed.

13

He left early the next morning, seeing no one but the servant who gave him fresh-squeezed orange juice and coffee.

Traffic on the LIE was hideous, and as it took over an hour to reach the Midtown Tunnel, he gave up on the idea of going home to his apartment. He went straight to the office and arrived just before nine thirty.

Within ten minutes he had a phone call. It was Cliff Widmore. "So I hear you've been visiting with the family," said the client.

"Hope you don't mind," said the detective. "It just seemed convenient to stop by. I was on my way home from Peconiquot."

"Mind?" said Widmore, with perhaps a shade more emphasis than he'd intended. "No, I don't mind. It's your show, Artisan. Do what you think best. Only, if I'd known you were going, I could've warned you what to expect."

"Did I need a warning? I had a very nice time. I really like your father."

"The old boy can be quite charming," said Widmore, though Artisan thought the tone was slightly grudging. "Did he bend your ear about that Scottish stuff? The old ways, the traditions?"

"A little bit. But what's the harm?"

"The harm? There is none, I guess. Unless he starts worshipping stones or going to the country club with his face painted blue . . . But what concerns me is that this is a very new obsession of his. It seems to have come from nowhere. I worry that it's a symptom of him losing his marbles."

"He seemed pretty lucid to me."

"You have to listen carefully. Believe me, Artisan, I've spent a lot of time observing the changes in my father. He follows scripts. It's what a lot of senile people do. There are certain things he talks about. Things he's rehearsed in his mind. But if he has to improvise, he's in trouble. Break the pattern and the seams show."

The detective thought that over. It was true that Arthur Widmore had not really engaged in the give-and-take of normal conversation. He had riffs rather than responses. Through the cross-currents of what others said, he'd essentially pursued a monologue. It was also true he'd gotten muddled in his sense of time, imagining that Artisan had known his daughter-in-law, already dead three months.

After a pause, Cliff Widmore said, "He still believe it was his idea to hire a detective?"

"He did mention that, yeah."

"While drinking heavily, I imagine?"

"Fairly heavily," said Artisan. "And very well."

"Well," said the son with undisguised exasperation, "that's another thing he shouldn't be doing. The doctors told him a few years ago he needed to cut way back. The damage to his insides . . . It doesn't show, Artisan. He's very good at having things not show. But he's in miserable shape."

The detective found himself resisting the dire assessment, and he couldn't quite tell why. Did Cliff Widmore have some reason to exaggerate the old man's frailty, or was he himself in denial about the mortality of this geezer who was not even his own relation?

Out of nowhere, Cliff asked, "Vivian come on to you?"

The detective was flummoxed by the question and could think of no reply that would not sound caddish.

Reading the hesitation, the client said, "You don't need to answer. Vivian's a bit of a slut. But, as you would say, what's the harm?"

"You don't like Vivian?"

"I didn't say I didn't like her. I said she's a bit of a slut. We've never been close, but actually I like her quite a bit. She's very sharp and sometimes very funny. She punctures my father's pretensions just enough. Most important, I know she'll never leave him."

"What makes you so confident of that?" asked Artisan. "The money?"

"No, not the money. The social standing. The aura of class. The chance to sit on charity boards with people even richer than oneself. That's why Vivian would never give up being Mrs. Widmore. The money she took care of with her first husband. He was very . . . let's call it colorful. She mention him at all?"

Artisan searched back through the fog of Scotch and wine and cognac. "Not that I remember. Just made some reference about a delay in becoming legally a widow."

Cliff gave a short dark laugh. "Ah. So you heard the 'living in sin' routine. They tell you what the delay was about?"

"No."

"The first husband was Jimmy Hoffa'd. He was disappeared. I think he was a gangster."

"Seriously?"

"Vivian denies it, of course. Says he was a legitimate business-man who was being muscled by the bad guys. His business happened to be running a cement company. Rather mysteriously, the cement company kept getting big jobs in Brooklyn and the Bronx. Then—just by coincidence, mind you—there was a power struggle in the Gambino family. Shortly after that, Vivian's first husband went to work one morning and never came home. The body was never found. Draw your own conclusions."

Paul Artisan pictured Vivian's regal posture and gracious manners and understated makeup. It was hard to imagine her as married to the mob. "I don't know," he said, "Vivian seems so . . . so Scarsdale."

"Scarsdale by way of Staten Island. Tottenville High. She's reinvented herself, and done a damn good job. Like I say, she's very sharp and she knows exactly what she wants. Don't ever underestimate my stepmother."

There was a brief silence, in the midst of which Paul Artisan was visited by an unbidden image of the light filtering between Vivian Widmore's soft but still shapely thighs. He remembered the heat of her first handshake and wondered if she would have come into his bed if he had called her bluff. He changed the subject to banish the vision. "Your father told me that he and Zander quarreled shortly before Zander left. He seemed upset about it, thought it might have been part of the reason Zander took off."

The dutiful brother didn't buy it. "Zander and my father *always* quarrel, and my father *always* imagines it's a big deal. After all these years, he still doesn't seem to get it that, from Zander's point of view, it doesn't matter what they're arguing *about*, it just matters that they're disagreeing."

"So you don't know the subject of the disagreement?"

"I do know, in fact. It's a personal thing and I very much doubt it matters."

There was another brief silence. The detective glanced around his office. Maybe it was because of the privileged precincts he'd recently been visiting, but he realized with fresh intensity what a dump it was. Promising himself to bring in a plant or a rug or something, he said, "I also talked with Moth."

"Moth?"

"Keith Baker. Zander's friend."

"Oh."

"He says that after the funeral he dropped Zander at Islip Airport. Thought he was probably heading to Key West. That make sense to you?"

With that rueful little laugh of his, Cliff Widmore said, "In a way. Key West is a dead-end place, right? Full of eccentrics and losers. I know my brother's spent time down there."

"Doing?"

"Who knows? Partying. Smuggling. He did once bring my old man a beautiful box of Havana cigars."

"You think he's spent time in Cuba?"

"No idea. But put it this way. People aren't supposed to go to Cuba, so chances are my brother did."

"I think I should go down to Florida," the detective said. "That okay with you?"

It seemed to be more than okay with the client. In fact, Paul Artisan had the vague impression that Cliff Widmore might be relieved to have him out of town, away from Locust Valley. "Do what you gotta do," he said. "Let me know when the expense draw is used up."

"Can you think of anything that might help me get started? Where he stayed when he was down there? Any friends, girlfriends?"

Cliff Widmore thought it over. Then he said, "The only thing I can remember is that one time he was down there, he mentioned he was hanging out with a yoga instructor. I remember because I was intrigued by the possibilities. Positions. You know. I mean, think about it: a yoga teacher. She had some hippie name— Moonbeam, Stardust, something like that. No idea if she's still around."

Paul Artisan stared at the world map that hung not quite straight on his crummy office wall. Manhattan was a speck and Key West was a speck and there was a fair amount of mystery and distance between them. "Moonbeam," he said, "Stardust. Okay, it's a start. I'll be in touch."

At six thirty that evening, Argos the ancient Labrador was rolling on his back on a grassy patch in Riverside Park, and the two men who loved him were trying not to notice that it was a bit of a struggle for the old dog to regain his feet. He pushed; he wobbled; he tried the opposite two legs. But if dogs, like humans, were prey to weakness and to pain, they seemed to be blessed strangers to suffering. Once up on his paws, Argos wagged his sweeping tail at everything and nothing; he followed his nose around on what was each new day a journey of discovery.

Artisan had been telling Manny Weissman all about Peconiquot and Moth and Locust Valley and the Widmores and the single-malt whisky and the marvelous Bordeaux.

His old professor said, "Sounds like something straight out of *Gatsby*. And please don't tell me you've only seen the movie."

"Sorry. But I did. Robert Redford, right? I didn't think it was that good."

"Frankly, the novel's overrated too. Nobody to like. The main characters are lushes, fornicators, and frauds. The narrator's a twerp and a suck-up. But that doesn't mean you shouldn't have read it."

The detective let that slide. Instead, he followed his wandering dog, and without looking at his friend, he said, "Manny, I'm worried."

"Worried?"

"I think I've gotten lazy. I'm afraid I've gotten dense. I've been doing all these trivial, bullshit cases, and now that I've finally got something with some guts to it, I feel totally out of my depth."

The old man knew enough to keep quiet and to let his young friend riffle through his thoughts.

"It's like my own instincts have started talking to me in a foreign language. I hear that inner voice but I don't know what to make of it. I can't figure out who to believe. I'm not sure I should trust my own client. It's making me dizzy."

Manny Weissman scratched his ear. With infinite calm he said, "Let's go through it logically. What's the problem with your client?"

Paul Artisan kicked at a bare patch of ground. "In some ways he's too good to be true. Responsible. Loyal to his family. Trying to take care of everyone, pick up everybody else's slack. On the other hand, he seems cynical and cold, like he hardly noticed his wife committed suicide three months ago. Zander's friend Moth thinks he's manipulative and phony. But then old man Widmore claims he's a very caring guy who hides his feelings so he can get on with things."

Weissman said, "What's so surprising, Paul? People are complex. It's only in movies and bad books that people are all one way or all the other."

"Fair enough," said the detective. "But it's the twin thing that makes it really complicated. Like a seesaw, one goes up and the other comes down. When I think Cliff is a good guy, I imagine Zander must be really evil—a spiteful psychopath driven to make himself and everyone around him miserable. But then, when it seems like maybe Cliff is actually a bad guy, I imagine that Zander is just a lost soul, harmless basically, looking for a way to feel okay about himself . . . I won't know which twin is which until I find Zander, and God knows if I'll ever find him."

Manny Weissman looked up at the sky. Mare's-tail clouds picked

up a pink tinge in the west, foretelling the end of this brief paradise
of perfect weather. "Has it occurred to you," he said, "that maybe
you've found Zander already?"

Paul Artisan said, "Excuse me?"

The half-blind dog knocked his head against a fallen limb.
Undaunted, he shook himself and continued on his sniffing
expedition.

The old professor held up his hands in a gesture of disclaimer.
"I'm not playing detective, okay? I'm following a logical exercise.
Tell me if you see a flaw or a gap in the reasoning.

"Go back six months, a year, whatever," he continued. "Zander
comes home from his travels. For the first time in his life, he goes
to work at the family firm. Learns the ropes, meets all the people.
He starts wearing business clothes—*Cliff's* clothes some of the time.
Why? Could it be that he's studying a role, rehearsing a part he'll
soon play?"

"Manny," said Paul Artisan, "this is diabolical."

"That's a value judgment," Weissman said, "and value judgments cloud analysis. Let's just continue with our exercise . . .
Given: that the brothers are virtually identical. If anyone could tell
them apart, who would it be? The wife, of course. And she conveniently dies."

"She killed herself," said Artisan.

The professor lifted a cautionary finger. "As I understand it,
that's an inference, not a fact. The only known fact is that she died
of drugs, booze, and carbon monoxide."

"You're suggesting she was murdered?"

"I'm not suggesting anything," said Weissman, "except that
with poor what's-her-name out of the picture, it would be a great
deal easier for Zander to take over Cliff's identity."

Paul Artisan walked in the park nearly every day. Now, suddenly,
the landscape seemed unfamiliar, almost eerie to him, the gently

sloping ground treacherous and unsteady beneath his feet. "What about the father?" he said. "He'd certainly recognize—"

"I think there's some question," said the old professor, "as to whether the father is truly *compos mentis*. Besides, there's a long and sordid history of sons fooling aged fathers when a significant inheritance is involved. Jacob and Esau, for example."

Value judgments cloud analysis. But at the same time, Paul Artisan's value judgment could hardly have been clearer. He did not want Manny Weissman's theory to be true. He didn't want to live in a world where people's identities could be utterly subsumed. It was way too creepy. He kept trying to punch holes in the argument. He said, "If Cliff is really Zander, then why would he hire a detective to find himself?"

Manny Weissman was unruffled. "It seems to me that the father's version of that story is entirely believable. *He* wanted to hire a detective. Zander—or Cliff if you prefer—stalled a month or more on doing it, to let the supposed trail go cold."

"What trail?" said Paul Artisan. Then he gave voice to the question he'd been dreading all along. "If Cliff is really Zander . . . then where's Cliff?"

Hearing that his friend was genuinely rattled, Manny Weissman said, "Hey, this is just a little thought-experiment, an exercise in logic."

"I know, I know," said Artisan. "So let's take the logic just a little farther. Where's the other twin?"

The sun went down behind the Palisades and Manny Weissman took a moment to slip into his cardigan. "I hate to say it, but logic would suggest that the other twin is dead."

Artisan just exhaled. The exhalation came out with a hint of a whistle and the old dog turned around to see if he'd been called.

"The friend," said Weissman. "Moth? He brings Zander to the

airport. But Zander doesn't take a plane. He picks up the car he's
left there. He drives to Cliff's house, where the new widower is
grieving. And he kills him. Then he dumps the body and takes
over his existence . . . I'm not saying any of this is true, necessarily.
But can you tell me that it isn't possible?"

14

Paul Artisan did not sleep well that night.

He was troubled by confusing dreams involving many mirrors. Sometimes a mirror held a grotesque image that was not the face it should have been reflecting. Sometimes a mirror seemed to swallow up a face and offer no reflection whatsoever. In other fragments of the dream, a mirror reflected nothing but another mirror, and in still other variations, what seemed a mirror turned out to be a window. But a window that led where?

The detective climbed down from the loft bed in his tiny bedroom, threw some water on his face, and made a pot of coffee. He was in a funky mood because he didn't want to do what he knew he had to do that morning. Resenting every moment, he showered, dressed, and headed out of the city, back onto the hated LIE, to the office of the Nassau County Coroner.

The office was in one of those squat and sterile municipal complexes that try so hard to be user-friendly that they end up being completely alienating and depressing. Handicap ramps and doughnut wrappers everywhere. Vapid art in primary colors, as at a grade school or a mental institution. Lots of fat security guards with handcuffs on their belts and lousy posture. Near the courthouse you could almost hear the ankle bracelets clattering and smell the lawyers' aftershave.

The coroner wasn't in. His gum-chewing receptionist told Artisan that he was doing an autopsy that morning. "You can probably find him at the morgue. You know where the morgue is, hon?"

Artisan said he didn't.

"You won't find lots of signs for it," she said. "Sort of discourages the patients, if you catch my drift. It's in the basement of the county hospital, other end of the complex. East wing. Sub-basement, really. Easier to keep things cool down there. You have a sweater?"

So Artisan walked through the shambling crowds of civil servants and the poor bastards who'd been called for jury duty to the county hospital. On the way, he wondered what kind of person strove to be a coroner. There seemed to be something essentially ghoulish about it, after all. Using poultry shears to cut through corpses' sternums and open up their chests like kitchen cabinets. Slicing dead stomachs and cold intestines to determine what a person's final meal had been. Measuring exit wounds and knife slashes, looking for poison or for bruises. Who aspired to a job like that?

In the lobby of the hospital there were people carrying flowers and stuffed animals and magazines and candy—all the standard emblems of good wishes and of hope. There were signs and arrows leading on to Pediatrics and Orthopedics and Oncology, but, sure enough, there were no directions to the morgue. This actually made sense; not many civilians proceeded to the morgue without an escort.

Paul Artisan found the east wing elevator bank. There were three cars going up but only one with a down arrow as well. He stepped into it alone, and pressed the button for the sub-basement. The doors closed with what seemed an unusual emphasis and finality.

The elevator ride seemed unnaturally slow, not exactly of a long duration but somehow outside of normal time. As time stretched out, distance became impossible to gauge. Was the descent twenty feet or was it miles down into the earth? And what had happened to simple notions of up, down, and sideways? This elevator ride did not feel vertical somehow. In Paul Artisan's suddenly jumpy stomach, it had more of the feel of a slanting, curving journey, a slow-motion lurch to a very different place.

The doors finally opened on a spotless, glaring hallway, a sort of pit stop on the way to eternity, a purgatory of bright white tile and fluorescent lights. The detective stepped out and approached a desk where a nurse was filling out a form. Her skin seemed slightly bluish in the ugly light; her uniform seemed as crisp as crackers. Artisan said, "I'm looking for the coroner, please."

"Dr. Edmonds is doing a procedure this morning. He should be just finishing up. Is he expecting you?"

"No. He isn't. But I'm happy to wait."

The nurse cleared her throat. It wasn't a loud sound but it seemed harsh bouncing off the tiles. "We don't have a waiting room," she said.

"Here is fine," said Artisan, though he wasn't the least bit happy to be there.

"As you like," the nurse said, and went back to her work.

Artisan stood there. He had never been prey to anxiety attacks, but gradually, with a strange detachment, as if it were happening to somebody else, he began to notice that he was feeling symptoms. His mouth was very dry. He was aware of his heart in his chest and his tongue in his mouth, and he didn't seem to be breathing except when he reminded himself to do so. His hands were clammy, and as if by instinct, his eyes sought out a window, an escape, an assurance that there was still a world beyond this glaring antiseptic chamber. There was, of course, no window.

The elevator that had brought him here opened once again. An orderly backed out. The orderly dragged a gurney, and on the gurney was a dead body wrapped in a sheet of Wedgwood blue. Artisan found himself riveted not by the corpse but by the folds and contours and draping of the sheet. It rose over the dead torso and fell away from the still limbs as gracefully as in a classic sculpture. Then the orderly destroyed the beauty of the composition by lifting up a corner to reveal a stiff and greenish human foot with thick and yellow toenails. He sang out to the nurse, "Need a toe tag, Eleanor. Name of Walter Sammler."

Paul Artisan leaned against the tile wall. His back was damp and the wall was very cold. At the back of his throat he was beginning to taste the morning's coffee mixed with bile. He didn't know how much longer he could stay here.

At the far end of the chamber, an automatic door slid open, and through it swept the coroner, Dr. Richard Edmonds. He was very tall and exceedingly thin, and his rubber-soled shoes seemed to gobble up the distance between the doorway and the nurse's desk. He dropped a file onto it. "Natural causes," he said. "Massive cerebro-vascular accident. The brain was just spongy with blood." He shook his head. "Forty-two years old."

The nurse nodded toward Paul Artisan. "This gentleman is here to see you."

The detective stepped forward and introduced himself. He hoped it was just the hideous lighting that made the coroner's face look so pallid and translucent, that put such a strange glint in his big rimless glasses and an odd gleam on his massive crinkled forehead. Shaking hands, Artisan tried to forget that these same fingers had just been poking around the inside of a corpse's skull.

"What can I do for you, Mr. Artisan?"

"It's about a case you handled about three months ago."

"I don't generally discuss—"

"Strictly off the record. Please. It's about Shannon Widmore."

At the mention of the name, the coroner frowned and looked down at his shoes. Then, in a tone of resignation, he asked the nurse to pull the file. Looking at his watch, he said, "I don't have time to go back to my office. We'll have to talk down here. Follow me."

He started walking with his giant steps back toward the automatic door. Artisan's feet seemed reluctant to follow; they seemed to realize what his mind was still fending off—that they were heading into the necropolis itself, the sanctum where the corpses were stored, where the bodies slated for autopsy were cut into and opened and probed, bits of their kidneys and livers buttered onto slides. The door slid open; the two men walked through. When it closed again, there was a slight *whoosh*ing sound, as if the worlds on either side of the door had different pressures, different atmospheres.

The coroner was, of course, unruffled. He seemed oblivious to the deeper chill and to the bleachy smell that made Paul Artisan's eyes begin to smart. The doctor leaned a shoulder against what appeared to be a giant version of an old-fashioned card catalog at a library. It was a file cabinet for dead people, one stiff per drawer.

Fiddling with the simple cardboard folder that held the data from Shannon Widmore's autopsy, he said, "We have a saying in my business, Mr. Artisan. 'What happens in the morgue stays in the morgue.' This conversation never happened. Are we agreed?"

The detective nodded yes.

Edmonds went on. "I take it you have some qualms about this suicide?"

"I take it you do too," said Paul Artisan.

The coroner frowned down at the file. "I'm not sure I'd go as far as to say that. I would say, though, that there was something of a rush to judgment in this case."

"Why?" asked Artisan.

"Please. Don't be naïve. The Widmore family is very powerful in this county. They didn't want publicity. They didn't want a mess. They wanted a fast pronouncement and a prompt burial."

"Who pressured you?" asked the detective.

The coroner didn't seem to grasp the question.

"Who in the Widmore family?" asked Artisan.

"That I couldn't say. Their lawyers talked to my bosses. Hints came down. . . . Look, don't misunderstand. I wasn't asked to falsify anything. I wasn't asked to cover anything up. But there were some gray areas I was encouraged to ignore, some questions I really wasn't given time to consider."

"Like?"

The coroner rubbed his giant forehead. "For example, there was no note. That in itself does not mean very much. The folklore has it that suicides always leave a note. That really isn't true. Some people kill themselves as a way of getting the last word in. *They* leave a note. Others kill themselves because they feel there's nothing left to say. It's just one hint among several."

"What else?" asked the detective.

Dr. Richard Edmonds riffled through his file. "There's a certain ambiguity," he said, "about exactly when and how she made it to the car she died in." He looked at his papers, scrolled down with a finger until he found the data he was looking for. "Her blood alcohol was point-twenty-three. That's fairly drunk but no drunker than some people who drive the LIE after happy hour. She had a considerable level of barbiturates in her system, but the effect of that is harder to gauge. It would have depended on her tolerance."

"I think this woman took a lot of pills," said Artisan. "I'd guess her tolerance was off the charts."

The coroner rubbed his chin and nodded thoughtfully. "My

impression also. So the point is this. I don't think the pills and
alcohol alone would have killed her. It was the carbon monoxide
that finished her off, probably quite quickly, as her respiration
would already have been extremely depressed. But there were no
pill bottles and no booze found in the car. Presumably then, to
put it in lay terms, she was pretty zonked before she *got* to the car.
In that state, would she have had the will and the presence of
mind and the coordination to seal the garage with towels and get
in and start the engine?"

Artisan thought that over, and was visited by a haunting image
of a lovely troubled woman sleepwalking toward death.

"Alternatively," said the coroner, "someone else took advan-
tage of her stupor and *put* her in the car."

"Were there any signs of struggle?"

The doctor looked down at his pages. "Neither here nor there,"
he said. "A small, fresh bruise on her shoulder, another on her hip.
Inconclusive. Could have come from anywhere. Besides, if someone took her to the car, it would most likely have been someone
that she knew and trusted."

Artisan narrowed his eyes against the bleachy sting and infernal glare of the morgue. Thinking aloud, he said, "Someone who
sometimes took her out for drives. Maybe when one or both of
them was drunk and stoned. Put her in the car half-conscious, say
he was going back for something he'd forgotten, leave her there
to die."

Unflappably, the coroner said, "It's plausible. A number of
scenarios are plausible. Which is why I wish they'd given me more
time." He gave a little shrug and closed the file. "It's a shame," he
said. "She was a very pretty corpse."

When Artisan was shown into the waterfront solarium at the Widmore home in Locust Valley, Vivian Widmore was talking on the

telephone. She was wearing shorts in a subdued plaid that looked quite fetching on her, and an open-necked blouse that only partly hid the breasts whose silhouette the detective could not help but remember.

She seemed unaccountably flustered by his sudden appearance. Artisan hadn't heard a word of her conversation on the phone, yet he had the distinct impression that her tone had suddenly changed. Sounding breezy but mostly sounding forced, she now said into the handset, "Ah, darling, I see we have a visitor. I'll have to call you back. Quite soon."

There was a bit of clatter as she dropped the phone back in the cradle.

"Ah, Mr. Artisan," she said, "how nice to see you again." Then, glancing toward the servant who was his escort, she added rather accusingly, "I had no idea you were here."

Apologetically, the servant said, "Mr. Widmore said to show him in, ma'am. Mr. Widmore is working in the garden."

Having recovered her studied poise, the third Mrs. Widmore turned back to her guest and said, "No matter. It's a pleasure. What brings you out this way?"

Before he could answer, Arthur Widmore appeared in the doorway. He too was wearing shorts. They looked far less good on him than on his wife. His legs were very pale and nude of hair, loose skin hanging where muscle used to be. He was also wearing a strange sort of green tunic; in his hands was clutched a rather dusty-looking pair of gardening gloves. He came in muttering. "Dammit, I just don't see why the heather doesn't grow here. It grows on bare rock in the Hebrides. It grows in the salt mist of Islay. Why does it fizzle on Long Island? Hello, Artisan. Don't shake my hand. I'm dirty as a peon."

"Arthur takes the idea of 'the old sod' quite literally," explained his wife. "He's had heather flown in all the way from Scotland."

"And why not?" the old man said. "It's beautiful. It's ancient." He glanced down at his watch. "Your uncanny timing continues, Artisan. Just about time for a nooner. Will you have something? Stay for lunch?"

"No, I really can't," said Artisan. He remembered the hangover that ensued the last time he started with the drinks and invitations at chez Widmore.

"A light something then. Drambuie on the rocks, perhaps?"

"Maybe just a beer," said the detective. "One."

"Ah, good. A Scottish ale. I'll join you. My dear?"

"A glass of Chardonnay." Looking at Artisan and mimicking him in that way she had, puncturing without quite giving offense, she added, "One."

The servant went to fetch the drinks. Another servant appeared with a hot towel for old man Widmore to clean his hands. She took the gloves and gardening tunic, and he sat down almost nimbly but not quite. "So," he said, "is this a purely social call?"

"Actually, no. I'm hoping to find out more of what happened right after Shannon's funeral."

"What happened?" said Arthur Widmore. "We buried the poor girl and everyone went home. What more should happen at a funeral?"

"Was there a gathering afterward? Did people come back here? Did people go to Cliff's house?"

"No, no," the old man said. "Nothing like that. It was a very small funeral. Immediate family and a handful of friends. Shannon's parents came down from Westchester, of course. They left immediately after. Everyone dispersed."

"The Widmores," Vivian added, "aren't exactly heart-on-the-sleeve type people, Mr. Artisan. You've probably picked up on that by now. When things get emotional, we tend to hide like wounded animals. We mourn alone."

"It's called dignity," said her husband. "What's the point of getting all weepy and snot-nosed and operatic?"

The drinks arrived. Arthur Widmore raised his glass of ale. If it was a toast, it was a pretty somber one.

"And Cliff?" asked the detective, after he'd sipped his foamy drink. "Did he go back to his house? Was anybody with him?"

"Clifford went back home alone," old man Widmore said. "I'm quite sure of that." Then, not impatiently but with genuine puzzlement, he added, "You're looking for Alexander, Mr. Artisan. What's it got to do with Clifford?"

The detective fudged. "I'm trying to learn about Zander's frame of mind. I'm wondering if he had words with his brother."

Sensibly, Vivian Widmore asked, "Then why not just ask Cliff directly?"

Artisan stalled for time by pulling at his ale. But, as in his troubling dreams of grotesque twins and mismatched reflections, the mirrors were doubling and warping and closing in on him. He couldn't very well tell the parents that he couldn't ask Cliff because maybe Cliff was dead, and maybe the person they believed was Cliff was really Zander. It was just a theory, after all, and like all theories, it could prove to be either true or crackpot or maybe even a little bit of each.

The detective tried a slightly different tack. "Since Zander's disappearance, has Cliff seemed different to you at all?"

Arthur Widmore put his glass down on a table. He rubbed his eyes. "Artisan, I'm an old man. I admit it. Maybe my brain isn't quite as supple as it used to be. But you're confusing me, Artisan. First you ask me about Alexander, and I can't see what it has to do with Clifford. Now you ask me about Clifford, and I can't see what it has to do with Alexander. Is there some connection you're not telling us about?"

Score one for old man Widmore, thought Paul Artisan. But he said only, "With all the stress, with everything he's taken on, I'm wondering how it's affecting Cliff. That's all."

"Clifford's fine," he said, as if by reflex, as if it were a point of honor rather than of observation. But then he paused to think it over. His flash of insight or lucky guess appeared to have taken something out of him; he suddenly seemed vague. He said to his wife, "Clifford seem different to you, darling?"

She crossed her knees and turned to Artisan. "We've hardly seen him, to tell the truth. We talk on the phone. Once in a while he stops by for a quick hello. But a meal or an evening, I can't remember the last time. He just always seems so busy."

"Busier than before?"

"Hard to say," said Arthur Widmore. "Hard to say." He sipped his ale, then frowned down at his hands. "Wish I knew why the heather does so poorly here. Sure you won't stay to lunch, Artisan? I think we've got cold lobster. Dandy with a bit of champagne."

15

He didn't stay, but for all he accomplished that afternoon, he might as well have lingered at the Widmores and enjoyed the unaccustomed luxuries of shellfish, sparkling wine, and the attention of a strangely alluring older woman. Instead, he drove to his office and searched online for anything more about the death of Shannon Widmore.

To his surprise, even the nosey New York media had written almost nothing about the passing of the young socialite; apparently the Widmore family's ability to squelch publicity ran wide and deep. *Newsday* published a terse account, saying only that Shannon Widmore had a history of depression. The *Post* ran one sleazy item that made innuendoes about decadence and drug use among the rich and powerful, but offered no suggestion of foul play. The *Times* printed a brief and dignified obituary, from which Artisan learned little more than that her maiden name had been Rogers, that she'd been educated at the Buckley School and Vassar, and that her father was a prominent surgeon from Larchmont.

Stymied, the detective sat at his desk and drummed his fingers on the places where the wood had already darkened from years of being tapped at. His mind wandered, and to his annoyance it wandered to Vivian Widmore with her mature and shapely legs crossed in her neat and classy shorts. Without question she was a lovely and engaging woman, graced with confidence and charm and what Artisan thought of as a kind of subtle power that went with ripe and patient carnal wisdom. That said, she was married and she was old enough to be his mother. Why was he so intrigued with her, and why was that intrigue tinged with wholly inappropriate desire? She had shown him her body and he could not believe the backlighting of her thin gown was an accident. Would she have come to his bed if he'd invited her? Or would she have laughed off the proposition, made some wry remark, and padded off to chaste sleep in her own room? It was the uncertainty, the *what if*, that was keeping Artisan preoccupied.

Trying to turn that preoccupation to productive use, trying to deny that what was spurring him on was simple prurient curiosity, the detective now directed his research to the wedding of Arthur and Vivian Widmore. It turned out they'd been married in St. Bart's church, the gorgeous edifice next to the Seagram Building on Park Avenue. In the rather gushy *Times* coverage, Vivian Widmore, who wore a classic Chanel suit in a rich shade of aubergine, was identified as the widow of a man named Monty Alban, deceased owner of a stone and gravel business. If hubby number one had been a mobster, the *Times* was too genteel to mention it; or maybe the Widmore family was powerful enough to disallow the mention. It would have been a nasty bit of gossip, after all.

"Fascinating subject, purgatory," Manny Weissman said, when his young friend had used the word in describing his weird, unsettling descent into the morgue, that glaring, sterile place where bodies languished while souls waited for release in a realm that seemed beyond the reach of time. "You've read your Dante, I hope?"

"Divine Comedy," said Artisan. "I read it for your course, remember?"

"I remember it was on the syllabus," said the old professor. "I long ago stopped equating that with confidence that the students actually read it."

They were following Argos down into the park. The old Labrador had sniffed out a female spaniel and was forgetting both his age and his dignity as he pinwheeled around, trying to get his nose against what would have been her private parts, if dogs *had* private parts. But they don't. All parts of a dog are public. This is one of the ways in which dogs are luckier and happier than humans.

"I read it," the detective said. "Though I can't say I remember much."

"Most of it, you wouldn't," acknowledged Manny Weissman. "The *Paradiso* is a total snooze. I mean, eternal bliss is probably a nice thing to experience, but as a subject for poetry, it stinks. Once you've made it to Heaven, what is there to talk about? As for the *Inferno,* it's got some great gruesome bits in it, but it's mainly Dante coming up with sadistic torments for all the people he didn't like. But the *Purgatorio*—that's an amazing and exciting piece of work."

They followed the dog in his winding course down toward the river. A thin blanket of clouds had moved in. Listening to Manny Weissman talk about the books he loved, that for him held the clues to truth and validation, Artisan remembered what a great lecturer he'd been, the rare electricity he'd created in the classroom.

"Purgatory," he went on. "That's where everything is up for grabs. The stakes could not be higher. There's suffering, but unlike on earth, the suffering isn't senseless and random. It has meaning and a purpose. Destinies balance on a knife edge. The slightest slip dooms you to perdition. Not just for a while. Forever. No more second chances. Purgatory *is* the second chance. The last chance. The hard road and the only road that can lead on to redemp—"

Just then Paul Artisan's cell phone started ringing.

His crescendo interrupted, his climax forestalled, Manny Weissman just shook his head.

The detective glanced at the phone's display. The area code was from the East End of Long Island. He had to take the call. He apologized with his eyes and flipped open the phone. "Artisan here."

"Paul? It's Moth. Zander's friend, remember?" The voice was pinched and quick and almost frantic, nothing like the mellow, stoned-out drawl of a couple of days before.

"Yeah, Moth, sure. What's up?"

A sharp and wheezy exhalation whistled through the phone. "I just heard from him. I'm scared. I think you're right. I think he's in trouble."

The detective had stopped walking and was filtering out the rattle of leaves, the voices of children, the hum of the city at his back. "Where'd he call from. What did he say?"

"He called from the ocean. You know, ship-to-shore. Said he was somewhere between Key West and Havana. Said he needed— *Oh shit! . . .*"

The words abruptly ceased and in their place a hell of desperately competing noises came roaring through the phone. Moth screamed as a groaning creak became a massive snap followed by a bellowing crash that gave rise in turn to aftershocks of clatter. Then there was nothing but a dead and awful silence.

"Moth? MOTH? Hello?"

Nothing.

Manny Weissman looked back at his friend. Artisan was staring numbly at the mute phone as if trying to squeeze an explanation out of it.

He said, "Something bad just happened. Something really bad, I think. I have to go out to Peconiquot."

"Now? We're talking here."

"Sorry, Manny. I really have to go."

16

It had been some days since Paul Artisan felt the need to pack his gun. Now he tucked the 9 mm into a neat holster he wore beneath a light, loose summer jacket and headed to Peconiquot.

Well before he'd driven the full length of the LIE, night had fallen and Moth's body had been found.

By the time he'd passed the vineyards of the North Fork and caught the ferry to the island, word of the tragedy had spread throughout the close-knit enclave. When Artisan reached the end of the road that led to Hap's boatyard and the bay, he found a cluster of pickup trucks and dune buggies. Men in jeans and flannel shirts milled and talked outside the perimeter of twisted yellow police tape that had been hastily slapped up. Here and there, randomly placed floodlights gave the scene a stagy and unnatural glow.

The detective walked up toward the barrier of tape. In a knot of burly locals he saw the fellow he'd first talked to on the ferry, the one who'd given him directions to this place. The ferryman saw him as well, and didn't seem at all pleased about it.

"What the hell you doing here?" he said.

Artisan took a deep breath and moved closer. In the phony

light he could tell that the ferryman's eyes were red. He'd been drinking and he'd been crying. Artisan answered the question with one of his own.

"What happened?"

The ferryman's mouth worked before any words came out, and then it seemed his voice might break at any moment. "Crushed. Cradle failed. Boat fell on him. Just smashed him all to hell." He hesitated, bit his lip. He also balled his fists. "It better not have anything to do with you."

With difficulty, the detective met his eyes. Five or six other locals had overheard their conversation. They seemed to be huddling closer together, tightening the half-circle around the outsider. They were working guys. In their pickup trucks they no doubt had things like sledgehammers and axes. Their island was dark, and heavily wooded, and something terrible had happened to one of their own. When bad things happened there was an impulse to strike back; and when bad things happened on an island, the impulse was to take vengeance on outsiders. Blaming outsiders was less unsettling than facing the possibility that the evil lurked within their very midst. Artisan was grateful for the weight of the pistol near his left armpit.

Trying not to flinch, he said, "Would I be here if it had to do with me? Don't make threats, okay?"

Uneasily, he turned his back on the group of angry men and ducked under the yellow tape. It took only a second for a flashlight beam to hit him in the face and a voice to shout out that he couldn't go there. By reflex he raised his hands and announced himself as a detective. He showed his license to a very young man in civilian clothes. The man seemed impressed and flustered that a private eye was on his island, as if it were a mark of glamour and distinction. Artisan asked to see whoever was in charge.

The young man led him into the enormous shed where Moth had worked and died, and where he still lay pinned—eyes open and arms outstretched, fingertips seeming to claw the ground—under several tons of fiberglass and teak. It would be morning before a crew would be able to lift away the wreckage of the yacht that had tumbled down on him; in the meantime there was no real way to cover up the body beneath the overhanging hull. Amid the stink of varnish and paint was a more visceral and haunting smell of the living substance that had been extruded out of Moth when his ribs and abdomen were crushed.

Closest to the body, sitting on the same stool that Moth had sat on just the other day, was a middle-aged man with short silver hair. He was wearing overalls, and Artisan was a bit surprised when the young man addressed him as chief.

He stood up politely and extended a hand. "Joe Ferrer," he said. Noting the visitor's surprise at his clothing, he added, "Police chief is a part-time job here. I'm an electrician mostly. Was swapping out a circuit box when the call came in." He motioned vaguely in the direction of the smashed boat and the sundered cradle and the dead man. "You know something about this?"

"I was on the phone with Moth when it happened. I heard him scream. I heard the crash."

The chief said, "You a friend of Moth's?"

"I met him once. We talked about a case I'm working on."

"What kind of case?"

"Missing person. I can't say more than that."

The police chief had a friendly face but now it tightened up between the eyebrows. "Don't pull that confidential shit on me. We got somebody dead here."

The detective let that pass. After a beat he said, "These cradles, what are they usually made of?"

The chief said, "The newer ones are steel. The old ones, like they got here, are made of hardwood. Oak or maple, usually. Maybe ash sometimes."

"They ever fail?"

He gestured toward the disaster that was nearly at his feet. "Seems they can, doesn't it? Though I don't believe I've heard of it happening before. Not on this island, at least."

"This one seemed just fine a couple days ago," said Artisan.

"There some point you're driving at?" said Joe Ferrer.

"I'm looking for someone Moth knew well. He had some information for me. He was passing it along at the moment he died. Maybe it was just an accident. Accidents happen. Or maybe someone didn't like that Moth was helping. Someone who doesn't want this person found."

The chief in overalls pulled at his lower lip. He seemed overwhelmed, way out of his depth, and Artisan empathized more than he would have liked to admit. Looking again at the wreckage—the sailboat with its keel askew like a dislocated limb, the broken rudder hanging by a cable—the chief said, "Goddamn cradle's nothing but splinters now. Be awfully hard to tell if it was tampered with."

Artisan shrugged. The forensics of the case were not his problem, though he had little doubt that when the county sheriff or the state police took over the matter of Moth's death, as they inevitably would from a part-time cop who was mainly an electrician, they would find evidence of sabotage. Sailboats didn't just fall on people at pregnant moments.

Apropos of nothing, the chief now said, "Moth was a funny guy. We were supposed to be enemies, I guess. You know, like in a cartoon. Me always chasing him around, him always escaping. Me the cop and him the guy that everybody knew was always smoking reefer. But I liked him, what can I say. The way a teacher likes the class clown, the troublemaker. You just felt there was something good there, something . . . I don't know . . . original maybe, trying to come out. Isn't gonna come out now, I guess."

Artisan nodded a silent amen to that but found that he had nothing more to say. He handed the chief a business card and turned to leave the shed.

Outside, beyond the yellow tape in the piercing bluish light that did not belong on a quiet island like Peconiquot, the men who'd been Moth's buddies were still gathered. They stood in shifting clusters and the detective noticed that their arms did not hang easy at their sides, but were slightly hiked up, shoulders hunched and rolled a little forward, muscles tense in rage and shock and bafflement. Maybe death was even more unsettling on an island. Maybe it seemed like an obscene visitor from the world beyond, an uncouth guest that carried not just a single tragedy but the threat of some horrible contagion.

Paul Artisan gave the men a wide berth as he walked back to his car.

Halfway down the gravel path, a large stone was thrown in his direction. It didn't hit him and it wasn't meant to. It was meant just to make him flinch, to call forth a quick shot of adrenaline. It was meant as a warning that he should not return.

Driving back to New York City, trying to parse out who might want Moth dead and why, Paul Artisan was suddenly assailed by a far more intimate notion. Somewhat belatedly, he realized that he had just lost his virginity.

He'd never worked on a case where people actually got killed.

In the course of his spying on people's infidelities and attempted frauds, he'd been spat at, slapped, kicked in the shins and in the groin, and once or twice punched in the face. In courtroom hallways he'd seen warring spouses forcibly restrained and disgruntled plaintiffs swinging at their lawyers. Those were acts of desperate, helpless violence, and sufficiently unpleasant.

But this was different. Not different in degree, but altogether different. What Manny Weissman had said about purgatory was also true of cases in which people died: Destinies were balanced on a knife edge; between life and death there was little room for error or time to recover from a stumble, and for some people, at least, there would be no more second chances.

It was also true that murder was an absolute offense. It could not be added on to. You couldn't double infinity, and you couldn't make murder more heinous by doing it twice, or twenty times. Which meant that there was no reason for someone who had killed not to kill again. If Moth was killed by someone who did not want Zander found, wasn't the next logical target the person who was looking for him?

Passing through the endless ribbon of suburbs and strip malls along the LIE, Paul Artisan tasted something metallic way back in his throat. It was fear, and no mistaking it. If it was humbling and distressing, there was also something bracing about it. Feeling fear was the beginning of finding courage. Courage *without* fear was just a macho pose, a snarling attitude, little more than practiced bravado. It was fear that gave nerve its stature, its dimension.

Feeling fear, and sensing that perhaps he'd be equal to the task of doing the right thing in the face of it, Artisan had the odd but wonderful sensation of burgeoning within his own familiar skin, becoming somehow larger as he swelled to fill in his own outline. There was pride in this new vision of bigness, a pride that he had longed to feel and had barely noticed he'd been missing.

A good feeling . . . but there was still the question of who killed Moth.

Zander had called from Key West. Or at least that's what he'd told his now dead friend. Should that be taken at face value? What if it was true that Zander was really living Cliff's life now, and in fact there *was* no second twin? The Key West story would be a convenient way of getting the detective off the track, and in a place where it might be easier to hunt him down.

On the other hand, if Cliff was Cliff and Zander really was in Florida, and really was in danger, then it was Artisan's clear duty to go down there and find him.

Was there one twin or two? Were the detective's nightmare mirrors adding or subtracting? There seemed no question that Artisan would have to go to Florida to find out.

17

Key West is a nice place to visit, but not in August.

Before Paul Artisan had even stepped through the doorway of the small plane that flew the last leg from Miami, the humidity hit him in the face like a dank and mildewed towel. Heat shimmered on the tarmac of the runway. Out over the Florida Straits, greenish clouds, knobby and lobed like cauliflowers, patiently waited to dump their next hammering and steamy shower.

The detective walked quickly though the tiny terminal. The A/C wasn't working. Instead of pushing cool air, it pushed grayish water that dribbled from the ducts and made small but treacherous puddles on the floor. Out at curbside, a short line of lethargic taxis was waiting. Some had their motors running and their windows closed, opaque with condensation. The lead cab had its windows open; the driver seemed asleep. He woke up grouchy when Artisan got in.

"Where to, bud?" he said.

"I need a hotel. Not too expensive."

"Take your pick, man. Town's empty. I been sitting an hour at the fucking airport. You on vacation?"

"No. I'm working," said Paul Artisan.

The feisty driver softened up as he realized he was talking to a fellow sufferer. "Okay. You got an excuse then. Been down here before?"

"Never."

They were driving on A1A, the ocean road. Coconut palms did a torpid little dance in the brief puffs of hot breeze. Now and then they passed fat guys in tank tops riding bicycles that were way too small for them.

"Sucks down here in summer," said the cabbie. "Hurricanes. Mosquitoes you would not believe. Mold? This is the place where mold was born. You wake up in a sweat. You take a shower. You put a T-shirt on. It's wet before your head comes through the top . . . You want ocean side or harbor?"

"Doesn't matter," the detective said. "Just so it's easy to get around."

"Everything's easy," the driver said. "Streets are dead. Thing with Key West in the summer, anybody who can afford to leave, leaves. The rich gays go up to Provincetown. The straights go to the Hamptons or the Berkshires. Who's left? The working stiffs. With a handful of unbelievably cheap tourists. This time of year they're either from Norway or from Georgia. Bubba or Sven, take your pick. It's a fifty-cent tip either way. You want a guesthouse or a big hotel?"

Artisan had a thought. "Any of the big hotels have yoga?"

"Yoga?" said the driver. He gave Artisan a probing stare in the rearview mirror. "You don't look like a yoga guy."

"I'm looking for someone," the detective said. "Someone who teaches."

The cabbie knitted his bushy brows. "You a bounty hunter, something like that?"

Paul Artisan had to laugh. "Bounty hunter? People usually ask if I'm a cop."

"Yeah? Well, this is Key West. We take things to a different level here. Usually a lower level. I'll bring you to the Strand. They got like a gazebo kinda thing out over the water. In season they have yoga, aerobics, shit like that. This time of year, who knows?"

The cabbie pulled into a driveway on the island's ocean side, in front of a three-story pink hotel. Artisan could not have said how he knew the place was practically empty; but there was something sad and uneasy about a dead hotel that you felt even from the outside. He slid out of the taxi and sucked a faceful of the turgid air.

Making it sound like an enormous favor, the desk clerk upgraded Artisan to an ocean-view room. A sleepy bellman showed him up to it on an empty elevator and through an empty hallway.

The curtains were closed and the A/C was blasting. The place was cold as the morgue and smelled slightly of rust. As soon as the bellman had left, the detective killed the fan and threw open the sliding doors to a tiny balcony. A cascade of humidity greeted him. Beyond, the ocean was flat as a lake. On a small beach where coral knobs poked up through the sand, there were two large women who seemed to have their tops off. In their case this was not a good idea. Feeling lonely, baffled, and already homesick (yes, it was absurd, he realized, but he already missed his dog and his walk in the park and his chat with Manny Weissman) the detective threw some water on his face, put on a fresh shirt that would not be fresh for long, and tried to get to work.

He went back to the lobby. There was a concierge desk but this time of year there was no concierge. He asked the front-desk person about yoga classes. Yes, they had classes out on the gazebo; it was wonderful starting the day with sun salutations out over the ocean. But no, they didn't have them in August, there just wasn't the demand. But if he wanted to do yoga there was another place he might try, more a locals' kind of place. It was called the Tea Shack. Just half a dozen blocks away. Did he want directions?

It was very late afternoon, an hour or so till sunset, when he walked out onto Key West's miniature streets. In front of clapboard houses whose shutters were painted turquoise and persimmon and mauve, huge banks of bougainvillea billowed down from porches and thick jasmine hedges poked between the slats of picket fences. Fat lizards clung to palm trunks. There were very few tourists gawking and it was easy to tell who the locals were: The men tended to be shirtless, with rosewood tans that seemed to go clear through to the sinews. The women mostly looked weathered and tough, a little like fish that been salted and dried. These were the people who didn't leave for hurricanes.

The Tea Shack turned out to be exactly that—a former warehouse on a side street, small, square, and tin-roofed, whose single room was now ringed with mirrors and paved with a new hardwood floor. A class seemed to be just winding down; Artisan stood outside the doorway and peeked in.

He was frankly envious of what he saw. The students were lying on their backs on mats, and a tall young woman, cooing softly about peace and stillness and focus on the soft *whoosh* of the breath, was padding silently among them, gently placing miniature sandbags over their eyes. *Must be nice,* he thought. Take the world away for just a little while. Blot out the light, silence the noise, smooth away the complications, and ease the dangers not by conquest but by an unashamed retreat. Standing in the heat, hearing the buzz of insects, he closed his eyes and drank in the singsong of the teacher's voice and tried to forget why he was there.

Then the class was over. People rolled their mats and found their sandals and headed for the door. Artisan watched them leave. They seemed to be a different subset of the locals from the salty, wiry ones out on the streets. These were the neo-hippies, people born too late. Artists without art forms. Dropouts without media coverage. Sweet people who'd kept their lives little and didn't seem to mind at all.

Inside, the teacher was tidying up blocks and blankets. For some moments Paul Artisan took an almost innocent pleasure in watching her move. She was wearing a lavender leotard with short blue tights beneath it. When she bent, it was with the smooth swoop of a dancer; when she straightened up, the chain of her vertebrae seemed to click in, link by link, between the muscles of her back. At length, in a mirror, she saw the stranger looking at her. With no great hurry or self-consciousness she turned to face him. "Can I help you?"

Artisan moved farther into the room. The woman he was talking to was slightly mussed but beautiful. Her brown hair was parted not quite in the middle and was damp from her exertions. She had green eyes with disconcerting flecks of yellow in them. Her shoulders were lean but very broad; her prominent collarbones strongly suggested an unstrung bow.

"I'm looking for someone," he said. "A yoga teacher. A friend of a friend."

"Oh?" The single syllable was freighted with a certain skepticism, but a skepticism tinged by humor rather than suspicion. "And what's her name?"

"That's the funny part," said Artisan. "I don't know her name."

"But she's a friend of a friend." This was not a question.

Artisan let it pass. "It's an unusual name, I think. Probably not given by the parents. Something astronomical. Sunspot? Starburst?"

The yoga teacher said, "You're a detective, aren't you? Private, I mean."

At that, Paul Artisan had to smile. He met her candid green eyes. "You know, you're the first person who's got that right all week."

"I have a certain gift," she said. "Now forget the yoga teacher with the funny name. Who is it you're really looking for?"

Artisan said, "You're the psychic. You tell me."

She could not suppress a cryptic little grin but she didn't take the bait. Instead, she said, "Sky."

"Sky?"

"There's a teacher in town named Sky."

"Can't get much more astronomical than that," conceded the detective.

"And you're looking for Zander Widmore," she said.

"Right again. I'm very impressed. And while we're on a roll, I'm guessing that your name is Sky."

"That's one for you. Two for me. But I can't guess your name."

"Paul," he said. "Paul Artisan. Will you help me find Zander?"

"I don't know yet. Will you buy me a martini?"

The detective's face took on a new expression, and the green-eyed woman with the certain gift read it perfectly.

"What?" she said. "You don't think yoga teachers like martinis?"

18

They walked over to the harbor side of town. The sun was sinking quickly through plump clouds. It would slide behind a cloud-top like a coin going down a slot; when it emerged at the bottom it was larger and redder than it had been before.

They went into a bar with a courtyard presided over by a scabby old mahogany tree. Sky ordered a Tanqueray martini—classic, nothing pink and nothing frou frou. It sounded splendid and Paul Artisan had the same. They clinked their big flared glasses, and the yoga teacher met his gaze with those disarming yellow-flecked eyes of hers. He wondered, if only for a heartbeat, if there were something intrinsically erotic about having a martini with a stranger in a city far away from home; or if it was the Key West air, freighted with a narcotic heaviness that was something like the aftermath of sex; or if it was simply that the yoga teacher was exceptionally lovely, with a posture that was at the same time completely self-possessed and unabashedly sensual.

He broke that pleasant but fruitless train of thought by munching on an olive and launching decisively into the business at hand. "I take it you've seen Zander recently?"

Sky was sipping her gin and held up a hand in a gesture like a

traffic cop. "Not so fast," she said. "I told you I haven't decided if I'll
help. You like to ask questions. I have some questions too. Like why
are you trying to find him?"

It was a simple query but the detective realized suddenly that
the answer had gotten rather complicated. "Depends who you ask,"
he said. "His brother is concerned that he's in danger. His father
seems to want a reconciliation after some big argument."

The yoga teacher's posture seemed to indicate that she wanted
more, but Artisan didn't know what else to say. He saw no point in
telling her about Moth's death or his unease about the purported
suicide of Shannon Widmore.

Sky fiddled with the toothpick that speared her olives. "That's
not exactly what I'm asking. My question is: Why are *you* trying to
find Zander?"

Paul Artisan did not quite get what he was being asked. Or
maybe he did, and the question made him nervous. With a slightly
awkward laugh, he said, "It's my job. Finding people is what I do."

"Ah," she said. "So you're doing it for money?"

His first impulse was to say, a bit defensively, that *of course* he was
doing it for money. What was wrong with that? But then a strange
thing happened. He realized that he wasn't. Not anymore. It was
very odd: People often used the highfalutin language of ideals to
mask the fact that their actions were based on purely pragmatic,
even cynical motives; here was the detective using the habit of cool
and practical detachment to mask the fact that he had fallen into
the grip of his own somewhat rusty ideals. Finding Zander had
started as a gig and now become a quest. Getting to the bottom of
the Widmore family story had taken on the urgency of a mission, a
stubborn digging toward something he could accept and understand as truth.

He looked over at the yoga teacher. She was staring at him without a single blink and he had the distinct impression that with her

special gift she had followed the strange but exhilarating progress of his thoughts; more than that—that she had led him to that progress. "No," he said. "I'm not doing it for money."

Gently, she said, "I didn't think you were . . . Next question. What will you do if you find him?"

Was it the gin or the humidity that made these very basic questions seem suddenly so problematic and so nuanced? "What will I do?" echoed the detective. "I'll tell him that his family wants to hear from him. If he's in trouble, I'll try to help."

"Will you drag him home?"

"Against his will? Of course not. I'm not a bounty hunter."

"Will you tell the family where he is?"

Artisan thought that over. "I think I probably should, don't you?"

Without hesitation, Sky said, "No. I don't."

She sipped her drink. The big glasses were almost empty. Artisan signaled for two more.

"I happen to believe," she resumed, "that people have a right to free themselves from toxic situations. What do you know about Zander? I'm guessing that most of what you *think* you know, you've heard from Cliff."

"Fair enough," said Artisan.

"Okay," the yoga teacher said. "So you think you know that Zander is a troublemaker, and drug-involved, and sometimes very spiteful, and occasionally a criminal. Yes?"

The detective only nodded.

"Well, all that happens to be true. But how did he get that way? I'll bet you didn't hear *that* from Cliff. About the lying and the manipulations that started practically when they were toddlers. Cliff stealing cookies and blaming it on Zander. Breaking windows, scribbling in their father's books, whatever. Lifting up girls' skirts, picking fights with weaker boys. It was always Cliff, but Cliff was quicker, a better talker, and Zander stood there mumbling, looking guilty, seeming to accept the idea that it must be all his fault. Why? Some mysterious guilt for being alive, for having the same genes? Eventually, Zander came to think he was as bad as his brother made him out to be."

Pecking at his second martini, more or less thinking aloud, the detective said, "So how bad *is* he? That's what I can't figure out."

With infinite forgiveness, the yoga teacher said, "Oh, he's pretty bad. I've never known him to be violent, though I couldn't swear he isn't. But I've seen him be dishonest, unfair, perverse, betraying. He certainly doesn't care about laws. At the same time, he's capable of being very good. Saintly almost. It's the yin-yang thing, isn't it? People capable of big evil are also capable of big goodness. Most people aren't capable of either. They're *blandly* good, just good enough to keep out of trouble. But if you think about it, that really isn't what goodness should be about, is it? . . . Anyway, I don't think family has a claim just because they're family. And certainly not because they happen to have a fortune. It's Zander's right to disappear. Agreed?"

A breeze rattled the mahogany leaves. Far off there was rumbling thunder, another tropical downpour on the way.

Paul Artisan said, "If I agree, do I get to ask a question?"

She sipped her drink and nodded.

"Okay. Agreed. So—is Zander in Key West?"

"Now? No."

"But he was here recently?"

"Yes. Just a few days ago."

At this the detective let out a deep breath of relief. At least now he knew that there were in fact two living twins, that he was not dealing with some especially eerie instance of identity theft.

"You saw him," Artisan said. It was not a question but it received a troubling answer.

"Well, no."

"You *didn't* see him?"

"Paul, try to understand. At times in the past, Zander and I have been extremely close. Some parts of some days I think I'm still in love with him. There's still this powerful, edgy thing between us. It's better that we don't actually see each other."

"So . . . what? You just spoke on the phone?"

"Yes. The phone. What's the problem?"

Artisan let that pass. The quiet thunder was rolling closer and there were beginning to be glimmers of muffled lightning in the sky.

"He say why he was in town?"

"Only that he was on his way to Havana to do some business."

"Havana," echoed Artisan. The word tasted exotic and illicit in his mouth, and the yoga teacher picked up on that immediately.

With a little laugh she said, "It's not a dirty word, you know. People from the mainland seem to think that Cuba is Timbuktu or the Evil Empire or something. It's a Caribbean island with great beaches and great music and hotels where Europeans go, and it happens to be ninety miles from here."

"And illegal for Americans."

"Please. Key Westers go there all the time."

"In private boats?"

"Sure. Sailboats, fishing boats, whatever. Decent powerboat, it's six, seven hours."

"So Zander would've hired someone to take him."

"Most likely."

"Know who that would have been?"

She swirled her drink and admired the oily sheen of the olive. "No. But I can tell you someone to talk to. Captain Jocko. Runs a fishing boat out of Garrison Bight. Real character. Hemingway look-alike. Considers himself the sort of unofficial dispatcher of the local fleet. He'd probably know who's been to Cuba lately."

"And back?" said Artisan.

"Excuse me?"

The detective was thinking once again of Moth's last words. The doomed man had said that Zander called from a boat between Havana and Key West. Unfortunately, he hadn't said which way the boat was facing. "Do you know if Zander's still in Cuba?"

"No idea," she said.

"And his business down there—you know what it was?"

She shook her head. "He would never tell me. I would never ask."

The detective looked down at his hands and blew some air between his lips. "Can I give you my number?" he said. "Will you call me if you hear from him?"

"You can give me the number. I'm not promising I'll call."

Handing her a card, he was suddenly depressed, weighed down by a feeling that was only too familiar: resistance to something that was difficult and only getting more so, an aversion to delving deeper into a dark and murky place. He would do what he had pledged to; he knew he would. Why then did he still, at every stage, feel so reluctant, so beset? Did it ever get easier?

Reading his thoughts one final time, the yoga teacher touched his hand. "I'm glad you're helping Zander. I know you'll do the right thing for him."

Thunder pealed directly overhead. A moment later, fat tropical raindrops starting pinging off of tin roofs and landing with sharp smacks on the leaves of the mahogany tree. The drops exploded into vapor that smelled of electricity.

"Let's go for a walk," the lovely woman said to Artisan. "You'll never feel a warmer rain in all your life."

19

They strolled through flat streets whose shallow curbs were quickly flooded; the little streams carried spent flowers whose petals twirled like small propellers.

The rain hammered down, tapered off, then roared again, bouncing off the pavement. By the time they reached Sky's cottage on a hidden lane, her leotard was pasted to her skin and wisps of hair ran down her neck. Water glistened in the hollows of her collarbones. For a moment she and Paul Artisan lingered on the streaming sidewalk that led to her front door, suspended in the eternal *what if* of a man and a woman standing close together in the dark, martinis in their bloodstreams and an evening's worth of conversation still spinning through their minds.

She gave him a quick hug. He felt the impress of her sodden bosom against his ribs; the warmth and the squeeze were withdrawn almost before they'd registered. She said good night and slipped away with supple steps.

The detective stood there, blinking up at streetlamps wreathed in yellow mist. Belatedly, he noticed the breadlike smell of the yoga teacher's hair when it had been so close to his face. Somewhere a cat screeched. He walked alone back to his empty hotel.

At seven thirty the next morning he was awakened by the ringing of his cell phone. He flipped it open and rather thickly said, "Artisan here."

The gruff yet almost shy voice on the phone said, "It's Joe Ferrer. From Peconiquot."

"Yeah, chief. What's up?"

"That cradle," he said. "The county guys came in. Decided to give it to state. The state guys lifted the boat away and dealt with what was left of Moth. They went through the cradle board by board. It was tampered with, all right. The forward support on the starboard side was practically sawed through. Thought you'd want to know."

"I appreciate your telling me," said the detective. He thought the conversation was over. He had a slight headache and he had to pee.

"But here's the thing," the electrician/police chief went on. "Even messed with like that, why did it pick that moment to fall?"

"I'm not sure I follow you."

"Ever chop down a tree, Mr. Artisan?"

"Can't say that I have."

"There's a wrong way and a right way to do it. The right way is you leave enough lumber so that you can control where and when it falls. Except it doesn't just *fall*. You push it."

"So you're saying—"

"I'm saying I think someone was in that shed with Moth. Hiding. Waiting."

There was a silence that went on plenty long enough to become awkward.

The chief went on. "I'm being straight with you, Mr. Artisan. I expect the same in return. There anything more you want to tell me?"

The detective said, "I don't know anything that would be of use to you."

Again, a pause. When he resumed, Joe Ferrer seemed to have taken on a new measure of strength and slyness; it was an old but true dynamic of the seeming yokel picking the moment to show his power and his savvy. "Mr. Artisan," he said, "I'm in a difficult position. The way we do things on this island, we like to clean up our own messes. I don't love having the state cops involved. At the same time, I don't like having private eyes hold out on me. What you and I have talked about, I'd like to keep it just between ourselves. Because if I tell the Staties about it, well, you know, they might waste a fair bit of your time. Start in with subpoenas, crap like that."

As threats went, this one was pretty cogent. Paul Artisan had his own issues with authority, and he didn't deal with cops if he could possibly avoid it. Some cops he liked, but most he found to be bullies and hypocrites. They upheld the laws, except for the ones that were inconvenient to themselves, such as the ones that protected people's privacy and allowed for client privilege and didn't assume that the government had the right to know everything just because it had the power to interrogate.

He said to the chief, "I hear you, okay? If I come up with anything helpful, I'll be in touch. I promise."

He hung up the phone and got out of bed. Not a great way to start the day—the threat of a subpoena. But there was something more fundamental gnawing at him as he threw cold water on his face and tried to settle back into his skin and get on terms again with the waking world around him: He didn't quite know where he was.

The sense of dislocation was not geographic; he knew he was in a hotel in the Florida Keys. His confusion, rather, had to do with a dizzy feeling that, in his recent island-hopping, he'd been traveling from tiny world to tiny world, and that in each new place he visited, the logic and the rules were different. He lived on the island of Manhattan. Moth had died on the island of Peconiquot. Last night he'd drunk martinis in the pouring rain on the island of Key West. Soon, perhaps, he'd be in Cuba. In this earth-size game of connect-the-dots, the dots were not markings on a page but outcrops of rock and sand where people lived their lives and blundered toward their destinies. What was called a crime in one place was not necessarily a crime in another. A tragedy here was a liberation there. One island's criminal was another island's hero. Where were the certainties and continuities of the mainland? Whose justice and which version of the truth was Paul Artisan supposed to serve?

Except for the fact that he had a fat gut and a full white beard, Captain Jocko didn't really look like Hemingway at all. His eyes were too close together; his lips were too flubbery and wide. But he seemed to feel that if he enlarged his presence by speaking in a big deep voice and keeping up a careful front of manly confidence, he could almost pass for Papa.

Paul Artisan found him at the inner harbor of Garrison Bight, where a rank of fishing boats were tied up stern-to at the dock, their tuna-towers glinting in the fierce sun. Jocko was sitting on a bench in the shade of a beach umbrella, at the center of a small group of charter captains drinking beer and eating coffee cake at 9 a.m. Seeing a potential customer, one of the captains called out, "Hey, bud, going fishing today?"

The detective said, "You might say that. I'm trying to find someone. Someone who went to Cuba the other day."

Captain Jocko sounded shocked. "Went to Cuba? From here? Isn't that illegal?"

Artisan said, "Sky said I should talk to you."

The shocked tone abruptly went away. "Ah," said the man who didn't really look like Hemingway. "The lovely Sky. How is she?"

"You nailed it. Lovely. Can we talk?"

Captain Jocko turned just slightly left and right; his companions drifted off. Artisan sidled into the shade of the umbrella.

"So," the big man said. "You want to find someone. Sometimes people would rather not be found. Key West is full of folks like that. Who you snooping for? Customs? Narcs?"

"I'm private. Working for a family with a missing son."

"Very touching. Why should I believe you?"

"Probably you shouldn't. But it's true."

"Want some cake?" said Captain Jocko. He nudged it along the bench toward Artisan with a finger that was none too clean.

"No thanks. I want some information."

Jocko sipped some beer and blinked off toward the milky green water. "I remember reading somewhere once that in the modern world information is the only real commodity."

"I'll buy some then. What's it cost?"

The bearded man declined to name a number. He said, "Man, business is really slow here in the summer."

Paul Artisan reached into his pocket and came up with a hundred bucks of Cliff Widmore's money. He handed it to Jocko.

Jocko looked at the bill a little sorrowfully, and said, "Customers or not, you still gotta keep the boat gassed up. Diesel's gotten fucking crazy."

The detective handed over a second hundred. Jocko tucked the money deep into his shorts. Not into a pocket; way down toward his crotch. Then he said, "A colleague of mine visited the fair city of Havana two, three days ago. I believe he might have had a passenger. You can find him two docks down, last slip on the left. His name's Crunch and his boat's called *Fish Lips.* He looks a little scary and he sounds a little mental, but don't worry. Once you get past the scars and the tattoos he's a very reliable guy. And don't worry about the spear-guns all over. Everybody needs a hobby, right?"

Artisan had nothing to say to that. Reluctantly, he abandoned the shade of Jocko's beach umbrella and emerged into the punishing sun. He walked the docks, stepping over tarry lines and now and then dodging men who were discarding reeking tubs of unused bait, until he found the *Fish Lips,* a thirty-eight-foot Hatteras that looked seaworthy enough if not exactly tidy. In its cockpit was a short but thickly muscled man, shirtless, who was tattooed in a sort of paisley pattern from the nape of his neck to at least the waistband of his fraying shorts. He was swabbing down his deck with soapy water, arms and shoulders bulging with each push of the mop, and when the water ran out of the scuppers it was red with blood.

The detective had a fleeting and cowardly impulse to turn around and go the hell back home.

Instead, he shaded his eyes and called out, "'Scuse me. You Crunch?"

The painted man stopped swabbing but didn't answer right away. It seemed he had a long habit of carefully considering what he would admit and what he wouldn't.

Artisan added, "Jocko sent me down."

Crunch gave a kind of grunt. "So what can I do for you?" From the tone, it seemed like the choices might be break your leg or wring your neck.

The detective hesitated. Even in Key West, it didn't seem politic to stand in a public place and shout about running visitors to Cuba. "Can I come aboard?"

The tattooed man said, "If you don't mind gore on your sneakers."

Artisan stepped onto the boat. Sure enough, the deck was tacky with some unspeakable mixture of lymph and detergent and blood that had toughened into half-coagulated strands.

By way of explanation, Crunch said, "Caught a bull shark yesterday. Sonofabitch was just a bag of muscle and blood. Mean too. Jaws still going with a bullet in its brain. But I don't think you're here for the fishing."

Artisan said, "I'm looking for someone who went to Havana the other day. I think maybe you brought him."

Crunch said nothing to that and went back to his swabbing. Artisan noticed the places where his tattoos were interrupted by raised pink scars from fishhooks or spears or knives.

"Guy around thirty-five, thirty-seven," the detective went on. "Sandy hair, blue eyes, trim build."

The tattooed man said, "How much did you slip to Jocko?"

"Two hundred."

"I'll take the same for now. Just put it on that little shelf under the compass."

Artisan did as he was told. It was a small investment to finally confirm that the second twin did in fact exist.

Crunch said, "Yeah, I took someone. Coulda been around that age. Sandy hair, no. This guy was bald or shaved. Wore a do-rag kind of thing."

Frustration made the detective squeeze the bridge of his nose and press hard on his sinuses. "The eyes, then. Really dark blue eyes, almost purple."

The muscular man stopped swabbing. "I'm a live-and-let-live kind of person, okay? But I don't look that close at guys, if you catch my drift."

Feeling certainty drift away once more, Artisan said, "His name's Zander Widmore."

Crunch said, "Have you noticed that I haven't asked *your* name? I wouldn't have asked his either. It's better that way, for everyone."

The detective squinted against the searing sun and tried to regroup. "Okay, you brought this guy to Havana. Did you bring him back here?"

"No."

"So he's still down there?"

"I didn't say that. I just said I didn't bring him back. I have no idea where he is."

"He say anything about why he was going?"

"I wouldn't've listened if he did." He finished up his swabbing and dumped his bucket of soapy water overboard. Then he smiled. It was a small smile, and quickly erased, but on the face of this menacing little man it was as surprising as if a pit bull had meowed. He said, "There's just one funny thing that I remember. He said, 'Get me there in time for breakfast at the Floridita.'"

Artisan said, "Sorry, I don't get why that's funny."

Crunch went back to his accustomed scowl. No one liked to explain a joke. Grudgingly, he said, "The Floridita's like the fanciest place they got down there. Famous bar and restaurant. Everybody knows they don't serve breakfast."

The detective thought that over. He said, "How much to bring me down there?"

Without hesitation, Crunch said, "Five hundred one way. Twelve-fifty round-trip."

The arithmetic made no sense to Paul Artisan, and he said so.

"Makes lots of sense to me," said the man with the tattoos.

"Unless your ass wants to rot down there in Cuba. When you want to go?"

Artisan said, "Today? Tonight?"

Crunch said, "I can do that."

The detective said, "In time for breakfast tomorrow at the Floridita."

20

"**T**he fellow you were on the phone with?" said Manny Weissman, when Artisan called him later that day. "He made the paper. Not the *Times. Newsday.* Said foul play is suspected. If it's true, it would be the first murder on Peconiquot in forty-seven years."

"Nice to be a part of history, huh?"

There was a pause, and the detective could imagine his friend plucking at the crease of his trousers or fussing with a button on his shirt. "Paul, I don't want to sound like an old Jewish mother, okay, but I'm getting a little worried."

The detective leaned over on his tiny balcony and looked out at the ocean, the unmarked road that led to Cuba. "You are a Jewish mother, Manny. Everybody should have one. And frankly, I'm a little worried too. That's life. How's Argos?"

"Fine. A little sluggish. Like he gets. It's muggy up here again."

There was another hesitation, which was rare in conversation between the two old friends. But neither wanted to speak his fears and neither could quite leave them behind. Weissman tried his best to change the subject. "You ever read a book called *Trent's Last Case?*"

"Sounds like a private-eye thing," said the private eye.

"It is."

"Manny, why would I read crap like that? Busman's holiday. Besides, I don't like the sound of this 'last case' stuff."

"He doesn't die," said the old professor, "he retires. And for my money, it's the most elegant mystery ever written. Way better than Sherlock Holmes or *Turn of the Screw*. Beautifully detailed. Perfectly logical. Deduction follows deduction, and you head for a completely satisfying solution to the crime."

"Sounds pretty standard to me," said Artisan.

"Yes, but here's what makes it special. You're hurtling toward the solution—and you realize you've still got half the book to go. You think, wait a second, this can't be. Turns out that, halfway through the book, the thing is solved with airtight reasoning—but the solution happens to be wrong. You see? The clues are all in place. The logic is fine. The deductions are sound—they just don't happen to match reality. Turns out there are *other* inferences, other deductions, that are equally correct. So the second half of the book *undoes* the first half, puts the pieces back together, and solves the crime even more brilliantly. It's a masterpiece."

Paul Artisan looked down at the water and at the beach where the brave though unattractive women were once again sunbathing topless. Feeling rather grumpy, he said, "Manny, from my perspective, that kind of sucks. You do the legwork, you figure things out—and then you've got to do it all over again?"

"Life is complicated. That's the point. It isn't like a string of numbers, you add them up, there's only one solution. Any number of possible outcomes can emerge from a single set of facts."

There was a pause, in which Manny Weissman grew painfully aware of his friend's preoccupation and of the distance between them—in miles, in age, in what they still had to accomplish in life, what they still had left to prove.

"But I'm just making chit chat," he resumed. "Trying to keep you on the phone. . . . Paul, listen, watch yourself down there, okay? Anything happens, find a way to call me. If there's a problem, you need bail, a lawyer, anything like that, I've got a little money put away—"

"Manny, please, it's just a ninety-mile trip, people do it all the time—"

"I know, I know. But I'm entitled to be worried."

"Okay, Mom. I'll call you when I'm back."

At 7:30 p.m., as instructed, Paul Artisan was back at Garrison Bight.

On board the *Fish Lips,* Crunch was rigging heavy-duty fishing poles, the kind used for sailfish and tarpon, and setting artificial baits on outriggers.

Trying to sound hearty, the detective said, "We gonna do some fishing?"

"Won't be time. Doesn't hurt to look like we are, though. Give the Marine Patrol a reason to ignore us. D'ya bring the money?"

Trying to sound firm, the detective said, "Five hundred now. The rest when we return."

Crunch shook his head. It seemed not to want to move much on top of his massive neck. "That isn't how it works. I got overhead. You'll see. Payment in advance."

Artisan thought of arguing but quickly decided not to bother. He knew that he would lose the argument. He knew that he'd lose *every* argument because Crunch worked by the law of the sea, and the law of the sea dictated that the guy who ran the boat always had the final say. It was harsh but it was clear, and there was relief in the clarity. There was relief, too, in surrender. The detective was putting his fate into the hands of a tattooed stranger who could shoot him with a speargun or stab him with a filleting knife and dump his body in the ocean and probably get

away with it. Living life meant taking chances. He handed over
the money.

Crunch made a point of not counting it, just stuffed it into the
pocket of his jeans. "Trust, you see? I'll bring you back. Trust me."

Since he had no other choice, Artisan decided that he did.

They pulled out of the slip. By the time they made it through
the cut at Fleming Key and out into the main part of the harbor,
one of those famous Key West sunsets was in progress. The water
was orange but with each moment it tended more toward copper—the amazing copper of new roofs. In the west, puffy clouds
went from pink to mauve; above them there was a swath of
improbable green in the open sky, and higher than that the jewel-
box blue of evening was already taking over. Sailboats meandered
here and there; the last of the snorkel cruises labored back from
the reef. They passed the enclave of scraggly liveaboards who
moored off of Christmas Tree Island, and soon were out in open
ocean.

An odd thing happened to Crunch once they'd left the land
behind; he grew relaxed, expansive, almost friendly. Like a bird
that was jittery and awkward on the ground but confident and
graceful in the air, he dropped his guard when he was in his native
element. He said to Paul Artisan, "You spent much time on the
water?"

The detective admitted that he hadn't.

"Best fuckin' life there is, man." He gestured out toward the
boundless horizon, where the last of the daylight seemed to be riding a slow wave toward the end of the world. "Look at that. Not a
fuckin' wall, not a fuckin' fence, no boundaries, no limits, there's
no place you can't go. That's freedom."

He reached down into a cooler behind the steering station and
came up with two beers. He popped one and gave the other to his
passenger. When he'd taken the first cold sip, he went on.

"I hear these politicians yammering about freedom on the news, I laugh my ass off. What the fuck are they talking about? Freedom to do what? To go to your job and sit in a cubicle? To buy a bigger TV set? To work your ass off to pay your mortgage? That's freedom? Oh, that's just grand. Thank you very much."

The boat plowed through the sea, gently rocking to a rhythm of wavelets that now could no longer be seen. The first stars emerged. Up ahead a lone light blinked.

Following his own train of thought, Crunch said, "Or take trade. That's another one that cracks me up. Free trade this, fair trade that. Trade is good, right? Except when it's with someone the government doesn't want you to trade with. Then it's smuggling. You know what it's like? Take a man and a woman. They're fucking. If they happen to be married, they're making love. If they aren't married, they're fornicating. But excuse me, it's the exact same activity either way, right?"

Artisan sipped his beer. He wasn't sure it mattered a damn if he spoke or if he didn't. But he said, "This boat big enough, fast enough for smuggling?"

"I don't smuggle, okay? Sometimes I trade. If someone wants to call it something else, they can. But yeah, a boat like this is perfect. Holds a lot of, say, cigars. Or square grouper."

"Square grouper?"

"Marijuana bales. They call 'em square grouper because they usually come in on fishing boats. But, you know, I deliver goods where they're wanted most. Like UPS. Auto parts wanted in Havana; fine, I bring 'em. Cuban rum wanted in Fort Lauderdale; no problem. Trade. Builds friendships and prosperity, right?"

The single blinking beacon had now resolved itself into a lighthouse, a sort of mini–Eiffel Tower in the middle of the sea.

"There's the reef," said Crunch. "Beyond it, we'll hit the Gulf Stream pretty soon. Gets a little rough. You get seasick much?"

"I don't really know," Paul Artisan admitted.

"Best thing," said his new buddy, "is if you can go to sleep. There's a settee down below. If you think you're gonna lose it, try to make it up on deck, okay?"

The raising of the subject was enough to give Paul Artisan the early signs of queasiness. But as he was heading below, he had a thought. "The guy you brought the other night—he also into trade?"

Firmly but without his land-side menace, Crunch said, "I don't talk about other clients. When you're gone, I won't say a word about you. You'll thank me for it someday."

21

To his surprise, Paul Artisan fell fast asleep. The placid ripples of the Florida Straits hypnotized him, and when the *Fish Lips* reached the deeper, wilder roll of the Gulf Stream, he felt that the cushion he was lying on had become a living thing and was rising up to meet him, to nudge his hip or rub his shoulder. He dreamed of sex and roller coasters.

Later, in what seemed the trailing edge of night, he awoke. The engine sound had changed; the motion had stalled. He heard the splash of another hull close by, and voices in a mix of Spanish and English. Then Crunch came down the companionway stairs. In the dimness, Artisan saw him open a compartment in the bulkhead and take out what seemed to be a case of booze. Seeing that his passenger was awake, he nodded toward the case and said, "Overhead, see? Good for international relations. A little cheer for the Cuban Navy and we're inside the three-mile limit. Next stop, Hemingway Marina."

The detective waited until the boat had gathered speed again and then came up on deck. Off to the east, the first hints of daybreak were peeking under the blanket of night. Ahead, the coast of Cuba was a tangle of mangroves and casuarinas. The time-frozen monuments of old Havana, the seawall and the battlements, were bracketed by new resorts destined to bring the fabled town into the world of Wi-Fi and McNuggets. But for now, at dawn, it still had the mystery of something like a casbah, a place where things could happen.

Crunch maneuvered smoothly past the breakwater and into the marina. Paul Artisan had expected . . . what? Crudely painted rowboats? Broken-down old tubs? No, there was wealth everywhere these days. Enough for cabin cruisers and catamarans and speedboats. Who owned them? Where did their money come from? Why assume it was illicit, that wealth could only be compiled here on stacks of dirty secrets?

Crunch tied up at a transient slip, then went below to fetch two more bottles of Johnnie Walker. Raising his left hand, he said, "Customs." Raising the right, he said, "Immigration. Saves a lot of paperwork. Be right back."

He returned in minutes with mugs of the thickest coffee Artisan had ever seen. Sipping it, he sensed that the caffeine and the sugar were in a footrace toward his brain, setting nerve-ends on fire as they went charging past. The sun came up. Not till its first rays hit him did the detective realize he'd been cold. He gave a single shiver. It might have been the residual chill of a night at sea or it might have been a tick of fear, a too-familiar impulse to shirk, a quickly erased fantasy of cutting and running.

He left the boat, stepped onto Cuba, and found a taxi that would take him to the Floridita.

Latin places, first and foremost, are places of the night.

They are most themselves in the hours after siesta, when the light is turning golden and the heavy air is languorous, and the women reemerge with their black hair freshly brushed and their eyes made up for sideways glances, and the men put on their open-

collared shirts and snuggest pants for strutting. The day sheds
its heat like a release from fever, and lights come on, and music
arises as if from nowhere, and the streets wriggle and squirm in a
dance that undulates between seeming chaos and a sort of loose
perfection.

But there is a counterpoint to the manic nights of Latin places,
and that is the sublime, extended quiet of their mornings. Driving
into central Havana in a taxi that was a 1957 Chevy, Artisan cruised
through silent streets where long shadows dragged fingers over
pastel stucco. Shutters closed like eyelids on buildings graced with
faded murals. Cats slunk, savoring the silence; here and there
people slept undisturbed in doorways.

Even Calle Obispo, where the Floridita was, was empty except
for the very occasional passing Buick or rusting Oldsmobile or two-
toned Dodge.

The detective walked up to the restaurant. Its big front window
was dark and there was a curtain pulled down over the glass panel
of the locked front door. He knocked. Nothing happened. He
knocked again, quite loudly.

The door opened a crack. A small man, a waiter, certainly less
than five feet tall, stood there in a short and starched white jacket
that reminded Artisan of something a chimp might wear on a comedy show. "We are closed, señor," he said. "Open eleven. There is a
sign."

"I have a meeting here," ventured Artisan.

The little man seemed dubious. "And who is this meeting with,
señor?"

The detective had no idea, of course. Instead, he said, "I was
sent by Zander Widmore."

If the name meant anything to the small fellow, it didn't show.
He said, "You wait one minute please."

He closed the door and locked it. Paul Artisan felt hot sun on his back. There was nothing gradual about the heat here. Once the sun cleared the treetops it was full and blazing day.

The little man in the monkey outfit returned. He ushered Artisan through the empty bar. The bar featured portraits of Hemingway and of bullfighters, and the detective would not have been surprised to see a woman dance by in a big hat festooned with fruit.

They went into the dining room. It too was empty except for one table made up with exquisite linen and old but sparkling glassware. The table was set for six but only one person was sitting at it. He was a dashing man in an elegant mint-green guayabera. His hair was jet black with flecks of wiry gray at the temples. His eyebrows and his mustache were combed and gleaming. Although he was alone at the table, he was flanked by two men who sat on bar stools just behind his shoulders. One of the bodyguards was white, one was black, both were very large. There was something classic, ancient, in the way the three bodies seemed to form a pyramid.

The seated man looked up from a beautiful plate of mango and papaya. In a soft but deep voice he said, "So, you are him."

Artisan said nothing.

With a suavely minimal lift of an eyebrow, the man signaled the waiter to pull back a chair so that the visitor might sit. The detective kept to the edge of the seat. "Coffee?" said his host.

"Thank you," said Paul Artisan.

The other man said, "I was not expecting you so soon. I compliment Mr. Widmore on his promptness. But of course you Americans are known for your efficiency."

The waiter brought the coffee. Artisan stalled by sipping it. If his table-mate was a criminal, he certainly was a polished one. His manners were courtly, his English was beautiful, heightened by just a touch of Spanish lilt.

With entire pleasantness, he now said, "You have brought what was discussed?"

The detective put his cup down and cleared his throat. He'd meant to do it very softly but the sound seemed harsh and ugly in the empty dining room. Straining to steady his voice, he said, "And what would that have been?"

"Excuse me?" said the suave man. It was all he said, and he said it quietly, but the bodyguards seemed perfectly attuned even to his slightest nuance. In response to the simple syllables, they seemed to puff up and lean forward on their stools, producing an effect like that of overhanging boulders.

Artisan breathed deep against a pinching tightness in his chest. He said, "Maybe we should start over."

The other man dabbed his lips on his napkin. "Yes. Perhaps we should. So who the hell are you and why are you here?"

Artisan told him. When he got to the part about the Widmore family fearing that Zander was in danger, the other broke into a hint of a sour smile.

"And you think the danger is from *me*? From *us*?"

"I didn't say that," said Paul Artisan. "That's what I'm trying to find out."

But his host was not to be deflected. He made a gesture that seemed to take in not only his bodyguards, not only the dining room of the Floridita, but the entire island of Cuba. "A rich American is in danger. *Of course* the threat must come from those Commies in the south. Their skins are a shade darker than ours. Their hair is shiny. Their leader is annoying . . . If you were *Cubano*, Mr. Artisan, you would see it quite differently. Danger does not come up from the south. It comes down from the north. Here we have known that for a long, long time."

Artisan settled farther back in his chair. Something odd had happened to him. He'd gone deep into his fear of being alone and helpless in this foreign place and had come to a state that was almost calm. He said, "Look, I didn't come here to talk politics. I have a job to do. A responsibility. I think that's something you understand."

The other man pushed away his plate of gorgeous fruit and slowly folded his hands. "A fine sentiment, Mr. Artisan. Bravo. But if your job is getting information from me, then I'm afraid that you will fail. Why would I help you? Mr. Widmore is a very valued associate of ours. Who are you? You are no one."

The detective soldiered on. "Zander Widmore met with you a few days ago."

"That much you have learned. Be content with it."

"What about? Why was he in Cuba?"

"Mr. Artisan, you are beginning to try my patience. That is not a good thing to do."

"Is he still here? Or where did he go when he left the island?"

The suave man in the mint-green guayabera didn't seem to move a muscle, but he must have gestured somehow, because suddenly the bodyguards were on their feet. They'd risen perfectly in sync, unlikely dancers, and they stood there with a mild but implacable readiness that was as disconcerting as any cruder threat. Their boss said, "I assume you've come by boat, Mr. Artisan?"

The detective said nothing.

"My men will bring you back to the marina."

Artisan looked up at the bodyguards. His fear returned at the thought of being captive in a vehicle with these two men in a country that they knew and he did not. He said, "That's okay. I'll get a taxi."

The other man said with finality, "My men will take you, Mr. Artisan. It is necessary that we see you leave our island."

22

Crunch was impressed when he saw his passenger emerge from the old but immaculately tended Cadillac, a flunky holding open the back door for him.

"Leave in a taxi," he said. "Come back in a limo. I guess your meeting went well."

"Not really," the detective said. "Let's get out of here."

"Don'tcha wanna have some lunch, see a little of the island?"

Hiding his hand with his body, he jerked a thumb toward the end of the dock where he knew the two goons in the Cadillac were still waiting. "We have to go," he said.

"Short fuckin' visit," said Crunch, though he'd gotten it by then. He started up the engine, cast off the dock lines, and headed north again.

They were back in Key West by late afternoon. Paul Artisan found it a little bit unsettling to realize it was easier to slip into U.S. waters in broad daylight than it had been to sneak into Cuba in the middle of the night.

He walked back to the empty pink hotel, gathered up his few things, and headed to the airport. It being August, there weren't many flights; then again, there weren't many passengers. He was able to book a seat on the next plane out, leaving in an hour and a half.

An hour and a half was way more time than he needed to think over what he'd learned in Florida and in Cuba. He went to the airport bar and ordered a beer; he'd come to the end of his accomplishments before the foam had died. He'd established that there really was a missing Zander—or at least it seemed there was. This was big. If there really was a missing Zander, then Cliff was really Cliff—and this, at least, suggested that the universe was still obeying its own rules, rules commanding that each person had one life to live and even twins had their unique existences, that people did not halve or double on a whim.

On the other hand, he still didn't know where Zander was. He didn't know what his business had been in Cuba. He didn't know who murdered Moth or why.

The list of things he didn't know seemed not to have an end, and the weight of all of it made him tired. Strangely, it also made him lonely, as if understanding itself were the best companion, and that, deprived of understanding, one could not help but feel isolated, alien, and vaguely paranoid. Moving through the world with an unsolved puzzle on one's mind was like walking down an alley full of looming shadows.

It was midnight when, two flights and a cab ride later, he finally made it home to his walk-up on Eighty-fourth Street on the very different island of Manhattan. He was exhausted, and gloomy, and really wished that he could pet his dog.

But sleep is an amazing healer, and in the morning he was refreshed and alert and almost optimistic. He had a quick shower and a cup of coffee, and he went down to the park to surprise Manny Weissman and the chocolate Lab they shared.

He saw his old professor before Weissman spotted him. It would grow to be a stifling day, but the sun was not yet high enough to top the buildings and spill into the hollow of the park, so Manny was wearing his cardigan. Below his baggy trousers, his heels turned slightly inward in his sneakers. He called them walking shoes, but they were sneakers, and Artisan felt an almost unbearable tenderness for this small detail: an old man trying to keep up and be comfortable in a world that would not stay still.

Argos was peeing on a bush, teetering as he strained to keep his leg uplifted.

Artisan called to him. The dog jogged over, nudged his head between the detective's knees, and wagged his tail. It was hard to say where the wag started or stopped; the old Lab's whole backbone undulated in a lazy sine wave.

Weissman turned. Artisan wanted to hug him. They shook hands.

"You're back," the old man said. "Good trip?"

"No. But I'm back. For a good long while, I hope. I've been sticking you with Argos way too much."

"Do I mind?"

"*I* mind, Manny," the detective said. "I miss my little life." With fresh appreciation, he glanced around the swath of park in front of him. In truth it was nothing very special. Its grass was patchy and its trees were undistinguished. What made it precious was that he saw it nearly every day. "Didn't think I would, or not so soon at least, but I do."

" 'The wise man stays at home,' " the old professor said. "That's from Emerson. Lot of truth in it."

"Not according to your hero Odysseus."

"Oh," said Weissman, "Odysseus came to see the wisdom of it. It's just that it took him twenty—"

Artisan's cell phone started ringing. He used to like it when that happened. It usually meant that some safe and easy work was com-

ing his way; he'd make a thousand, fifteen hundred bucks and feel
busy for a little while. But in recent days a ringing phone had come
to carry with it a hint of dread that registered in the pit of his stomach before it traveled to his brain. Unconsciously bracing, he
flipped open the phone and said hello.

"Paul? It's Sky. From Key West."

As if there could be any other, the detective thought. But the lovely
yoga teacher did not sound good at all. "Nice to hear your voice.
What's up?"

There was a hesitation, an awkward beat that was not in keeping
with Sky's poise and grace and balance. At last she said, "A boat
blew up last night. A fishing boat. In Garrison Bight. It's in this
morning's paper."

Artisan reached up and rubbed his forehead. Bleakly, he
said, "You're the psychic, but I bet I know what boat it was. The
Fish Lips?"

"That was it."

"Anyone on board?"

"The skipper. A man named James Hennessey. Went by the
name of Crunch. He lived on the boat. He was killed."

"Christ."

The yoga teacher said, "Boats blow up sometimes. Usually it's
propane stoves."

"And usually it's weekend boaters who don't know what they're
doing."

"The cops are calling it an accident for now. They've asked to
hear from anyone with information. I'm guessing you'd rather
not get involved."

"That's an excellent guess," said Artisan.

There was a pause. The detective thought of Crunch, the way
he changed, absorbed contentment, from the open grandeur of
the ocean. But life was for those with warm blood coursing in their

veins, and in the next heartbeat he caught himself wondering if Sky had already taught a class that morning, if her leotard would be just slightly damp from exercise, her hair just barely frizzed with moisture against the nape of her neck.

She said, "I take it you didn't find Zander."

"No, but I found the man he was down there to see. Very impressive. Could've been the Godfather, or a counter-revolutionary warlord, or the Minister of Justice. I couldn't read him at all."

"Paul . . ."

"Yeah?"

"I had a crazy thought this morning. I don't know why I thought it and I don't know why I'm saying it, and maybe it's a terrible thing to talk about when someone's just been killed. But when I heard about this poor guy on the boat, alive one second and dead the next, I sort of wished I'd made love with you the other night."

"I sort of wish that too. I also wished it then."

"Things go too fast sometimes. But so does life. That walk in the rain—it was wonderful, wasn't it?"

"Yeah, it was wonderful."

"You be careful, okay?"

"Okay. Thanks. Stay in touch, okay?"

He closed the phone, looked off toward the river, and let out a long slow breath.

Manny Weissman said, "You want to talk?"

Artisan said, "Jesus. Where to start? The guy who took me to Cuba just got killed, and a beautiful woman I met in Key West now tells me she wishes she'd taken me to bed."

Unflappably, the old professor said, "Eros and Thanatos. Love and death. Another pair of mirror-images for you. Death seems to make people amorous—have you noticed? Why? Seems morbid at first, but I don't think it is. Love's the closest thing to an antidote for mortality. Or maybe it's just the DNA screaming to be passed along while there's still time."

The detective had no reply to his friend's musings, and even Manny Weissman's thoughts seemed really to be elsewhere. The two men watched as the old dog salvaged a hairless tennis ball from the tangled base of a forsythia.

In a very different voice, the old professor said, "Paul, I know I urged you to stick with this job. And maybe I was wrong. You're allowed to walk away, you know."

Artisan didn't answer and for a few moments he looked away. Then he met his friend's gaze squarely. "Manny, do you remember a talk we had, oh, in eighty-nine probably, in your office, when I was deciding to leave school?"

Almost bashfully, Manny Weissman nodded. "I remember."

"I remember too. I remember word for word. You said there was a kind of truth that could be found in books, and a kind of truth that could be found in deeds. And that if a person, deep down, had a yearning for the kind of truth that came from deeds, then he would never be completely satisfied with the truths that came from books. Do I have that right?"

Weissman didn't have to answer.

"That's why I can't walk away from this. I wish I could, believe me. This woman in Key West? She made me realize this isn't just a job. I'm not doing it for money. But you know what else? I'm not doing it for this crazy messed-up family either. I'm doing it for me. I'm looking for something, digging for something, and I don't even know what it is . . . I gotta get to the office. I'll take Argos to my place later. That okay?"

***

23

Paul Artisan's dusty premises had never seemed dustier, or punier.

He paced from the anteroom to his desk, around his desk to the grimy window. The airshaft view—brick and steel and blankly reflecting glass seeming to lean in from all sides—made him feel even more confined than just sitting in his chair. Where were the wide ocean vistas in which a person could hope to clear his head? Where was the broad horizon where the eye could rest and hope to find some balance and some peace?

Already in a feisty mood, he picked up the phone and called Cliff Widmore's office. A secretary answered. He asked to speak to Mr. Widmore. Could she tell him who was calling? The detective gave his name. The secretary vanished from the line, then came back and told him Mr. Widmore was in a meeting.

It was the most familiar brush-off in the world, but today it made Paul Artisan angry. He was just the hired help; Cliff Widmore was the client and the boss—fair enough. But people were dying and truths were being buried, and these were things from which a person couldn't hide behind a secretary. Artisan said, "How long will he be in his meeting?"

"I really couldn't say, sir."

"It's urgent that I speak with him today. Please tell him that I'll be at his office in half an hour. I'll wait as long as necessary."

The secretary sighed and asked him to hold on a moment.

Cliff Widmore soon got on the line. He sounded harried and charming in equal measure, and for some reason that Artisan could not identify, the mixture grated on him. "Artisan? How's it going? Making progress, I hope? Listen, I've got an absolutely hellacious day. How about we talk tomorrow?"

The detective said, "You've heard about Moth?"

Absently, Widmore said, "Yeah. I saw it in the paper. It's a shame."

Artisan said, "The man was killed, Cliff. And you're telling me *tomorrow?*"

The client seemed surprised at the detective's vehemence. Paul Artisan was a bit surprised by it himself.

Trying to keep things affable, Widmore said, "Hey, aren't you the laid-back guy who goes to work in tennis clothes?"

"Not anymore. Not when people start getting murdered all around me."

Perhaps not sounding quite as surprised as he might have been, Cliff said, "People, plural? Are you telling me there's more than one?"

"I was in Havana . . . Jesus, it was only yesterday. The guy who took me, his boat blew up last night. We have to talk, Cliff. Today."

"Shit," said Widmore. "I've got a board meeting at ten."

"You told me your father's still chairman, right? He'll be there too?"

With grudging resignation, the heir said, "Yeah, he'll be here."

"Good. I'd like to talk to both of you. What time is the meeting over?"

"You're being a pain the ass, Artisan."

"Sorry. What time is the meeting over?"

Cliff Widmore had said eleven thirty, but at ten till twelve the detective was still waiting in the CEO's big office. He'd been made comfortable enough, with Pellegrino and glossy magazines and a view that was almost oceanic in its scale—except that waiting was never comfortable.

When the father and son finally appeared outside the office doorway, they were bickering. Or rather, the father was bickering and the son was humoring him in a way that would have seemed quite obvious to anyone other than the old man himself.

"You ask me," Arthur Widmore was saying, "the board's getting too damn democratic. Everyone has an opinion. Everyone's full of advice."

"Dad, that's why we have a board."

"Then why do we have a chairman?" the father countered. "I'll tell you why. Because, at the end of the day, someone has to be in charge. This dirty word, *hierarchy*. What's wrong with it? Someone has to be accountable, and you can't ask someone to be accountable while denying him the right to do things as he sees fit. The Old Laws, in their wisdom, recognized that."

"Dad, those laws might have worked in feudal Scotland—"

"Damn right, they worked! And that new fellow from Hanso—Mudworm or whatever his name is—"

"Mittelwerk," his son corrected him.

"Whatever. I don't trust him. I think he's sneaky. I much preferred having Alvar on the board. Alvar is a gentleman."

"Really?" said Cliff. "What makes him a gentleman? The fact that you made a ton of money together? If that's the definition, I think Mittelwerk's a gentleman. He's got ideas, ambition—"

"Everything but morals," the old man interrupted. "Everything except a conscience."

"And who's Alvar?" said Cliff. "Jiminy Cricket? . . . But look, we have a visitor."

Paul Artisan rose from the settee, and for a pathetic moment Arthur Widmore looked at him as though they'd never met before. In that same moment, the detective's vague mistrust and growing ambivalence toward his client sharpened into something close to active dislike. Why was he so condescending to his father, and why didn't he help the old man out? It would have been so easy to say, "You remember Artisan, Dad."

But he didn't say it, and the old man stood there trying not to look like he was tottering above a precipice of confusion and embarrassment. He was wearing a solid dark suit with a vest and bow tie of tartan plaid; the outfit was just on the cusp between natty and absurd. His silver hair was perfect but his eyes were slightly dull and his neck was loose and stringy where it protruded from his collar.

After a few seconds that seemed very long, Artisan stepped forward, hand extended, and reintroduced himself.

A neuron fired, and relief that he couldn't quite hide spread across the old man's face. "Of course, of course. The detective. Sorry, I still had that completely pointless meeting on my mind. Nice to see you again. Have you found Alexander?"

"Actually, no," said Artisan. "It's turning out to be pretty complicated. That's why I wanted to talk to you both."

Motioning for everyone to sit, Cliff Widmore said, "What, you need more money?"

"I'm not here about money, Cliff. If I need more I'll let you know." To the old man, he said, "Mr. Widmore, you've heard about Moth?"

"Moth?"

"Keith Baker, Dad. Zander's hippie buddy from Peconiquot."

"Ah. Interesting fellow. Strong opinions."

Cliff Widmore made a dismissive gesture.

"You've heard about his death," said Artisan. It was not a question.

"His death? He's dead?"

"Sorry, Mr. Widmore. I thought you knew."

The old man became exasperated. "How would I know? People don't tell me things. You see, this is what happens when you're old. People leave you out. You lose control. There's less and less you can decide for yourself. You don't get the information you should have and so of course you seem confused."

Artisan gave Widmore senior a moment to calm down. Then he said, "It's pretty certain he was murdered."

"Murdered? Why?"

"That's what I'm trying to figure out, Mr. Widmore." The detective told him about the phone call from Moth, and his own trip to Havana, and his meeting with Zander's mysterious associate, and the death of the man who'd ferried him to Cuba. "So I'm looking for a thread," he concluded. "What might Zander be involved in that would link Peconiquot with Havana?"

Cliff Widmore said, "Shipping drugs in? Running guns?"

His father said, "Clifford, why do you always assume the worst about your brother?"

"Why? How about past experience?"

There was a brief silence. Paul Artisan took the opportunity to look out at the uncluttered green swath of Central Park. Then a phone started ringing. It was a ring that seemed to come from nowhere or from some muffled place—inside a wall, underneath a pillow.

With that condescending tone of his, Cliff Widmore said, "Dad, that's you."

"Is it?" said the old man, and he started slapping at his pockets. "I hate these damn things."

He found the phone and looked at the display. "Hell," he said, "it's Vivian. Woman can't live without me for an hour."

He flipped open the device and his first words were, "Yes, darling, I miss you too . . . What? What's that? Hang on a minute."

Holding the phone away, he said to Cliff and Artisan, "She's just heard from Alexander. He called from California."

The detective quickly slid to the edge of the settee. "Where in California?"

Arthur Widmore relayed the question to his wife.

"That little town he goes to, that retreat or whatever," the old man reported. "Vivian says he sounded upset."

"Upset about what?" said Artisan. "What did he say?"

"What did he say, dear?" Arthur Widmore passed along.

He listened intently then moved the phone away again. "Didn't say a lot," he related. "Didn't have time. Said things weren't going very well and then he got cut off."

"Cut off how?" asked the detective. "Was there a noise? Did she hear anything in the background?"

Arthur Widmore passed along the question.

He closed the phone before he spoke again, and his old and handsome face seemed to grow a little paler above the plaid bow tie. "She said she didn't hear a thing. He was just cut off. Like suddenly not there."

All the doormen at Manny Weissman's building knew Paul Artisan, of course.

They knew the funny dance the two men did, passing their shared dog back and forth. They'd seen them in the lobby many times, by day or night, in rain or snow, transferring half-full bags of kibble, or a scrap of blanket that had become the old Lab's favorite bed, or a chewed-up plastic hamburger that was his favorite toy that week. They all knew where Artisan lived, and they had his phone number on file somewhere, and they knew he was the person to call if there was ever an emergency with the nice old man who lived alone in 11-J.

This afternoon it was Hector who was on the door. Hector was a huge guy with an enormous neck, a neck for which no collar was ever big enough. This was a problem because the co-op board decreed that doormen must wear ties. So Hector wore a clip-on that attached to one side of his open collar and dangled sideways at a jaunty angle.

"Manny in?" Paul Artisan asked him.

"Pretty sure," said Hector. "I'll let him know you're coming up."

The old professor was standing in his doorway when his friend stepped off the elevator. "You okay?" he asked. It was unusual for the detective to show up in the middle of a working day.

Argos came squirting out between Manny Weissman's ankles and went skidding down the hallway in his eagerness to sniff Artisan's feet and get his head scratched.

"I have to go to California," the detective said. "Now. I can't fucking believe it."

"California?" said Weissman, and he led the way into the apartment. It was an apartment that Paul Artisan loved. If one could feel nostalgia for a place that still existed and that had never been one's own, he would have felt nostalgia for it. It was a perfect place for a certain kind of New York intellectual, the sort of shabby-tweedy person who used to live in all these buildings before the prices got too high. Bookshelves everywhere. Rugs of no great value with their tassels all askew. Coffee tables stacked high with journals and newspapers and generally untidy manuscripts by students and friends. Amid all the archaic print, a laptop that Manny had resisted and resisted, but which had by now become an alien but welcome companion, a miraculous compression of library and post office.

And of course the apartment was replete with a homey if not exactly delicious smell of dog.

Dropping into a well-worn easy chair, Artisan said, "Zander called from there. Called looking for his father. Just a little while ago."

Slowly, carefully, Manny Weissman sat down on the sofa opposite and tried to figure out why Artisan seemed so grumpy. He said, "But that's a good thing, isn't it? That Zander was heard from? That you know where he is?"

Grudgingly, the detective said, "Yeah, it's a good thing. If he's okay, if he's really there."

The old professor said, "You want a cup of tea?"

"I really don't have time. My plane's at five fifteen."

Manny looked down and plucked at the crease of his trousers. "Something else is bothering you, isn't it? I mean, something besides having to go to California."

"Yeah, something is," admitted the detective. He dragged his fingertips along the plush arms of his chair and pulled in a long slow breath. "I'm starting to think my client is a real scumbag."

"He's a rich and powerful man," said Manny Weissman. "Power doesn't often correlate with niceness. Remember *Lord of the Flies?*"

"Not really," Artisan admitted.

Manny said, "It's about how thin the line is between survival of the fittest and survival of the cruelest. Winners sometimes can't afford to be decent."

"That sounds just like Cliff," said Artisan. "This woman I met in Key West? She says that, right from early childhood, Cliff was setting Zander up to fail, always making trouble then lying so that Zander took the blame. Then there's the dead wife, Shannon. Maybe there was foul play involved, maybe not. Even if there wasn't, I feel like he made her miserable, in some way drove her to the pills and booze. And, even though he's always talking about how he wants to protect his father, he's sort of awful to the old guy. In a polite way that I find completely creepy. He's slighting. Dismissive. Almost like he's trying to convince the old man he's way more senile than he is."

Manny Weissman crossed his hands against his modest paunch and took that in. Then he said, "Paul, the world, unfortunately, is full of very insecure people, people who can only keep themselves propped up by holding others down. That doesn't mean . . ."

He let the words trail off and reached down to pet the dog.

"Mean what, Manny?"

The old professor waved off the question like he was shooing away a curse. "Nothing. It was just a crazy thought, reckless."

The detective was not inclined to let it drop; he scooted forward in his chair. "Doesn't mean that he could be a killer? Don't think I haven't thought it, Manny. I mean, the guy seems to *destroy* people. Where's the line between character assassination and actual killing?"

"Legally, the line is pretty clear."

"Sure," said Artisan, "but if I was fascinated about legally, I'd be a lawyer. I'm talking morally. I'm talking about what's possible for a given person, a particular conscience—or lack of conscience, as you suggest. The problem is I don't see a motive. Cliff's already head of the family business. His brother, by his own choice, has taken himself out of the mix. What does Cliff have to gain?"

The question dangled for some seconds, but Manny Weissman moved the conversation elsewhere. "What's the father like?" he said. "I'm curious about my own contemporaries."

In spite of everything, Artisan had to smile at the recollection of Arthur Widmore in his crazy tartan vest and bow tie. "You know, I really like the old guy, but it's awfully hard for me to think of him

as your contemporary. He seems about six hundred years older—
like some medieval duke or laird or something. He's off-the-charts
right wing, but I think he's really honorable. He is who he is, no
excuses and no apologies. He's obsessed with his Scottish heritage.
Today he started spouting off about the Old Laws . . ."

"Now, that's really interesting," Manny Weissman cut in.

"What is?"

"Old Scottish law. It's really a unique code. Not Roman. Not
English. A third strand, a legal backwater suited to that one
society."

Paul Artisan just shook his head. "Manny, how the hell do you
know this stuff?"

"How should I know how I know it?" He gestured toward a
solid wall of books. "I pick things up here and there. Maybe it was
in some gloss on *Ivanhoe*. Who remembers?"

The detective glanced down at his watch then sprang up from
his chair. "I gotta pack some things and go. Guess you get the dog
again."

"Bring an extra sweater," said his old professor.

"It's August, Manny."

"Nights get cold in California. Bring an extra sweater."

24

It was a grimy orange dusk when Paul Artisan's plane landed in Los Angeles, but by the time he claimed his rental car, it was night. Feeling very Californian, he hit a chicken drive-through called Mr. Cluck's and munched some greasy drumsticks while heading up the 405.

Taillights snaked in an endless procession in front of him, tracing out the undulations of a city improbably dropped into a shifting landscape of hills that broke and canyons that caught fire and ravines that became waterfalls when it rained. Famous exits slipped past: Wilshire Boulevard. Sunset. The names breathed glamour, romance, endless possibility. But in the meantime there was traffic.

The road climbed up to a cluttered ridge that afforded a vast if hideous vista of the San Fernando Valley, then descended along the backside of the mountains to an endless gridded plain. All right angles now, stripped of contour and of context, Southern California stretched gigantically away in all directions.

The detective got onto the 101 and headed north. If the traffic was less heavy now, it was also more manic, and Paul Artisan experienced a feeling that was becoming grimly familiar but without getting any less uncomfortable. It was the feeling that he was barreling full speed ahead with virtually no idea where he was going or what he would find when he got there. He was proceeding on blind faith—and this was strange, because faith was something he hadn't realized that he had.

All he knew about his destination had come from a couple of derisive comments made by Cliff and a five-minute online search he'd managed to do while waiting to board the plane.

He was heading for a tiny town called Luna, about two hours up the coast, then a dozen or so miles inland on a narrow road that wound into a steep and secret valley, and dead-ended at the base of a massive mountain built up of beautiful striped sediments. Not being on the road to anywhere else, Luna was little visited; no one went there by accident or discovered it by just passing through. It was one of those places that people spoke of in hushed tones; knowing of Luna, having been there, created among people an instant bond.

Decades before the New Age crowd started searching for energy vortices, or electromagnetic nodes, or vantages from which the planets lined up in a certain way, Luna and its gorgeous valley were perceived, or imagined, to have special properties. Some thought that the original local Indians, the Chumash, had left behind some vestiges of shamanistic magic when they'd vanished. Others believed there were curative powers in the mineral-rich waters that mysteriously spouted from springs in the stony hills. Still others felt that Luna was simply a beautiful and quiet and accepting place in which to escape the pressures of the outside world—a sort of landlocked island embedded in a continent that barely noted its existence.

Whatever the reason, the area had long been a haven for spiritual seekers, philosophical foundations, cults that ran the gamut from the utopian to the apocalyptic. Over the decades, Luna had

been home to gurus and swamis, yogis and prophets, as well as a
certain ratio of exploiters, frauds, and crackpots, people whose
hideaways were raided in the middle of the night by the IRS or the
DEA. Its hills had seen experiments in free love and in radical
celibacy, in voluntary poverty and the odd contemporary phenom-
enon of using the jargon of the spirit to prop up good old-
fashioned greed. Peyote-eaters and vegans lived there side by side.
Rich kids from disastrous families took on Sanskrit names or grew
their hair in dreadlocks and lived on protein derived from seaweed
and from mung beans.

Driving in by night, Paul Artisan saw almost nothing of the
winding creekbeds, the graceful ridgeline, the spreading live-
oak trees with their amazing canopies. But even without the
visuals, he had a vague but undeniable sense of the power of this
valley. He felt somehow *nestled* in it, caught up in its quiet and its
isolation as in a room made all of cotton puffs. He found a
motel on the edge of the little village and fell into a serene and
dreamless sleep.

In the morning he awoke to a basket of muffins and a thermos of
coffee left outside his door, and to a view as austerely beautiful as
anything he'd ever seen. Folded, graceful hills, sun-baked and
yet full of life, rose up on three sides. Where the trees stopped
there was an endless mat of chaparral; from the level of the valley, the vegetation appeared to be a tweed of blue and rust and
silver mixed in with a dozen different greens. The sky was so
clear it seemed purple at the zenith, and the air was spiced with
eucalyptus.

Sitting on the tiny porch outside his motel room, sipping coffee and watching a red-tailed hawk ride the morning thermals,
Paul Artisan found it deliciously easy to forget altogether about

the complex and troubled world beyond this valley. Then his cell phone rang.

It was Joe Ferrer, the part-time police chief from Peconiquot, and he had a simple question. "The name Alexander Widmore mean anything to you, Artisan?"

Keeping secrets and hoarding privileged information were central parts of the detective's job, of course, but he'd never been any good at outright lying, and a direct question disarmed him every time. Seconds ticked away as he tried to frame a suitably evasive answer.

Joe Ferrer responded to the silence by saying, "I take it that's a yes."

"Yeah, chief, it is," Artisan admitted.

"Why don't you tell me what you know about him?"

Artisan squinted toward the gorgeous hills. As if offended by this intrusion of the outside world, they seemed somehow to grow more distant and less vivid, their magic suddenly less available to him. The detective braced himself for a negotiation. "Why don't you show me yours first? Why are you asking me about him?"

The cop saw no reason not to tell. "The Staties got a warrant to go through Moth's things. They found half a pound of marijuana and a ton of books on philosophy and politics. They also found a round-trip ticket to Key West and a power of attorney given to him by someone named Alexander Widmore. Gave him access to bank accounts, brokerage accounts, the works."

Paul Artisan said nothing. He was wading through thoughts of his own, and progress wasn't coming easily. The mysterious Cuban at the Floridita had presumed that he was someone else, someone sent by Zander and not expected quite so soon. It now seemed that Moth had been meant to be the errand boy. But what was the errand?

Joe Ferrer said, "Widmore's the guy you're looking for, isn't he?" The detective had no choice but to acknowledge that he was.

"Isn't there a Widmore family that owns a bunch of real estate? He part of that same clan?"

"Right again, chief."

Joe Ferrer let out a soft sound that was somewhere between a whistle and a sigh. "A power of attorney from someone like that— that's putting a lot of money up for grabs."

"I'd say," said Artisan.

With a hint of local pride, the chief said, "Guess he really trusted Moth."

"And I guess someone really didn't like what the two of them were cooking up."

There was a brief silence. The detective sipped some coffee.

Joe Ferrer said, "The Key West part. You know anything about that?"

"Yeah, I do," said Artisan. "But I want something in return for the information."

The chief seemed amused at the detective's belief that he could bargain. "Oh, really?"

"The Widmore connection—I want it kept out of the papers."

"Look, I can't just—"

"Publicity won't help the case, believe me. And the father of the family—he's a nice old guy and he's got more than enough to deal with. What's wrong with sparing him some pain?"

Joe Ferrer said nothing, and Artisan understood that was as much as he would get.

In return he said, "Forget about Key West. Moth's real destination was Havana. I've been down there and I learned exactly zilch. And the guy who brought me there was later killed."

"What?"

"Back in Florida. His boat blew up. Last I heard, the cops were calling it an accident. It wasn't. And now you know everything I know."

The Peconiquot chief took a moment to let that settle in. When he spoke again, his tone had become a shade more collegial and more rural and more wry. He said, "Shit, Artisan, you're finding out more than I am. Still, it isn't very much, is it?"

"No," the detective agreed. "It isn't very much."

25

He closed his eyes and pressed them with the heels of his hands, creating golden starbursts and phosphorescent pinwheels behind the lids. He hoped that when he looked out at the mountains once again, their intimacy and their nestling nearness would have been restored.

But it didn't quite work out that way. The outside world had insinuated itself with its violence and its hidden tawdry motives; the lovely illusion of *awayness* could not be so easily restored. The detective showered and dressed and prepared to resume his giant game of connect-the-dots that would somehow link Peconiquot and Key West and Havana to this California town with its mystics and its wackos.

He went to the front desk to ask the whereabouts of the Helios Foundation. According to Cliff, that was the place where Zander had spent time.

"Helios, Helios," said the woman at the desk. She was sixty or so with long gray hair and a big sweet smile. "Let me think which one that is."

"How many do you have here?" asked Artisan. "Foundations, I mean."

"Oh, quite a few. There's New Eden and the Spirit Friends and the Noah's Ark Foundation. Quite a few. Price of land up here, I'm not sure how they do it. Anyway, Helios, right. That one's in the upper valley. Go to where the road snakes up, then, when it flattens out again, you'll see a big walnut grove on the right and an apricot orchard on the left. Beyond that there's a pasture with some llamas, then a corral with miniature horses. Just past it, between two cypress trees, there's an unmarked road that goes back into the hills. Takes you right to it."

Paul Artisan said, "You seem to know this valley very well."

She flashed that beatific smile. "Lived here all my life," she said. "Why would I leave?"

He thanked her, checked out, and followed her directions.

The road between the cypresses went on quite some distance, past orange trees and an avocado orchard. Then the land got rougher, strewn with boulders and dotted with cacti. Beyond this wasteland, a patch of cottonwood forest suddenly appeared, the beneficiary of water flowing underground. At the edge of this copse the road broadened into an unpaved parking area filled with Jeeps and beat-up Volkswagens, but also with a smattering of BMWs and Jaguars. Beyond the parking area was a metal fence, and in front of it, serving as a kind of gateway, was a one-room wooden office. Artisan went in.

A young woman with wide eyes and very thick brown hair was sitting at a wicker desk. She was wearing one of those gauzy Indian cotton shirts that you could see right through, and the detective tried not to look at her breasts.

"Welcome to Helios," she said. "How can I help you?"

"I'm looking for someone," said Paul Artisan, still not looking at her breasts, which happened to be rather large, yet held high and steady by young taut muscles. "I don't know if he's still here."

With entire pleasantness, the woman said, "I'm sorry, but we don't share information about our guests and members. We respect their privacy. I'm sure you understand."

"I do understand," the detective assured her. "But it's very important that I find this person. Like life and death important. Is there someone else—a director, a boss—I can talk to?"

The slightest hint of disapproval crept into the woman's voice. "We don't have bosses here," she said. "We do have an Adviser. His name is Elio. If you'd like to speak with him, I'll bring you in."

The detective said he'd appreciate that.

The woman pointed through a side door that led on to a little shed. "Okay. You can leave your clothes in there."

Paul Artisan said, "Excuse me?"

"You can leave your—" she started to repeat, then interrupted herself. "We're a naturist community. Were you unaware of that?"

Artisan let that settle in a couple seconds. Then he said, "You mean, like, a nudist colony?"

The woman said, "We don't like the word *nudist*. There's something salacious about it, don't you think? It suggests that being naked is some deviation from the norm, when in fact it's just the opposite. Clothing is unnatural. So we leave it behind here. There're flip-flops in the shed. I suggest you wear some. We do have animals on the property."

The detective blinked. Zany and anarchic thoughts were racing through his head. He felt extremely silly for having tried to sneak a peek at this woman's boobs when they soon would be entirely naked. . . . But what if it was just a hoax? What if he stripped off all his clothes, then, as in that universal dream, suddenly found himself surrounded by people who were dressed as usual?

Not without difficulty, he left the office, went into the little shed, and got naked to the skin. The young woman slipped out of her gauzy shirt and loose-fitting shorts and they strolled together like Adam and Eve into the Helios Foundation.

The place seemed, in fact, a facsimile of Eden. Fruit trees were growing everywhere: persimmons, pomegranates, tangerines. The silver of an olive grove glimmered on a higher slope. People walked innocently naked, unmindful of their pubic triangles; unmindful, as well, of their un-flat tummies and spreading buttocks and rounded shoulders, all the candid imperfections that make each of us a rough draft of some impossible ideal.

They walked through a shady lane of trees to a small house mostly made of glass. In front of it, a man in sunglasses, and with tangled but exuberant gray hair not only on his head but also on his chest and shoulders was sitting in a redwood tub that captured warm water from a spring. The young woman introduced the man as Elio, first name only, and he produced a soft wet hand to shake.

The naked detective introduced himself.

Elio said, "Welcome, Paul. You look uncomfortable."

"I am."

"It's not uncommon when people first arrive at Helios. But gradually you realize that, in our essence, we're all naked anyway."

Artisan said, "I'm sure there's something deep in that. But as a purely practical matter, we usually wear clothes."

Elio let that pass. "How can I help you?"

"I'm looking for someone who's been here recently."

Elio didn't seem too happy with the answer but he remained resolutely cheerful in the face of it. Behind the cheer, however, there seemed to be a layer of caution, a worldly vigilance that was slightly out of keeping with the edenic setting. Gesturing around him, he said, "We have nothing to hide, as you can see. All consenting adults here, legal age. No drugs or weapons on the premises. Who is it you're looking for?"

"Zander Widmore."

"Ah." Elio let the syllable dangle there a moment. Then he

asked the woman who'd escorted Artisan to leave the two of them alone. He asked if the detective would like to join him in the tub. "Very relaxing," he said. "Water's full of iron and magnesium."

Reluctantly, Artisan climbed in. It seemed preferable to standing buck naked in full daylight.

Elio said, "So. I don't think you're a cop. Even in Luna, cops usually object to taking off the uniform and getting in the tub. So why are you looking for Zander?"

"I'm working for his family. They want to know that he's okay. That's all."

Elio scooped some water and rubbed it on his head. "And what if he isn't okay? Would they want to know that too?"

Artisan said, "I'm not sure I follow you."

"My point," said Elio, "is what do people really mean when they say that someone is *okay*? Usually it means that they're behaving the way other people want them to. It's not about well-being. It's about doing the expected thing."

"I think," said the detective, "that Zander's family gave up on that version of *okay* a long time ago. At this point they'd settle for living and breathing."

Droplets flew as Elio vigorously scratched his hairy chest. "By that modest standard, he was okay as of a day and a half ago. That's the last time I saw him."

"Do you know where he was headed?"

"I'd rather not lie to you, Paul. So I think I just won't answer that." He paused, then went on in a tone that was almost professorial. "Paul, how well do you know Zander?"

"I don't know him at all. In fact, the more I try to figure him out, the less I feel I know him."

"I think I know him fairly well," said Elio. "He's been coming here from time to time for years. Just dropping in, then vanishing again. No pattern. Seems chaotic. But we have a saying here, maybe you've heard it: Not all who wander are lost. There's a reason, a value, in the wandering, the journey—"

More by reflex than reflection, Paul Artisan raised his hands out of the water in a fending gesture. "Elio," he said, "I'm sorry, but I'm not from California—in fact I'm from New York, and I don't have a lot of patience for this *journey* bullshit."

The Adviser didn't rattle. "That's fine," he said. "We don't preach or proselytize. We don't have a doctrine. We believe that people should find their own way to happiness. You familiar with a philosopher named John Locke?"

Somewhat impatiently, Artisan said, "Only as a name."

"Fascinating guy. Seventeenth-century Brit, amazingly advanced. Huge influence on Thomas Jefferson. Locke argued that the highest goal of our intelligence is the careful and constant pursuit of true and solid happiness. Think about that! He's not talking about religion or science. He's not talking about rules or authority. He's saying that the best use of our reason is in learning to be happy."

"Very interesting," the detective said. "But about Zander—"

"That's exactly what I'm getting to," said Elio. "When Zander first came here, he knew nothing about true and solid happiness. Self-indulgence, yes. Following whims, yes. Real happiness, no. The closest he came to happiness was in rebelling. But here at Helios he had nothing rebel about. We've tried to get rid of hierarchy. We have no rules except the rules of common decency and common sense. So Zander had to work pretty hard to offend us."

"But I take it he managed," the detective said.

"Yes, he did," said Elio. "Hurtful sexual behavior. Bringing in amphetamines, cocaine. Even petty theft."

"You kicked him out?"

"Of course not," the Adviser said. "We put up with his nonsense until he realized it wasn't getting our attention. Then he stopped behaving badly. Then he was ready to move on."

"But he came back again."

"Oh, yes. Several times."

"Why?"

"Interesting question," Elio said. "Why does anyone go back to a situation in which he's behaved badly, embarrassed himself? Looking for forgiveness? Redemption? Or just to have another go at testing the limits in a place that really has no limits?"

Paul Artisan settled deeper into the warm water of the redwood tub. It was silky and relaxing, but for all of that, something was bothering him. Something seemed a little too easy about Elio, a little too glib. One moment he sounded like a guru, the next his affect was more like that of a salesman with a hot new product. The detective said, "Elio, you keep saying there's no rules here, no authority. But someone's in charge, and someone's saying what goes and what doesn't, and that someone happens to be you."

The other man's sunglasses had fogged. He wiped them on a scrap of towel. "Fair enough," he said. "But as heads of state go, I'm pretty damn benign. Look, hippie communes fall apart because no one wants to be in charge. The Helios Foundation is not a hippie commune. We are what the world would call a going operation. We pay our way."

"How?" said Artisan.

"That's confidential."

"You sell things? Run a business?"

"Paul, we're not a charity. That information isn't public."

"Wait a second," the detective said. "We're sitting here naked in front of your glass house, you're telling me you've got nothing to hide—except some things are still secrets?"

Elio smiled. It was a slightly different smile from the ones Artisan had seen from him so far—a little less nice-guy but possibly more spontaneous. He said, "Paul, I like talking with you. You're a challenging son of a bitch. We don't get a lot of those here. You say you're not from California? Me neither. I'm from Jersey. Elio's not my birth name. I took it because I like the sound of it. My birth name's Eddie. Eddie Ippolito."

He waited for a reaction, and he got one. There was a well-known Ippolito family in the Jersey Mob; their official businesses were road-paving and construction, and they were considered to be just one notch below the ruling echelon.

"Aha!" said Elio, really seeming to be having fun now. "Now I've got you. You're wondering: *those* Ippolitos? Or one of the thousand others that are teachers, dentists, electricians? You're thinking: If it *is* Mafia, what's the scam here? Money laundering? A place for fugitives to hide? Or is all of this just an elaborate way for a dirty old man with ill-gotten funds to surround himself with adoring naked women? Is that some of what you're thinking, Paul?"

The detective didn't answer.

Elio went on. "You're a suspicious person. Or maybe it's just your job. But that's fine. Suspicion is . . . well, in Jersey we might say suspicion is the ass-end of curiosity. And curiosity's a good thing. So live with the suspicion and see where it takes you."

Paul Artisan sat there in the silky water and wondered how he'd been put so thoroughly on the defensive. Trying to take back the momentum, he said, "Did you know Zander had just been in Havana?"

"He told me that."

"You know why?"

"Possibly."

"Cuba, here—I'm trying to figure out the connection."

"Can't help you there," said Elio.

"Can't or won't?" asked the detective.

"Bottom line's the same. No."

There was a pause. In the sudden quiet, the low drone of hummingbirds could be heard as they hovered to suck nectar from a jasmine hedge. Their throats flashed brilliant red when they turned them toward the sun.

After a moment Elio resumed. "I'm not sure I should do this, Paul, but I'm going to tell you where Zander went from here. Two reasons. The main one is that I'm seriously worried about him. He was different this visit. He was focused and seemingly together but there was a kind of desperation to it, a sort of frenzy waiting to happen. He just seemed like someone who was running out of time."

The hairy man paused, scooped water, and rubbed it on his neck.

Then he said, "The second reason's about you, Paul. You say you don't like *this journey bullshit.* That's fine. You don't have to like it. But whether you like it or not, you're on one, my friend. Zander's in Australia."

26

Paul Artisan didn't even try to think until he'd put his clothes back on.

But once he'd dressed and said good-bye to the woman in the gauzy blouse and gotten back into his rented car, it seemed clear to him that what he needed to do next was get in touch with his client. Driving back toward the village of Luna, he dialed New York. This time Cliff Widmore willingly took the call.

"Artisan!" he said, with that wry, hale tone that the detective no longer trusted. "How goes it? Have you made it to California?"

"I'm there now."

"Have you found that nut-farm where Zander hangs out?"

Strangely, Artisan found himself resenting the comment. "I'm just leaving it," he said.

"And was my brother there? Meditating? Levitating?"

"He left a day and a half ago."

"Figures," said Cliff Widmore. "And let me guess: No one knew where he was heading."

The detective said, "As a matter of fact, someone did know. That's why I'm calling."

And he passed along the few details, or guesses, that Elio had shared with him during their last moments in the redwood tub. Elio was pretty sure that Zander had flown to Sydney, where he hoped to see some former associates with whom he'd once tried to launch a business in black pearls. Then—or so Elio believed—he would probably head up to the Barrier Reef, to an unnamed island some ways out into the Coral Sea, where he said he had an appointment.

Cliff heard out this recitation, then was silent for a moment, waiting for more. Finally he said, "Oh, great. That's it? That's all you know?"

"That's it," admitted the detective.

The client said, "Seeing some old associates, whose names we don't know, in a city of I don't know how many million people, then taking a meeting on an unnamed island in a place where there are thousands of islands . . . Artisan, are you really convinced this is even worth pursuing?"

The question took the detective completely by surprise. It had never for a moment occurred to him that he might abandon Zander's trail—not at this stage, certainly. He'd already endured his crises of shirking, and somehow he had crossed the line that divided the half-assed from the committed; he wasn't bailing now. He said, "Cliff, this is real progress. We started with the whole wide world. We've narrowed it down to one small continent."

The client sounded unpersuaded. "If you had a name, a contact. If you had some idea where or when this meeting was—"

Paul Artisan didn't want to hear about the difficulties, about the preposterous thinness of what he had to go on. Cutting in, he said, "Is it the money, Cliff? I know it's a long way—"

"It's not the money," said the heir, seemingly by reflex. "Of course it's not the money."

"Well, I'm going," the detective said with finality. "I just wanted you to know."

There was a pause. The pause lasted about two deep breaths, and at the end of it Cliff Widmore, sounding resigned rather than enthusiastic, said, "All right, Artisan, since you're so determined. Tell you what—I'll ask our travel person to make arrangements for you. Call my secretary in an hour. You want one way or round-trip?"

"Cliff, I plan on coming back."

"Sure. People always plan on coming back."

Driving toward Los Angeles, from which he'd been booked on a midnight flight to Sydney, Paul Artisan dialed Manny Weissman's number in New York.

In a world where it was nothing to cross continents or the equator or the date line, where a million cell-phone waves were bouncing off of satellites and into speeding cars and anonymous cubicles, it was a great comfort to dial a familiar number and to know the room where the phone would ring. Tearing down the 101 just inland from Malibu, the detective was picturing Manny's apartment, the end table strewn with books and magazines, and somewhere amid the mountains of pages, an old single-line desk phone, a near-antique from an early generation of touch-tone.

Manny picked up on the third ring and said hello. Hearing it was Paul, he asked how things were going.

"Great," said the detective. "I spent the morning at a nudist colony."

The signal wasn't perfect on the freeway. Manny Weissman said, "A Buddhist colony?"

"Nudist. Nudist," said his friend. "I'll tell you all about it when I see you. How's everything there?"

"Fine," said the old professor. "The dog seems happy. And I was just thinking about *King Lear.*"

This was vintage Manny. It was just before five, New York time. Most people were still at their jobs, but tired and antsy and dis-

tracted, thinking about sex or happy hour or the baseball game
that evening. Some were in dentists' offices reading *People* maga-
zine. Manny was home on his sofa thinking about Shakespeare.

"Amazing piece of work," he went on. "And for God's sake,
don't tell me you only saw the movie."

"Actually," said Artisan, "I saw the play. Years ago. Must've been
in the Park. James Earl Jones. Creepy daughters plotting against
their father, right?"

"Close enough," said Manny. "But that's not where the trouble
starts. And that's not what's so heartbreakingly brilliant about the
story."

Three thousand miles away, Paul Artisan drove his rented car.
Shopping centers and brown hills streaked past, but Artisan was
seeing the view through Manny's window.

"It's a play about old age," his friend continued. "About the
choices and the diminishments of age, and the grace and wisdom—or lack of it—that old people bring to the few decisions they
still have to make. Lear is old, and failing, but he's still a king, still
supposedly in charge, still accustomed to having his own way. Little
by little, he feels his importance waning, his influence shrinking.
Time is passing him by. There's less and less he can control."

Paul Artisan said, "Sort of like Arthur Widmore. Except instead
of king, he's chairman of the board."

"Very good, Paul," said his old professor. "He's my contemporary, after all. It's not so hard for me to think my way into his skin.
But let's stay with Lear for now. What's the one thing he still has
power over? His own estate. His wealth and land. He can still say
who gets what. He cherishes that power, that remnant of his status
as patriarch. But, in his vanity and his far from perfect wisdom,
Lear makes a calamitous decision in dividing things among his
children. And everything that happens after—all the misery, all the
deaths—comes back to that unwise decision."

Paul Artisan had snaked across three lanes of traffic and pulled onto the shoulder of the freeway. His engine idling, he said, "But that's Lear. As for Arthur Widmore, we don't know anything about how he's dividing his estate."

Manny said, "That's true. But I've been thinking. Those things you told me about his obsession with his heritage, the old Scottish laws. What's that about? I think he's trying to recreate a world that makes more sense to him, a world in which he matters more. A lot of old men do that—trust me."

"Okay, but how does that connect with—?"

"I've been doing a little research," said Manny Weissman. "Are you familiar with the phrase *law of primogeniture?*"

"That's about inheritance, right?"

"Exactly. More specifically, it's a system that favors first-born children at the expense of other siblings, to prevent estates from being broken up. Scotland had a particularly stringent version. Had to, because the land was too poor and the climate too harsh to support a bunch of small farms. So younger children basically got nothing. That's why there were so many Scottish emigrants and missionaries. There was nothing left for them at home."

"But Manny, that was Scotland. This is America."

"Exactly. And which does old Mr. Widmore seem to prefer? He walks around in tartans and drinks single-malt whisky and talks about how much better the old ways were. He's trying to go back to a lost world."

"But it would be crazy—"

"What? To leave everything to one son? Any crazier than what Lear did? Old people get stubborn, Paul. And sometimes wiggy. Cliff thinks his father is senile, right? You think he's charming and eccentric. Well, maybe the truth is somewhere in between. He's with-it enough to have strong opinions and to make decisions consistent with them, but that doesn't mean that they're wise or even sane decisions."

Traffic whizzed by. Paul Artisan felt an itching in his scalp, but when he went to scratch it he found it was really in his brain. He said, "Even if Arthur Widmore is really following this primogeniture thing, we still don't know—"

"Which son is the first-born?" put in Manny Weissman. "As a matter of fact, we do know. I've been in touch with the Nassau County clerk's office, division of birth records. Zander is older. By twenty-three minutes. But they actually have different birthdays. Born just on either side of midnight."

The detective sat there in his rented car. Through the silence, Manny Weissman seemed belatedly to realize that his musings had thrown his friend into a complete, befuddled turmoil.

"Look," he said, "it's just a theory."

"True," said Artisan. "But it would certainly give Cliff a motive for wanting to get rid of Zander."

Weissman said, "And that's the piece that was missing, right? But forget it, it's probably all wrong. You coming home tonight?"

"Actually, that's why I called. I'm flying to Australia."

"Australia?"

"Supposedly that's where Zander is. But, Manny, all of a sudden I don't know why I'm supposed to be finding him."

His friend said, "You'll find him because you said you would."

The detective said, "But why? So his younger twin can kill him?"

27

There are people who see it as their due to ride in the forward compartments of jetliners, who are blasé about the myriad small luxuries that pertain in first- and business-class. Such people barely notice the big leather seats that cradle buttocks and shoulders and allow for legs to be stretched out almost normally; they take in stride the civilized amenities like pre-flight champagne served not in plastic cups but actual glasses, and prettily printed menus that inform you what there'll be to eat.

Paul Artisan was not one of those people.

For him, business-class was a rare exotic treat. He had no idea why he was seated there. Had he tweaked Cliff Widmore's pride by suggesting that maybe the client was too cheap to send him to Australia? Or had the travel department simply goofed, imagining, maybe, that they were sending some big executive? No matter. Sitting at the gate at LAX, pitying the coach-class passengers who trundled by with their awkward carry-ons, he was already enjoying the passage. A lovely flight attendant with bobbed hair and enormous eyes was lavishing attention on him—bestowing smiles, topping up his bubbly, bringing him cashews and Brazil nuts not in a sad little packet but a handsome porcelain dish.

With a graciousness that could not seem otherwise than sexy, she leaned close to serve him. Her nameplate said CINDY; her perfume said wild. This, he thought, was living.

His sense of his good fortune increased exponentially when he saw his seatmate.

She was a tall, lithe woman, thirty, give or take, dressed in black slacks and a neat blue sweater with a short black jacket over it. Her hair was dark and trim, practical but not severe; her eyes were gray and widely spaced. When she reached up to put her attaché in the overhead compartment, it was with the sure, efficient motion of an athlete.

Sitting, she flashed Paul Artisan a smile. It was a pretty smile, an open smile; above all, it was confident, the smile of a person who expected good treatment from the world and who would have no problem dealing with situations in which the world failed to meet her expectation. She fastened her seat belt and took out a mystery novel. In fact, she took out *Trent's Last Case*.

In a minute or two, Cindy came by to offer her champagne and to top up Artisan's yet again. Now that they both had glasses, she turned to him and said, "Cheers. It's a deathly long flight. We may as well make friends."

They clinked glasses.

"Cheers. I'm Paul."

"I'm Pru."

"As in Prudence?"

"Exactly. A nice old-fashioned name, yes? Given me by a nice old-fashioned family. But the power of suggestion doesn't seem to have worked."

"Meaning you're not prudent?"

She sipped her bubbly. "Not very."

The plane was pushing back and Paul Artisan was savoring his seatmate's accent. Unmistakably Australian, it featured crisp, clipped consonants counterbalanced by leisurely breathy vowels.

She said, "Have you made this trip often?"

"No, I've never been to Australia."

"Oh, you'll love it. Everybody does. Friendly. Outdoorsy. Lots to do." She'd noticed, as women tended to, that he wasn't wearing a wedding ring. "You're single?"

"Very."

"Straight?"

"So far," he said.

"You'll be very popular in Sydney."

"I appreciate your confidence."

"Australian women are mad for American chaps."

"Nice to hear that someone is," said Artisan. "Why?"

"Oh, American guys actually seem to enjoy the company of women. They're sensitive. They talk about their feelings."

"Really? That's not an opinion I've heard before."

"Maybe it's just all relative. Our chaps are such blockheads. All they want to do is play rugby or sit in the pub with their mates. Why don't they just hop into bed together and get it over with? I'm guessing that we'd all be better off."

"So I take it you're single too?"

"Firmly," she said. "Decisively. I'm not the type to do the shopping and wipe the baby's nose while Mr. Wonderful is off surfing with his pals. Thank you very much, that's not for me. Are you on holiday?"

"No. Business," said Paul Artisan, and in that moment he realized he hadn't bothered to concoct a cover story for what was bringing him to Sydney. Somewhat lamely, but at the same time hoping to create a bit of intrigue, he said, "Nothing very interesting. And you?"

"Coming home from business," Pru said. "I work for a little

Aussie biotech that's doing amazing things with derivatives of eucalyptus."

"Ah. You're a scientist."

"Not really. Me, stuck in a lab all day? With artificial lighting and microscopes and little bits of gooey things on slides? No, I'd go berserk. I need sunshine and people. I'm in the marketing end, building partnerships. Shall we have some more champagne?"

She waved her empty glass toward Cindy, who by now had just a hint of matchmaking mischief in her eyes.

When their bubbly had been refilled, Pru said, "You know, they all say drinking makes the jet lag worse, but they're awfully skimpy on advice for surviving the flight without it. Cheers."

They clinked again. Once airborne, she went back to her book. Artisan read a newspaper and now and then glanced at her profile. She had a beautiful strong jaw line and her nose was very slightly upturned.

She read awhile, then marked her place with an index finger and turned back toward her seatmate. "This is most peculiar," she said. "The detective is about to solve the crime and I still have all these pages left to go."

Paul Artisan casually pointed at the book. "I don't want to spoil the surprise," he said. "But I will say that's one of the cleverest mysteries ever written."

Pru said, "You see? That's another refreshing thing about American men. They read." She glanced at her watch. "Oh, Christ," she said, "only thirteen more hours to go. Want a sleeping pill?"

Artisan hesitated. They'd had quite a bit of bubbly by now.

Pru read his thoughts. "I know, I know. Do not mix with alcohol. But I told you, Paul, I'm really not that prudent."

He shrugged and accepted the pill. They clinked glasses yet again and washed the drug down with champagne. When they fell asleep her head was on his shoulder.

———

The Pacific Ocean is the biggest thing in the entire world.

When Paul Artisan woke up again there was still a fair bit of it to go; there was no hurry to stir. Pru's head was still on his shoulder. He liked it there. Her hair smelled of mint and loose strands of it tickled his neck. After a while she opened her wide gray eyes and gave him a sleepy smile. There was intimacy in waking up together, even fully clothed and in an airplane seat.

They washed and stretched and had some breakfast. As the coast of Australia was drawing nearer, Pru asked Paul where he'd be staying. He named the hotel where he'd been booked by Cliff Widmore's travel person.

Pru shook her head. "Boring, if you don't mind my saying so. It'll be full of bustly Asian businessmen wearing pagers, and tables full of middle-managers trying to decide whether to shake hands or bow. Why don't you stay down in the Rocks?"

"The Rocks?"

"Great neighborhood," she said. "Oldest part of town. Right down by the Bridge and the Opera House. Great restaurants. Funky small hotels."

"Sounds nice," said Artisan, "but—"

His seatmate said, "Look, is there anything you absolutely have to do today?"

At that the detective could not help sighing. What he'd been planning to do was to find Sydney's jewelry district and track down merchants who dealt in black pearls and try to locate the people that Zander Widmore had once had an abortive business with. It was not a scintillating prospect and probably futile to boot.

Pru who was not prudent did not wait for him to answer. She said, "Why don't I show you the Rocks? Have some lunch, a stroll along the Quay. You up for that at all?"

28

A page had somehow fallen off the calendar, and when they reached Sydney it was midmorning of the second day out from Los Angeles. Traveling light, they grabbed their carry-ons, freshened up in the terminal, and caught a taxi into town.

When they pulled up to the address Pru had given, Paul Artisan said, "Wait a second. This isn't a hotel. It's a brewery."

"Brewery downstairs, hotel above," she said. "How Australian is that? Let's get you checked in and then go have a stroll, eh?"

Late August was the end of Sydney's brief winter. Trees were coming into bud. Patches of grass were going green practically before one's eyes. Sunlight twinkled on the enormous harbor; ferries tugged zipper-like wakes behind them; people strolled with the sweaters they no longer needed slung around their shoulders.

They walked the narrow streets of the Rocks—streets hemmed in by squat buildings made of sandstone blocks hewn by early convicts—then broke into the open air of Circular Quay, the horn-tooting, whistle-blowing crescent from which the entire city seemed to rise. Passing the Opera House, Pru took Paul Artisan's arm. "Tired?" she asked.

"Exhausted, yes. Discombobulated, yes. Tired, not at all. This is gorgeous."

She said, "Where do you stand on raw and strange and somewhat slimy seafood?"

"Can't get enough."

"Good. I have just the place for lunch."

She led the way to a harborside building that was really just a shed, but whose outdoor tables offered a drop-dead view of the water and the sailboats and the gigantic Bridge. They ordered oysters and octopus and tuna that was just barely seared along the edges, along with a local Riesling so dry that it all but sizzled on the tongue. A splendid brunch in an upside-down city at ten thirty in the morning.

Oyster-shells, sucked dry of their sea-like juice, accumulated on a shared plate. Artisan watched with pleasure as Pru fastidiously dabbed her lips with a corner of her napkin. They drank wine, and gradually the view shrank down to a close-up of each other's faces.

When the plates were cleared and their glasses topped up with the last of the Riesling, Pru said, "Ah. Yum. Now I suggest we play a little game."

Paul Artisan said, "Uh-oh."

She went on undeterred. "Let's tell each other one true thing about ourselves. Something you never tell anyone and maybe haven't even thought out in words before."

"Dangerous game," said the detective.

She shrugged and said, "So what? You first."

He looked down at his hands, briefly at the twinkling harbor, then back at Pru's gray eyes. "Okay," he said, "here goes. I sometimes feel like I was born out of my own time, or maybe I'm just a little weird, because my best friend is almost eighty, and I'm not usually very interested in people my own age, or in what they care about or do. I'm interested in fuddy-duddy things like calm, dignity, peace of mind. Sometimes I think I'm just a young old fart."

Pru considered that and sipped some wine. Then she said, "Or maybe just a serious-minded person."

He said, "Thank you for the benefit of the doubt. It's a leap of faith, believe me. Your turn."

She took a deep breath, exhaled a nervous laugh, and said, "Oh, boy, why did I start this?" She sipped some wine. "Okay, okay. I consider myself a very strong person and an extremely independent one, but I sometimes worry that there's something, I don't know, a little brittle or a little forced about my precious independence. I don't know how to say this very elegantly, so don't laugh, okay? It's like I've become as tough and smooth as a nonstick pan, and if something wonderful touched me it would slide right off because I've forgotten how to be in love."

Paul Artisan was staring at her. Her face had flushed, her skin had tightened at the hairline, she was fanning herself with her hand. Sipping wine, she said, "Phew, that was difficult."

It took her a moment to realize that her new friend's eyes had also welled up and reddened. Surprised, she said, "Paul—"

He said, "Pru. I think you're really beautiful. Not like a nonstick pan at all."

She shook her head and gave a little laugh and looked away. When her eyes returned they pinned him fair and square. "Would you consider making love with me?" she said.

Her mouth tasted of wine and ocean; their kisses had the sweet sharp tang of beaching waves.

She was bold, deliberate, unafraid to show her body. Without frenzy, they folded back bedclothes, rearranged pillows, made of the room an altar to the possibility of finding passion around the corner or at the far ends of the earth.

Her skin was soft, the flesh beneath sinuous and firm. Her hands were cool and confident on his back and neck, and when she lifted her loins to meet him, the arch of her back and the grip of her thighs made a cradle in which he was rocked and coddled and tossed and teased and nestled and wrestled and finally quelled.

They slept awhile, having no idea how long or what time it had gotten to be. They awoke with a baffled gratitude to be in each other's arms, and were making love again before they were quite certain that they weren't dreaming.

Then they rested, their heads propped up on pillows, their voices changed to a soft hum of coos and relieved exhalations that were almost giggles. Since they'd last paid much attention to the light, the sun had pivoted across the sky. It now filtered in through slatted blinds with a viscous golden glow both sensuous and melancholy.

Pru kissed him on the neck and got up to use the bathroom.

He rubbed his eyes and looked around the room. It was ordinary enough—a couple of worn chairs, a pair of lamps, an old-fashioned armoire with a mirror that didn't fit its frame quite perfectly. Then something happened to the light, some accident of glare and angle and reflection.

A slice of sun slipped between the blinds; it put a flash of yellow-orange in the mirror; and the mirror suddenly reflected something shiny in Pru's handbag, which had been left slightly open on a chair. The shine drew Paul Artisan's eye. For an instant he imagined that what he was seeing was just a lipstick tube or a metal case for sunglasses; then, with a certainty that made him feel slightly dizzy and a little sick to his stomach, he understood that he was looking at a gun.

He got out of bed and grabbed it from Pru's bag. It was a nickel-plated .32 caliber revolver.

He was sitting naked in a chair and pointing it at her when she came out of the bathroom.

Seeing it, she gave a quick whimper and froze. Then, oddly, suddenly modest, like Eve cast out of Eden when innocence was finished, she moved to cover up her breasts and loins. She said, "What the hell are you doing with that?"

He said, "I think I get to ask you first."

For a moment she said nothing. Her eyes went to the chair that held her open handbag. She said, "You went through my things?"

"I didn't go through your things. If you have such a shiny gun, you shouldn't leave your purse wide open."

"Guess I was thinking of other things when I put the bag down."

"That's very flattering," he said. "But you need to talk to me, Pru. What the hell is going on?"

She was silent. He kept the gun pointed at her solar plexus. Her taste was still on his lips, suddenly seeming a delicious poison.

He said, "Look, we came in on a plane together. Neither of us had checked luggage. How'd you—"

"An associate slipped it to me at the airport. In the ladies room outside of customs."

"An associate?"

"Paul, I don't work for a biotech, okay?"

"Yeah, that much I picked up on."

"And I know why you're in Sydney. I know exactly why. You're not the only detective in the room."

He said, "But who—?"

"I'm working for Cliff Widmore, Paul. Through Intercontinental . . . Please, can I sit down?"

He didn't lower the gun, just wagged it. She sat on the edge of the bed and pulled a sheet across her shoulders.

He said, "Cliff Widmore hired you to tail me?"

"Yes."

"And to fuck me?"

She lifted up her wide gray eyes. "Paul, please don't talk like that. I never in a million years imagined this would happen. I was just supposed to keep an eye on you. Please, can you put the gun away?"

He didn't. He was still trying to sort things out and the confusion and the jet lag were making him dangerously jumpy. He said, "Wait. Let's back up a second. Widmore hired you and got you on a plane in the time it took for me to get to LAX?"

"I was already working for him, Paul. On something else."

"What else?"

"You know I can't tell you that."

"I also know a gun trumps professional ethics every time. What were you doing for Widmore?"

"Something completely routine, okay?"

"No, not okay," said Artisan. "What is it?"

She blew some air between her lips. "His stepmother's having an affair. I follow her to the little downtown hotel where she meets the boyfriend, usually on Thursday afternoons. I get some pictures. End of story."

Artisan was visited by a lewd remembered image of Vivian in her backlit nightie. He wasn't surprised she had a paramour, but he didn't quite get why her stepson gave a damn. "Why does Widmore care?"

"How should I know? Wants to have something on her, I guess."

"Another happy family," said Paul Artisan. "But enough about them. Why did Widmore have you tail me?"

She squirmed and tugged the sheet that was awkwardly arranged between her thighs and over her torso. "Paul, would you please put the gun away?"

"Why so nervous, Pru? Guilty conscience?"

She mustered some indignation. "No. Not at all. It's because you aren't going to like this, Paul. And I don't want you to take it out on me."

They locked eyes and after a moment it was Artisan who flinched. He put the shiny gun on a small table that was next to him. It gleamed an infernal orange in the dying light.

"Paul, why do you think Cliff Widmore hired you?"

Artisan wasn't sure he understood the question. "Why? He hired me to find—"

"No, Paul. Why did he hire *you*? Why not Intercontinental, where he already did business, which has agents all over the world?"

"Because he didn't want—"

"Publicity?" she cut in. "I'm sorry, Paul, but that's not it. There's no one more discreet than we are. Paul, he hired you because he didn't think that you could do the job."

The detective's body processed that bit of news more quickly than his mind. He felt like he'd been kicked in the stomach. With what was left of his breath, he muttered, "That son of a bitch."

Pru said, "Agreed. Believe me. He doesn't want his brother found. His father insisted on hiring a detective. He picked one that he thought would fail."

Artisan found that he couldn't speak. Humiliation choked him, and he hadn't yet discovered the anger and defiance that would give him oxygen again.

His new lover said, "But you surprised him, Paul. You turned out to be the real deal. And that got him worried. So he sent me to keep on you, to give him some notice, at least, if Zander was going to be found. You mind if I get dressed?"

He didn't answer, didn't even nod. She got up from the bed and found her clothes. He watched her absently but with an ache as her beautiful skin was hidden away from his sight.

Still barefoot, she squatted next to the chair where he inertly sat. "Paul," she said, "I'm sorry. I should have told you sooner. We never know what's going to happen, do we?"

"No," he said, "we never do."

She said, "I've just resigned the Widmore job. You can believe that or not, but it's true."

He reached over to the little table and handed her the shiny gun.

"Keep it," she said. "You're likelier to need it than I am."

She retrieved her purse, took out a pad and pen and scrawled down some numbers. "This is where I'll be. I have a sister here in Sydney. She's the one who works in biotech."

She kissed him on the cheek and left.

29

He fell back into the bed that was still faintly redolent of Pru's skin and hair, and as the room grew duskier he slipped into one of those dead exhausted sleeps in which one's torpid body seems to be sinking through the mattress, through the floor, down into the mantle of the earth.

He awoke, disoriented and starving, in the middle of the night. His body clock had melted, as in a Dali painting; he found a twenty-four-hour restaurant and gorged on eggs and bacon and potatoes, all washed down with too much coffee, and then he strolled to the waterfront to watch the sun come up. Standing in the predawn chill between the Erector-set geometry of the looming Bridge and the spinnaker curves of the Opera House, he thought about his new lover; and yet he couldn't decide which version of her to fix on. The bold and lovely woman who'd seduced him? The resourceful colleague with a gun in her purse who, quite literally, was on his case? Or the purportedly contrite new friend who had supposedly come clean?

Replaying the scene in the hotel room, he could not avoid confronting again the humiliating revelation as to his hiring. Hired to fail. Picked because he was a lightweight. The recollection of it infuriated him now, put a crawling itch along his hairline. But along with the pique and the resentment came a more useful realization that led him to one of those rare amazing moments that are the punctuation of a life, that divide things into how they were before and what they could only become after.

He understood that Cliff Widmore, that shrewd, manipulative bastard, had been right to hire him.

Standing half a world from home, his nerves rubbed raw, his habits and defenses stripped away, the detective now saw himself more nakedly and truly than people for the most part allow themselves to do. He understood what Cliff Widmore had seen when he looked at him: someone essentially uncommitted and unserious, someone limited and diminished by a profound and basic holding back. And he understood that Widmore saw him that way because he, Paul Artisan, saw himself that way.

Or had, until now.

Looking out at the softly twinkling water of Sydney Harbor, sniffing the cool salt air, the detective realized that his eyes were wet. But the tears he was crying were not soft tears; he felt strangely new and strong. What was making him weep was the pain of transformation, the struggle out of a cocoon. In a rush of wordless understanding, he saw the coolness and the distance and the lack of commitment that had kept him small and held him back from life. He saw those things, and with a sudden solemn joy he knew that he could cast them off.

He would not hold back and he would not fail. He knew that now. The sky began to turn a pale yellow in the east. He headed back toward his hotel to get to work.

Striding along Argyle Street, he passed sleeping restaurants with their chairs propped upside down on their scrubbed tables, and hip boutiques, their display windows now mute and dim. The orange light from streetlamps grew grainy and didn't quite seem to mix with the wan illumination of the dawn. The streets were practically empty; somewhere a garbage truck groaned.

A couple of blocks ahead, a small delivery van turned onto the street. *A comforting urban sight*, thought Artisan; delivering hot bread or fresh delicious pastries for the morning's early customers.

But this van did not move at the stately pace of a truck making local deliveries. Having made the turn, it shot forward with a screech of its spindly tires. Its headlamps were switched onto high beams, sending forth a sweeping, blinding glare. *A drunk, no doubt*, the detective thought; some fool hurtling toward a daredevil ending to a wasted night.

He felt no more intimate misgivings until the speeding van was half a block away and suddenly angling toward the sidewalk.

A jolt of adrenaline fired deep inside Paul Artisan, carrying with it the miraculous power to make time go slowly. He saw the van's front tires hit the curb, the impact compressing them down to the rims. The little truck bucked like a horse, found its balance, and charged straight toward him. The detective felt the fatal impulse to freeze, to go past panic, past survival, to a perhaps serene, passive death. Now he could read the rivets and small rough scratches on the van's front fender.

He begged his muscles and sinews to work and he dove into the shallow shelter of a doorway. The van streaked past him, rocking and snorting. Sparks flew and there was a hideous scraping as the truck's fender glanced along a stone facade; fish-tailing, the back end took out a display window. Glass rained down and splattered and a burglar alarm began to wail.

Then the van was gone. The street was empty again. Paul Artisan sat crumpled in the doorway, and for some moments his legs refused to lift him up. Finally, unsteady as a toddler, he rose. Side-stepping glass, moving slowly at first then breaking into a breathless jog, he went back to the hotel above the brewery. He reached his room just as the sirens were cranking up.

He threw cold water on his face, then called the number Pru had given him.

A woman's voice answered the phone, a voice so thick with sleep that he couldn't tell if it was his new lover or the sister who worked in biotech. He asked for Pru.

The voice said, "Christ, do you have any idea what time it is?"

"Actually, I don't," the detective admitted. "I'm sorry. But, please, it's important. Is she there?"

Rather grudgingly, the sleepy woman asked him to hang on. After a moment, Pru said hello. She sounded a lot less groggy than her sister.

"Pru, it's Paul."

There was a moment of baffled silence. Then she said, "I'm happy to hear from you, but it's awfully—"

"A truck just tried to run me down."

"What?"

He told her about the careening van, the desperate dive into the doorway, the breaking glass, the sirens.

She said, "Jesus. You're okay?"

"I'm fine. But I'm shook up and I'm pissed off and I guess I needed to hear your voice."

There was a pause, then a sharp, affronted intake of breath. Pru said, "You needed to know that I was home. You needed to know it wasn't me."

Artisan considered that. Adrenaline put a glary wash on everything; he hadn't yet had time to ferret out the details of his fear and his suspicion. But here was this woman who had lied to him, who had already once successfully pretended to be a very different person than she was, who had made love to him with a revolver in her purse. He said, "Yes. Sorry. But I think I've earned my paranoia."

She said, "I wouldn't hurt you, Paul."

He heard himself say, "Then, would you help me?"

There was a pause. She didn't seem to understand the question, and Paul Artisan himself wasn't yet quite sure what he was asking.

"Look," he went on, "I can do this job, but I'm not sure I can do it alone. There's too much I don't know. I don't know your city. I don't know your country. I want you to help me find Zander."

She seemed to think that over, but not for long. "Paul, think what you're asking me to do. Cliff Widmore is an important client of our agency. I can make some excuse and drop this assignment, but I can't just jump sides and work against—"

"Pru, listen. There's a lot that I don't know, but there's a few things you don't know. You think of Cliff as a rich bully who would blackmail his own stepmother. I happen to believe there's a very real chance that he's a murderer."

"A murderer? You're serious?"

"Serious as cancer. Think about it. Cliff hires me to find his twin. Why? The story I get is so he can be joyously reunited with the father. Then he hires you to spy on me. Why? To know when or if I'm getting close, to get some advance word on Zander's whereabouts. Why does he need advance word? I don't think it's so he can plan the homecoming party. Now, who's the guy in the van, Pru? Either he's with you, which I prefer not to believe, or he's yet another layer put in place by Cliff to make sure that Zander never reaches home."

Pru said, "But why—?"

Artisan said, "I'll explain. I need to see you. I need your help."

"I really shouldn't do this."

"It clearly isn't prudent," said Paul Artisan. "But you're not a prudent person, are you? Zander was supposedly meeting some people in the black pearl business. Is there anything like a jewelry district in this town?"

She sighed, and named a café on Pitt Street, and said that she would meet him in an hour.

30

Over tea and scones he told her about Moth and the power of attorney, and about Crunch and the mysterious Cuban, and about the purported suicide of Shannon Widmore.

She heard him out, then said, "But couldn't it all be just exactly the other way round?"

"Please," said Artisan, "let's not even go there."

She went there anyway. "You're suggesting that Cliff is behind the deaths. But Moth could have been killed because he was involved in something criminal with Zander. Crunch might have died because someone didn't want him snooping into shady goings-on in Cuba. And Shannon could as easily have been taken out by one twin as the other, or could have killed herself out of guilt for an affair with her husband's brother. Isn't it just as logical with Zander as the bad guy?"

He rubbed his neck and pictured her on the plane with *Trent's Last Case.* He dreaded the possibility that he might have to rip apart all the logical connections he'd painstakingly put together, and be forced to reassemble them from scratch.

Trying not to whine, he said, "I *started* with Zander as the bad guy. The druggy. The thief. The guy who made trouble just for spite. If you knew how many times I've gone back and forth on this . . . This twin stuff, this mirror-image stuff—it's enough to make you crazy. If one twin's good, the other must be bad. It's like this primordial battle between good and evil, darkness and light."

Pru broke off a piece of scone and said matter-of-factly, "Or they could both be sons of bitches. If one twin's awful, that doesn't mean the other one's a prince. From what I've seen, the whole family's pretty miserable."

Paul Artisan picked up some crumbs with the flat part of his thumb. "The stepmother, you mean?"

"Yeah," said Pru, and she flushed quite prettily with indignation. "With her sordid little Thursday afternoons. Okay, she's still got a healthy libido and she married an old man. So get yourself some fresh batteries, dearie, and draw a nice warm bath. I mean, she made her choice. Why can't people honor the choices they've made?"

Idly, Artisan said, "This Mr. Thursday—who is he?"

"We've got photos," Pru said, "but haven't been able to ID him. He doesn't really seem like grade-A gigolo material. Probably around sixty, okay-looking but no matinee idol. Nice suits, salt-and-pepper hair. He arrives and leaves in taxis. Her too, separately."

Artisan shook his head. "I feel bad for old man Widmore. Have you met him?"

Pru said that she hadn't.

"He's sort of like King Lear. A bit of a blowhard but basically a decent guy who can't understand why things are no longer going his way. Tries to do the right thing while his family either falls to pieces or turns against him."

Pru touched the back of his hand and smiled. "You see," she said, "that's why Aussie women fall for American guys. Our chaps don't cite Shakespeare."

He wasn't sure if it was the compliment or the touch of her

hand, but he suddenly wanted to make love with her right then and there. He deflected the thought by saying, "Zander supposedly came to Sydney to talk with some people about pearls. Black ones. Do you know much about black pearls?"

"Only that they're expensive and trendy. And that there are a lot of just so-so ones around and the really good ones are hard to come by."

He sipped some cooling tea and heard himself say, "Like women."

"More like men, actually," she countered.

"Guess it depends on your point of view," he said. "One more question. Do you agree that we're never going to figure out which possible version of the truth is true except by finding Zander?"

"Yeah," said Pru, "I agree with that."

"So let's go find him," said Paul Artisan.

To the visiting American it felt like that drowsy time in the second half of afternoon, but in fact it was around nine thirty in the morning and the upscale shops on Pitt Street were just opening for business. The two detectives ducked into an elegant boutique that specialized in emeralds and sapphires and opals.

They were greeted by an eager young salesman. His hair was moussed, his collar was crisp, his manners were impeccable. They told him they'd like to see something in black pearls.

"Ah!" he said, completely delighted by the request. "Come this way. Just got in the most amazing double-stranded necklace. Stunning pearls. Totally stunning."

He reached into a vitrine and came up with the necklace, pinned against cream-colored velvet to set off the rich hues of the pearls. They were black, yes, but they also held a mysterious sheen-less silver and a moody green like the bottom of the ocean and a comforting blue-violet that was like the endless, embracing dark of deep space.

"Magnificent, isn't it?" said the salesman. "Not cheap, I'm afraid. Fifty thousand dollars. Would you like to try it on?"

Pru waved away the offer. "Thanks, but it would be too sad to take it off again."

Paul Artisan made bold to finger a pearl. It was wonderfully cool and he imagined it would stay that way even on a woman's neck. "Where do they come from?" he asked.

"These particular ones," the salesman said, "come from an island between the north coast and Bali."

Pru said, "They're farmed, yes?"

"Oh, yes," the salesman said. "Have to be. Far too rare in nature. One pearl in a thousand is a black pearl."

"Guess that's why they're pricey," said Paul Artisan.

The salesman made a clicking sound with his tongue. "But you know, even at these prices, most of the producers barely make a profit. It's a horribly difficult business."

"How so?" Pru asked.

"First of all," the salesman said, "it's incredibly labor intensive. To get a single pearl, you basically have to perform surgery on an oyster, put this tiny pellet in just the right place in the ovary. Don't get it exactly right, the oyster dies and you've got to start over. Even if it works, you've then got to babysit the oyster for a couple years, checking its progress and health. So many things can go wrong. The water has to be pristine. A change in salinity or temperature can be deadly. Plus you've got the constant threat of piracy—"

"Piracy?" said Artisan. The word shot through him as if he'd stuck his finger in a socket. If the bad version of Zander were the true one—if he was a reckless adventurer and self-destructive thrill-seeker—what could be more romantic than playing pirate?

"Oh, yes," the salesman placidly went on. "You see, the oysters are attached to ropes, and they just sit there in the open water. The producers build cages and nets and such, but it's virtually impossible to really safeguard the crop. Pirates come in with a fast boat, some sharp knives, and a couple of scuba tanks, and they can steal tens of thousands of dollars' worth of oysters in twenty minutes."

Pru said, "And the stolen pearls are sold to retailers?"

The salesman said, "At a tempting discount, of course. *We* would never deal in pearls of questionable provenance, but plenty of merchants do."

Paul Artisan said, "Anyone producing pearls up at the Barrier Reef?"

"Not that I'm aware of. Conditions would be perfect, I suppose. But it's become almost impossible to do anything up there. Land is wildly expensive. Everything is strictly regulated. I did recently hear a rumor, though."

Artisan tried to keep his feet in his shoes. "Yes?"

"Supposedly some chap with more money than is good for him was trying to buy a little cluster of islands and turn the whole thing into a sort of pearl farm and reserve."

Pru said, "Know anything about the fellow?"

"Not really. American is what I heard. Then again, the loonies with the big ideas and unlimited funds usually are. No offense, of course."

"Of course," said Artisan.

"What part of the Reef?" asked Pru.

The salesman grew a little cautious. "Look, it's just a rumor."

"Understood," said Pru. "What part of the Reef?"

"Pretty far north is what I've heard. Out from Lizard Island, that area."

Paul Artisan looked sideways at his colleague and lover. To the salesman he said, "Well, thank you. Thank you very much."

The salesman gestured down at the gorgeous necklace. "Can I show you something else, perhaps? Something less expensive?"

The two detectives were already heading for the door.

31

Pru held the taxi while Paul gathered up his few things and checked out of the hotel above the brewery. Then they drove to Paddington, where she ran up to her sister's flat, emerging in five minutes with a shoulder bag and a medium-size suitcase.

Nodding toward the luggage, Artisan said, "How long are we staying?"

She said, "We'll need to check a bag, won't we? For the—" She dropped her hand below the level of the seat and made a trigger-pulling gesture.

"Right," said Artisan. "That little thing."

"*Those* little things," she corrected.

With just a touch of lingering unease, he said, "Oh, you have one too?"

"You didn't think I'd come along without one, did you?"

He didn't answer that, just tried to keep his face as neutral as could be.

She said, "Still a little suspicious, Paul? Live with it. It'll give an extra bit of excitement to our time together."

He looked over at her, at her graceful neck and sculpted

shoulders and elegant jawline and generous lips. "I don't need any more excitement. I'm in knots for you as it is."

She liked that. She squirmed a little and her mouth moved in what was half a smile and half a puckering-up to kiss.

Inside the terminal, they bought their tickets for Cairns with a connection out to Lizard Island. Then, at the gate, waiting to board, Pru took out her laptop to check her e-mail.

"Oh, great," she said. "I'm on probation."

"Hm?"

"I e-mailed my boss yesterday," she said, "quitting my surveillance of you. I just said I had pressing family matters here in Sydney. Now he tells me that's unacceptable and unprofessional, and I'm on probation until I explain myself more fully."

"Bosses suck," said Artisan.

"Easy for you to say."

"Yeah, it is," he admitted.

"I don't think I'd have the nerve to go off on my own," said Pru.

"Doesn't take nerve. Takes pigheadedness and a lifelong tendency toward insubordination. Mind if I check mine?"

She handed him the computer. He had just one message that was of interest. It was from Manny Weissman.

Manny had been continuing his research into old Scottish laws and traditions. Now he had a question: He wanted Paul to guess when the feudal system had been abolished there. Artisan passed the question on to Pru.

"Oh, boy," she said. "Like fiefs and vassals? History's my worst subject. But I'd say the 1600s."

"I'd guess just a little later," Artisan said. "Maybe around the time of the American and French Revolutions."

He scrolled down for the answer. It was 2004. November 28, to be exact.

Manny Weissman had written *Scottish feudalism lived into the twenty-first century! These people seem to take the old traditions very much to heart.*

Pru said, "Interesting. How does it connect?"

He told her about the birth order and the law of primogeniture.

She could not hold back a slightly wicked chuckle at the thought of Cliff Widmore, with his custom shirts and five-hundred-dollar loafers, being cut off from his inheritance. She said, "But primogeniture, in this day and age—it seems a little far-fetched, doesn't it?"

"It's just a theory," said Paul Artisan. "But Manny's theories have a way of being right."

The flight to Cairns was uneventful, but the hop to Lizard Island was breathtaking. Flying below the scattered, fluffy clouds, the little plane threw its shadow over water that was a hundred shades of green and turquoise and indigo, and over ribbons and patches of coral that were mustard yellow and burgundy red and the lavender of freshly opened lilacs. The Reef seemed to go on forever, following the bend of the earth at each horizon.

Pointing out the window, Pru said, "Biggest living thing on the planet. And the only one visible from the moon."

The landing strip at Lizard was a slightly rough affair, crushed coral held together with imperfect mortar. But once the rattling and the bumping were over, and the engine had been quelled, and they'd stepped down from the little staircase that was so much more romantic than a Jetway, all was peace. Lizard Island smelled like hot seashells and cool water. Palms swayed and rattled; the sound was like maracas.

There was only one resort on the island. It was the sort of place where they met you in a golf cart and handed you a glass of some

fabulous tropical juice, then swept you off to a waterfront bunga-
low full of bamboo this and rattan that, with a big inviting bed
above which twirled a lazy and mesmeric ceiling fan.

Checked in and heading for their room, Paul Artisan thought,
*Whatever else happens here, we've come to paradise together. This is no
longer just a passionate collision of strangers. We're arriving as a freshly
minted couple.*

It was way too soon to be falling in love but he suspected that
he was.

He wished he could forget that she had packed a second gun.

Inside, he said to her, "I think I've discovered a new side effect of
jet lag. I want you at the oddest hours."

She said, "We have work to do." But even as she said it, her
shoulders took on a certain softness that suggested recreation.

He pointed out the window. Beyond it was a strip of fine white
sand and then an emerald lagoon, a calmly twinkling pool perfectly framed by fringes of the Reef. He said, "I don't see how we
can resist a swim, at least."

She said, "No, I don't think we can resist a swim."

He said, "But then I won't be able to resist making love to you
while your skin is still all cool and salty."

She looked at him and, unconsciously, her tongue flicked out
just the tiniest bit to lick her lips. "Are you always so frisky?" she
asked.

"Actually," he said, "it's been a long time since I've been this
frisky. And that's the truth."

Later, they strolled the beach with its happy assortment of kayaks
and Sunfish and Hobie Cats, then went to the concierge desk in
hopes of finding a way to explore the out-islands where it was just

possible that Zander Widmore was scheming to install a pearl farm.

Sitting behind a bamboo desk, the concierge was a perfect Aussie. He was sunburned; he was freckled; he was broad and he was friendly. He said, "Right. Exploring the empty islands. Fabulous idea. Amazing snorkeling out there. If you've got a taste for it—not everybody does—you can go right out to the edge of the Coral Sea, where there's a mile drop-off into the Pacific. That's where you can swim with the marlin and the big sharks."

"Not too sure I feature that," Paul Artisan admitted.

"Right," said the concierge. "Just as you like. We do have a private launch for hire. Problem is, one of our other guests has had it booked it all week." He looked down at a ledger on the desk. "For the next three days as well, I'm afraid."

"Ah," said Pru. "That's rather disappointing."

There was a pause, one of those classic hotel standoffs where the staff can't help but the guests won't go away.

"I have a thought," said the concierge. "Perhaps the other guest would be willing to share the charter. I can't speak to that, of course. But he appears to be on his own and he seems an approachable fellow."

"That might work," said Artisan.

"What's his name?" asked Pru.

Only a heartbeat went by between the question and the answer, but in that tiny increment there was time enough for Paul Artisan to say his own version of a prayer, to send forth a silent plea that he would finally catch a break, that all the goose-chasing and blind alleys and befuddled moments would open up at last into the sunshine of clarity and success, and that the guest's name would be Zander Widmore.

It wasn't.

"Purdue," said the concierge. "Mr. Cameron Purdue."

Some air came out of Artisan. He felt his shoulders sag.

"He's been coming back with the launch around five, five thirty," the concierge went on, "and he's usually in the bar for a sundowner by six. Just go introduce yourselves. We're completely casual here at Lizard Island. Everybody talks with everybody."

32

The bar was faux Polynesian, with heavy varnished posts holding up a roof of thatch. Somber carvings flanked the entrance, but any suggestion of solemnity was quickly dispelled by the red and yellow and green drinks served to people on bamboo stools or at little wicker tables. There were no walls, no windows; the soft moist air of the tropics wafted through with the sensuous melancholy of a remembered kiss.

It was just six when Pru and Paul walked in. The sun was low, back in the direction of the Australian mainland—but no mainland could be seen, just vague low outcrops of coral and mangrove, punctuating a sea whose myriad colors were now reduced to a uniform gold as the late light skidded on its surface.

The two detectives casually looked around for a man sitting by himself. They didn't see one. There were couples huddled with their faces close over fancy cocktails served with straws. At the bar there was a group of Aussie guys, fishing buddies—the type, no doubt, that Pru couldn't stand—sucking beer and lying about fish that they had caught.

Not till they had scanned the whole place did they see a man alone. Sitting at a table with a glass of wine and a bowl of nuts, half-hidden by a post, he had his back to everyone and was facing out toward the water and the sunset. Artisan studied him a moment, though he could not have said what he was looking for or what he imagined a stranger's back could possibly teach him.

Still, he sensed in the man sitting by himself something that was other than ordinary loneliness. Something in his posture suggested self-exile, a willful aloneness with a conscious purpose; a cleansing mission, maybe; or even a sort of self-invented purgatory here in the midst of paradise. He wore a loose linen shirt whose collar only half-covered his sunburned neck. On his head, he wore a silk do-rag knotted at the corners; it was impossible to tell if he had hair.

Slowly, with an anticipation that was very much like terror putting electricity at the backs of his legs, Paul Artisan guided Pru toward the solitary stranger. Just before they reached his table, Pru said, "Mr. Purdue?"

In answer to her engaging voice and lovely accent, he swiveled in his chair.

Paul Artisan blinked and swallowed and felt himself grow slightly dizzy—less a physical dizziness than the kind of unmoored feeling that sweeps over people in the presence of the uncanny. Every human face on earth is purportedly unique, but this was a face that mocked that comfortable assumption. This face was a double, a face not truly owned by anyone because it was shared by two. The deep-set eyes were so blue they were almost violet. The chin was square but not heavy or aggressive; a perfect chin. The face was spared from mere prettiness by a slight thickening at the bridge of the nose and some worldly weathering at the corners of the eyes.

"Yes?" said Zander Widmore, or Mr. Cameron Purdue.

With a steadiness that Artisan could only admire, Pru said, "The concierge suggested we talk to you. I hope you don't mind."

He smiled and said, "Of course not. What can I do for you?"

The smile was Cliff's smile, beautiful teeth behind lips that curled just slightly asymmetrically. The voice was Cliff's voice, or nearly. It had the charm but maybe not quite the facetious edge.

Pru asked him about the possibility of sharing the charter of the launch.

Zander/Cameron blinked off toward the lowering sun. He said, "You're totally welcome to come along. As my guests, of course. But I don't think it would be very interesting for you. I'm not sight-seeing or diving or anything like that. I'm actually looking at real estate."

Artisan took the opportunity to jump in. "There's property for sale out here?"

"Only under very special circumstances. You're American."

"Yeah," said Artisan. "From New York. And you?"

"Oh, a tiny little town in California. Probably you've never heard of it. Called Luna."

"Ah," said Artisan, and he wondered about the alias and the phony version of where he came from. Was it simply that he hoped not to be found, or was there some deeper drive to shuttle off the person he had been, to divorce himself from the identity that had only seemed half his, and to emerge redeemed, a different man?

Zander/Cameron said, "On vacation?"

Some spark of playfulness or tactics led Pru to blurt out, "Actually, we're on our honeymoon."

The lonely man seemed genuinely pleased for them, as decent people always are when others find a mate. "That's terrific," he said. "Congratulations." He gestured toward the vermilion sun that was now just a hand's breadth above the Coral Sea. "I'm sure you want to savor this romantic sunset. If you want to come along tomorrow, be down at the dock at seven thirty."

They all shook hands. The sun went down. The stars came out. Pru pointed out the Southern Cross.

When they sat down to dinner, they found a bottle of champagne already chilling in a silver bucket on their table. It had been sent by Mr. Cameron Purdue.

Next morning there was a gauze of red cloud in the east. Low tropical sunshine diffused behind it, staining the water with a tinge like drying blood. The breeze was already warm and carried with it a tang of iodine.

When Paul and Pru reached the dock, the launch skipper was just laying in a cooler full of drinks and sandwiches. Another poster Aussie, he was hale and red-haired and wore a neat safari shirt with epaulettes on the shoulders. Looking up from the cockpit of the boat, he introduced himself as Brian. "So," he said, "you're friends of Cameron's?"

"Just acquaintances, actually. I'm Pru."

"I'm Paul."

"Well, welcome aboard. Here, let me take your bag."

Pru handed him the beach tote she'd been carrying. To his surprise, the weight of it deflected Brian's beefy arm. "Heavier than it looks," he said.

Pru just gave a little shrug.

Then Cameron/Zander came rambling down the dock. His walk was forward-leaning, purposeful. He wore a smile that was wide but tight, and suggested to Paul Artisan less a simple happiness than a kind of quiet mania. "Ah," he said, "the honeymooners. You've decided to come along."

"Wouldn't miss it," said Pru. "And thanks for the champagne."

He waved away the thanks. "Well, I hope you won't be disappointed with the expedition." He stepped aboard with the ease of someone who'd spent a lot of time on boats. To Brian, he said, "All right, mate, let's get out there and hunt for paradise."

Paul Artisan couldn't help thinking: *Hunt for paradise? Weren't*

*they there already? And what were the chances that anyone who had to look
so hard for it would ever find it?*

The launch eased out from the dock, was funneled into deeper
water, then roared up onto plane, heading north and east toward
the outer limits of the Reef. The clouds burned off and the sun
blazed down. Brian zigged and zagged to avoid yellow and purple
coral heads in the shape of giant mushrooms and enormous cauliflowers. Nurse sharks swam by lazily; eagle rays with eight-foot
wingspans glided along like some unearthly bird designed for flying underwater.

After a while, above the loud whine of the engine, Pru shouted
to Zander/Cameron, "Are you thinking of building a house out
here?"

"For myself?" the other man shouted back. "Oh, no. Wouldn't
be allowed. It's all marine sanctuary."

"Then why—?" said Artisan.

Zander/Cameron cut him off, but gently. "I don't mean to be
mysterious, but I can't talk about it. Very superstitious. Tell a wish,
it won't come true. This is just a fantasy I've had for a long time.
But sometimes fantasies happen, right?"

Pru offered a vague nod of support. Then she reached into her
bag and came out with a tube of sunblock. She rubbed some on
Paul's neck. He rubbed some on hers. He loved having license to
touch her.

They roared along for an hour or so, then, still far in the distance, they could see where the water changed. The shallows, with
their hundred nuanced hues, abruptly ended. Beyond, a gorgeous
blue like an ideal of denim stretched forever.

Perhaps a half mile before the change, there was a cluster of several small islands. Brian steered toward them. He throttled back;
the launch came down off plane, its deep-V hull now slogging
through a sea that suddenly seemed viscous. He nosed between

two outcrops, brought the engine down to idle, and turned his attention entirely to Cameron.

"You see," he said, "out here is good if you need water circulation. There's some mixing in with the Pacific, though less than you might think, because the temperature differential makes a kind of boundary."

Zander/Cameron nodded thoughtfully.

"The downside," Brian went on, "is that you're way more vulnerable to storm surge."

The other man said, "Good sites for the settlements?"

The skipper said, "Prevailing winds are easterlies, so you'll want west-facing beaches and bays. Here, I'll show you what there is."

Steering vigilantly, he weaved between the islets, pointing out breaks in the mangroves and natural clearings fringed with casuarinas. Rounding one outcrop, he dodged a ribbon of coral and headed in to examine the next.

That's when Pru spotted the other boat.

It was far off in the distance, tiny and elusive as a satellite in the night sky. Still, it was strange to see another craft at all in that immensity of sea; they hadn't seen another boat since five or ten minutes out from Lizard Island. And why, of all possible trajectories in the trackless ocean, did this new craft seem to be headed directly toward them?

She caught Paul's eye and steered it toward the possible intruder. In turn, he glanced down toward her beach bag. She nodded. In unconscious sync they each drew a deep breath and exhaled very slowly. The other boat was perhaps two miles distant. It seemed to be traveling very fast and its course did not waver for a second.

Brian continued with his survey of the islets, pointing out possible locations for piers and cisterns and dwellings.

The other boat kept coming. It could be seen now that it was a speedboat, Cigarette-type, with a high, wide spoiler and a hull as black as death. It held course like a rifle shot and a plume of spray rose up behind it.

The launch idled placidly along. Zander/Cameron asked questions.

Pru decided they could wait no longer. She bent down and reached into the beach tote. She came out with the nickel-plated .32 as well as a 9 mm she'd retrieved in Sydney. She gave the pistol to Paul and kept the revolver for herself.

Brian saw the guns glint in the brilliant sunshine. He said, "What the bloody hell—"

Paul Artisan said, "Look, we're on the same side here, okay? We're a little worried about that other boat."

For the first time, the skipper looked out at the oncoming craft, now maybe half a mile away. "It's just some silly rich man's toy," he said.

Artisan said, "It's had a bead on us for miles. That seem usual to you?"

The clattering roar of its oversize engine could now be heard. Brian and Zander/Cameron shared a look.

Pru said, "I don't imagine we can outrun the thing?"

"In here? No way," said Brian. Then he gestured toward the rolling swell of the indigo Pacific. "Out there we might have a chance."

Artisan said, "I think we ought to get our asses out there."

Brian finally looked worried. He glanced at his client. Zander/Cameron nodded. The skipper edged toward open water and gunned the engine. It seemed maddeningly sluggish now, slow to get up on plane.

The other boat closed relentlessly. Behind its glaring windshield two figures could be seen. No details, no faces; just malevolent silhouettes getting nearer every second.

The boundary between the Coral Sea and the Pacific seemed to keep receding. The speedboat chased the launch's stern, then finally deviated just enough to come up along its flank—the wide part, the biggest target, like when you stalked an animal. Paul Artisan did not yet see weapons, but he saw a certain posture, a readiness, an unmistakable intent.

In tandem, he saw two thick arms beginning to be raised.

Beyond thought, he shouted, "Zander! Get down!"

Then the shooting started.

Quick bursts blazed forth from the speedboat. Pru and Paul braced against the gunwales and fired back. With the speed and the chop and the rocking, shots went high and shots went wide and shots knifed down into the water. The windshield of the launch was shattered; glass spilled into the cockpit.

Finally they reached the seam between two seas. The shallow-bottomed speedboat hit the swell like a skidding car sliding up a snowbank. Its nose lifted, it did a half-twist, it slammed into a trough and resumed its grinding, angry progress. Its passengers kept shooting, shots now random in the percolating chop.

Pru wedged herself for balance between the console and the gunwale. Paul Artisan dropped to his knees and braced his elbows on the transom.

Broadside to the waves, the speedboat dipped and rolled and showed its belly, and Artisan squeezed off a lucky shot that found the death-black hull just where it sheltered the big gas tank. The bullet tore through, ripping shards that carried sparks; the sparks brought forth the fury in the fuel. There was an eerie *whoosh* as the nascent fire sucked for oxygen; then a pregnant hesitation; then the speedboat did not so much burst into flame as become flame.

For a grim moment it crackled and hissed. Then it exploded. The explosion seemed to happen in extreme slow motion. A small red mushroom cloud lazily rose up. In it was a pair of fire-licked bodies, somersaulting almost gracefully.

The bodies fell; the flames subsided; the pieces of the fiberglass speedboat were already melting into the bottomless Pacific.

Suddenly it was very quiet. In the launch, a mix of fear and awe seemed to make it impossible for anyone to move. Finally, Brian said, "Everyone all right?"

The voice broke the spell. People straightened up. Like survivors of any disaster, they felt the need for touch, for contact.

Paul and Pru threw their hot guns in the ocean.

As they headed slowly back toward calmer water, Paul Artisan reached into his pocket and said to Brian, "I hope we can all agree that nothing unusual happened here today."

The launch captain said, "They fired first. You don't need to pay me off. But maybe it's time you all left Lizard Island."

Then, for the first time since the shooting started, the man whom Paul Artisan had called Zander finally spoke. His deep blue eyes flicking back and forth between Paul and Pru, he said, "Who the hell *are* you people?"

33

The three of them were on the next plane off of Lizard Island, but they didn't have much opportunity to talk until they'd reached the airport at Cairns. Walking into the terminal, Zander said, "I could use a drink and I'd really like some explanations. Anyone like to join me for a beer?"

They ducked into a concourse bar and found a quiet table beneath a giant television showing cricket. The beers arrived in enormous frosted mugs; they tasted fabulous after the salt and hot sun of the Reef, after the fear, after the stink of burning gasoline and human flesh and plastic. Paul Artisan took several gulps before he started talking.

When he finished his recitation, Zander Widmore said, "Wait. Let me make sure I have this right. My brother hired you to find me because he was quite confident that you wouldn't."

"Correct," said Artisan.

The twin now turned to Pru. "And he hired *you* to spy on *him*, once it appeared that he was actually getting close."

"Right," said Pru. "Exactly."

"And you gather from this," said Zander, "that he wanted word of where I was so he could have me killed?"

Neither detective answered the question. It seemed better in that moment to let the Widmore heir live with it a while.

After a pull on his beer, he shook his head and went on. "I don't buy it. Look, my brother Cliff's a real prick, pardon my French. He's manipulative, he's phony, and I don't doubt for a second that he'd rather I'd never been born. But actually killing me—no. He's too smart to be a criminal. Too smarmy too. That's his great talent. He gets his way without actually breaking the rules."

Artisan shared a secret glance with Pru. Denial was a powerful thing, and it was hard even to imagine the difficulty and pain of acknowledging that one's own twin, one's own genetic double, had murder on his mind.

Zander seemed to wrestle with the notion for a moment, then went on. "Besides, think about it: I'm his *twin*. The other half of what we started from. Unfortunately, I'm him and he's me. Could he hate himself that much?"

As gently as he could, Paul said, "Zander, there's some things you probably don't know about. Your buddy Moth. You know he's dead?"

He drank more beer before he answered. "Yeah, I know. A friend from Peconiquot got word to me."

"You know that he was murdered?"

"Murdered?" said Zander. "He wasn't murdered. A boat fell on him. It was an accident."

"The cradle was tampered with," said Artisan. "It's being treated as a homicide."

"Jesus Christ."

"He had a power of attorney from you," the detective said.

For the first time, Zander Widmore looked suspicious. His posture stiffened, his eyebrows moved just slightly, his voice took on an edge. "How do you know about that?"

"The cops found it. They had a warrant to go through Moth's things. Why'd you give him a power of attorney?"

Zander looked away and bit his lip. "I'm not ready to talk about that."

Pru ventured a guess. "Your superstition again? Tell a wish, it won't come true?"

"Something like that."

Paul Artisan said, "Have anything to do with your friend down in Havana?"

Zander put his glass down a bit harder than he needed to and stared at the detective. "For Christ's sake, why am I getting the third degree here?"

Pru said, "Zander, we're on your side. I think you know that by now."

Artisan said, "Don't worry, he didn't tell me anything. Not even his name. But the guy who brought me from Key West? He was killed. And the other night in Sydney, someone tried to run me down. And today out at the Reef . . ."

He reached out and gripped the other man's arm before continuing.

"Zander, it isn't a pretty thing to think about, okay? But if we didn't happen to be there, it's an excellent bet you'd be dead by now. Eaten by the sharks or pecked apart by gulls. I'm sorry, but will you please understand that we're talking life and death here?"

He seemed to take that in. But if it shook him, the effect was very understated, registering as little more than a slight flush of the forehead and some quick blinks behind his sandy lashes. When he spoke again, the words were either very stoic or shockingly impersonal. He said, "It really doesn't matter. Except that I have work to do."

He raised his glass as if toasting his own labors.

Pru said, "Zander, you're older than Cliff, aren't you?"

He nodded. "Fifteen, twenty minutes."

She said, "Has your father ever talked about inheritance? About how things will be divided?"

"Not the kind of thing that he would talk about. Very déclassé to talk about money."

Paul Artisan said, "Has it occurred to you that you might be sole heir?"

"Excuse me?"

"By the law of primogeniture."

In spite of everything, Zander Widmore could not suppress a quick percussive laugh. "Primogeniture? But that's medieval!"

Artisan said, "With due respect, so's your father."

Thinking that over required another round of beers. Zander signaled for them.

Then he said, "Look, that would be crazy. My father's eccentric. He's gone a little ga-ga with this Scottish stuff. But he wouldn't take it that far."

The fresh beers arrived. Pru said, very quietly, "You sure?"

Zander sipped through foam and thought that over. "Sure? No," he admitted. "Not entirely."

Paul Artisan said, "Just before you left Locust Valley, the evening before Shannon's funeral, you and your father had a rather bitter argument, yes?"

Zander glanced down at the table that was splotched with broken rings of condensation. The memory of the quarrel seemed to cause him pain. He nodded, then said, "The old man tell you what it was about?"

"No. He said it was just between the two of you."

At that, Zander flashed a rueful smile that Artisan had seen before. It was the same exact expression of family love and family sorrow, thwarted affection and well-nourished regret, that he'd seen on the face of Cliff. It was the one mannerism and perhaps the sole emotion in which the mirror-image twins were perfectly equal partners.

He said, "Ah, Dad. He's so old-school. Of course he wouldn't tell. Though it wasn't exactly just between the two of us. Vivian and Cliff were also there. It was quite the family argument."

Pru said, "So what was it about?"

"Nice try," said Zander. "But if Dad's enough of a gentleman not to broadcast family matters, I think I should follow his lead."

"Actually," said Artisan, "I have a message from your father. It's why he wants you to come home."

The words had a strange effect on Zander Widmore. Almost instantly his jaw softened, his forehead smoothed, his eyes grew tender and needy. He leaned forward as if wanting to close the distance between his father's message and himself. He seemed suddenly like a small boy hungry for kindness, hoping for a warm hand on his shoulder.

Artisan said, "He says that, after you left, he thought about the argument and decided you were right."

Hands on the table, eyes on his hands, Zander very softly asked, "He said that?"

"He wanted me to tell you."

There was a pause. Overhead, the mute cricket game continued on the giant screen. Vaguely the white noise of the airport filtered in—the PA voice in several languages, the beeping of the carts that carried the infirm.

Finally, Pru said, "Zander, will you come back to the States with us? Will you let us bring you home?"

34

At the Oceanic counter, Zander bought himself a ticket to Los Angeles by way of Honolulu, with a connection on a domestic carrier on a red-eye to New York. He paid for Paul and Pru to change their Sydney tickets. Then they eased into the dull, familiar airport game of waiting, waiting, waiting.

But once they were en route across the South Pacific, drinking red wine from actual glasses, the Widmore twin became extremely chatty, animated, almost manic.

If he'd ever really grasped the danger he was in, and remained in even now, he seemed conveniently to forget about it. All that seemed to matter was that he was going home. Going home because his father wanted to be reconciled. Going home because, after a lifetime of feeling that everything he did was wrong, his father now acknowledged that the wish that meant the most to him was right. Relief and vindication dwarfed everything else he might be feeling, even mortal fear.

Suddenly, apropos of nothing, Zander said to Paul and Pru, "You're not religious, are you?"

The detectives acknowledged that they weren't.

"Me neither," Zander said. "But there are certain things I

believe in. Spiritual things. Like good and evil. How can I say this? They're not just adjectives. They don't just describe things. They *are* things. Good exists. Evil exists. They're opposites—but opposites have almost everything in common. You see?"

"Like twins," said Pru.

Zander sipped more wine. "Fair enough," he said. "Like twins. Plus two and minus two. Positive charge and negative charge. If they weren't *nearly* identical, they wouldn't be opposites. That's why it's so easy to confuse them."

He swiveled in his leather seat, fiddled with his do-rag, warmed to his subject. "Of course, with human opposites or human twins, it's hard to make it cut and dried, because humans are so damn complicated. I mean, speaking for myself, I've been bad, really bad. But at least I've known it, okay? I've chosen it. I've wallowed in it. With Cliff, it's always been different. He's bad while pretending to be good. Which is worse? You tell me."

Without hesitation, Pru said, "It's worse to be a hypocrite."

Zander said, "That's what I think. But look around, look at the people who run things—the world prefers a hypocrite every time. Still, at the end of the day, you have to choose. Am I going to be a good person? Or am I going to be a selfish scumbag? The hard part is that you don't choose only once. Okay, maybe if you're a great saint or a mystic, you have some amazing breakthrough and you never have to deal with it again. But most of us have to *keep on* choosing. Day in, day out. Year in, year out. Good or bad—which way are we going to go?"

Paul Artisan said, "That's the whole idea of purgatory, right?" He was playing to Pru, of course, still wooing her with the tidbits he'd picked up from Manny Weissman. "Like in Dante. People suffer, but there's a point to it, a purpose. It's a last chance to cleanse your sins, clear your conscience, so you can qualify for heaven."

"Exactly!" Zander said. "But what if there is no heaven? No hell either. No afterlife at all."

Pru drained her glass and said, "I'm not quite sure I follow that."

Zander said, "If there's no afterlife, no eternal reward to shoot for, then purgatory is *now*. I don't mean that to sound gloomy. Not at all. I mean that *this* is our chance to get it right. First chance. Last chance. *Only* chance. But that's exciting. Beautiful. Right?"

"And very difficult," said Artisan.

"Sure it's difficult. So what? Our work in *this* life is to choose good over evil, to be fair, to be kind. And there *is* a payoff, though it doesn't have to do with harps and wings. The payoff is peace of mind. That's what redemption really is."

He paused, seeming almost in a kind of trance.

"Redemption," he said again, slowly, breathily, lovingly. "Most beautiful word in the language, isn't it?"

No reply was called for and the detectives didn't answer.

Zander went quiet after that, savoring the thought, drained by the passion of his argument.

The miles slipped by. They crossed the date line. They dozed. Artisan felt Pru's head on his shoulder once again, remembered the thrill of first contact, the smell and tickle of her hair. The vast Pacific went on and on.

The stop on Oahu was mercifully brief, but after it there were still five hours of ocean to go.

Zander Widmore's moods flickered like a candle in a drafty hallway. One minute he seemed exorbitantly happy at the thought of going back to Locust Valley, receiving the blessing of his old and fading father. The next minute a kind of sourness crept in, as though he were recalling other times when he'd let himself imagine that acceptance was forthcoming, that the roles within the family were finally being reinvented, only to be smacked down by his brother's dismissiveness, his father's disapproval.

Paul Artisan, too, ran a gamut of conflicting moods. He was proud of himself. He'd persevered where in the past he'd shirked; he'd succeeded where the smart money had expected him to fail. He'd found the missing twin half a world away, and with the help of a wonderful colleague who was now his lover, he was bringing him safely home.

But was that the good news or the bad news?

If Cliff Widmore was in fact intent on the murder of his twin, then Artisan was delivering the prey quite literally to his doorstep. Was he playing the part of a guardian angel for a joyful reunion between a father and a son, or was he the dupe who was leading a victim to the slaughter?

At LAX they cleared immigration and customs, then sleepwalked to the gate for the flight to JFK.

In California it was evening. They'd been traveling for sixteen hours. Their clothes were rumpled and their minds were rumpled. Alcohol and caffeine had chased each other through their bloodstreams in a sequence that now seemed wholly random. They were bored and they were hyper, they were tipsy and exhausted. There were two hours before the New York flight.

Pru took out her laptop and checked e-mail. There was a message from her boss at Intercontinental. He was surprised and disappointed not to have heard from her, and she was docked until they'd spoken. Pru quietly cursed him out, then passed the computer to Paul.

He logged in and a moment passed. A completely ordinary moment in an airport. People arriving and people leaving. The joy of reunion, the ache of parting. The bustle that seemed to deny mortality or at least to provide a distraction from it.

Then Pru noticed that Paul's face had gone very slack. His skin had paled, his eyes grown enormous and glassy. "What is it?" she said. "What is it, Paul?"

He couldn't speak for a little time, and when he did, it was not to Pru but Zander. He said, "I'm so sorry. I can't believe I'm the one who has to tell you this. There's been a death."

Bad news, like a stain on fabric, takes a while to sink in. Zander seemed to hear the words as empty sounds and only gradually understood that they had meaning. Then his heart went into mourning before his mind had quite come around to the concept of grief. The grief took on form as a silent inconsolable scream that repeated again and again the wrenching phrase *too late*. After the decades of battling and flailing and searching desperately for a way to love each other, he'd be coming home too late to hug his father. Too late to talk with him. Too late by mere hours. Hours that would cheat them forever of the understanding that would redeem them both.

His voice choked down to a hoarse and shaky whisper, he said, "When?"

"Earlier this evening," said Artisan. "In his own house. Shot. Bungled robbery, it seems."

Zander said, "Shot? My father, shot?"

Now it was Paul Artisan's turn to have a lag in comprehension. He squeezed down with his eyes, then turned his face toward Zander Widmore.

"No. Not your father. Your brother, Cliff."

_____

35

The e-mail was from Manny Weissman. He'd just heard the item on the radio, the Metro New York news. It wasn't in the papers yet; details were sketchy.

Apparently the Widmore heir had come home to find a burglary in progress. His alarm system had been successfully deactivated; some drawers and closets had been ransacked. The burglars had presumably panicked at his unexpected homecoming, and Cliff had been shot twice in the chest. He was dead when police reached the scene. Evidence was being gathered, neighbors being interviewed.

And that was it. There was nothing else that Paul Artisan could pass along to Zander, and nothing that would have made the slightest difference anyway. Death erases nuance, blots out even meaning. The questions that remain are only riddles for the living, ambiguities to ponder as a pale distraction from a loss. To the dead themselves there is nothing consequential, nothing to be said and nothing to be asked.

In the waiting area at LAX, Zander Widmore seemed to have slipped into a state of passive shock that took him far away from everyone and everything. There was both a sag and a stiffness in his posture, as if a soft nudge on the shoulder would be enough to push him over. There was a silence around him so absolute that it seemed it could last the biblical span of forty days.

After a long quiet, Pru gently put a hand on Zander's knee and offered him her phone. "Perhaps you'd like to call your father," she said. "It might be good if he heard from you."

The surviving twin blinked at the phone as if he didn't in that moment quite know what it was. Then he shook his head. In a whisper, he managed to say, "I can't. I can't right now."

Onboard, he took a sleeping pill and washed it down with vodka.

He was soon asleep, and after a while the rhythm of his breathing was interrupted by a rattling catch, a sort of quiet whimper, and Paul and Pru realized he was sobbing. Sleep had eased away the barriers, skirted the defenses. Or maybe it was that Zander's bones and sinews realized only now that they had lost their other half, the half that had lived inside a different skin but was the selfsame substance nonetheless. Or maybe Zander needed dreams to go far back to a time before the hurts and frustrations and belittling, when he and Cliff had been just kids together, brothers, pals.

Not wanting to disturb him, Pru spoke very softly. "At least, with Cliff gone, Zander's out of danger."

Whispering in turn, Paul Artisan said, "You don't actually believe that, do you?"

She looked down at her lap and sighed. "No. But I was sort of hoping you would."

He shook his head. "Not for a heartbeat. If burglars are smart enough to disable an alarm system, they're smart enough not to rob a house just when the commuters are coming home. They were laying for him. You agree?"

"Unfortunately, yeah, I do."

There was a pause. The turbines hummed. Zander's grieving breath rose and fell.

Pru went on, "But the other deaths . . . the van in Sydney, the guys in the speedboat . . . if it wasn't Cliff behind all that—"

Paul cut in and finished the thought. "Then we've got to think the whole thing through again. Just like poor old Trent."

It was dawn when they landed in New York.

At the shops and newsstands along the airport concourse, the morning papers were being unbundled. Cliff Widmore's picture was on the front page of the tabloids, beneath lurid headlines telling of his death. Paul Artisan bought a *Newsday* and a *Daily News*. The vendor didn't seem to notice that the dead man's twin was standing right in front of her. This was New York; strangers didn't meet each other's eyes.

Strolling through the mostly empty terminal, Artisan skimmed the coverage of Cliff's death. It was still being described as a burglary gone sour. But of course the Nassau County cops were not privy to the other pieces of the puzzle, and partial truth was seldom true at all. Partial truth made fools of those who settled for it; either you got to the bottom of something or you'd accomplished nothing.

On the sidewalk, heading for the taxi line through humid air that seemed as tired as the end of summer, Zander turned to Paul and Pru and, through his lingering grogginess, thanked them for all they'd done.

Paul Artisan said, "Don't thank us yet. We're going to stay with you awhile."

That didn't seem to register right away with Zander. He paused, then said, "Look, that's very nice, but you really don't need—"

"Zander, listen," the detective said. "I don't want to make this any harder for you than it has to be, okay? But your brother wasn't robbed. That story makes no sense. He was murdered. Like you were almost murdered yesterday. Someone wants both heirs gone, Zander. And whoever it is, it seems like he's in a hurry."

The surviving twin's forehead clamped down, veins stood out on his neck like he was lifting boulders. And in fact he was wrestling with a heavy burden of exhaustion and grief that held him back from seeing things clearly. Fumbling after words, he said, "But the person who wanted to kill me . . . You told me it was Cliff."

Artisan said, "It seemed to be Cliff. I thought it was Cliff. I was wrong. I'm sorry."

Zander looked away as his eyes were filling up. He whispered, "Don't be sorry. I'm glad you were wrong. I'm really glad."

Pru said, "Your father's money, Zander. Where would it go next?"

36

"**N**ice place," said the cabbie, with classic New York understatement, as he pulled up to the gate of the waterfront mansion in Locust Valley. "How do I get in?"

"Just punch in the code," said Zander Widmore. "8-1-5-1-6."

The gate slid open, and the taxi crunched over the white gravel of the long driveway.

Pru said, "Funny, isn't it, the way there's certain numbers you remember your whole life."

"That's an easy one," said Zander. "My and Cliff's birthdays. Strange, huh? I was born just before midnight, he was born just after. Our birthday parties used to last two days . . . But shit, I get nostalgic, I'm going to dissolve."

It was just after 7 a.m. The red clouds in the east had faded and congealed into a uniform gray haze. There was no refreshment in the morning air; leaves hung downward on the trees, limp as sleeping bats.

The big front door was opened before the visitors had even climbed the steps. A maid appeared in a black dress with a white apron, a maid whom Artisan had seen before. But in Zander's presence she suddenly became a person, she had a name and thoughts and feelings.

She said, "Alexander! Thank God you've come home."

He said, "How are you, Mary? How's my father?"

"We're all in shock," she said. "Entirely in shock. Your father had an awful night. He paced. He mumbled. Honestly, he didn't always make the best of sense. A few hours ago he finally went to bed."

Inside the grand foyer, introductions were made. Mary and Artisan renewed acquaintance. Almost as an afterthought, Zander said, "And Vivian? How's Vivian?"

The maid's face tightened by a barely perceptible increment. She took a moment to choose her words, then said, "Steady. Mrs. Widmore has been quite steady, I would say."

Zander said, "Ah. Composed. Appropriate. As ever."

Mary said, "Well, it isn't quite the same for her, is it? Not flesh and blood, I mean."

"But Mary, it isn't flesh and blood for you either."

Her eyes had filled; she turned them away. "No, but it feels like it is. People are different, aren't they? What they feel. What they show . . . Mrs. Widmore is having coffee in the sunroom. Shall I tell her you're here?"

Before he could answer, Paul Artisan cut in. "Maybe it would be better to surprise her."

Mary made bold to say, "Perhaps there've been enough surprises."

But the detective had captured Zander's gaze, and the sole remaining Widmore son agreed. He led Paul and Pru through the enormous silent house, through the gallery of Scottish forebears, past fireplaces, sitting rooms, bay windows that faced out on splendid lawns. At length, they reached the end of a carpeted hallway and saw Vivian Widmore sipping coffee, gazing out at the placid waters of the Sound.

Her back was to them; they paused a moment to study her. For Pru this was particularly odd and almost dizzying: The handsome woman she knew only as a furtive adulteress who slipped in and out of hotel lobbies wearing big sunglasses and a kerchief on her magnificent head of hair was now transformed into the lady of the manor, legitimate, domestic, regal. She was dressed in black slacks and a loose black blouse, the elegance of which somehow worked against the semblance of mourning. Her posture was serene and her hand was firm as she raised her cup to her softly pursed lips.

"Hello, Vivian," said Zander.

Paul and Pru gazed at her intently as she turned in answer to the voice. But if they'd hoped to see some classic sign of guilt in her reaction, they were disappointed. She didn't spill her coffee, or blanch white as though she'd seen a dead man walking, or even rattle her cup against its saucer. She registered a level of surprise that was fitting, neither more nor less, and when she rose from her chair she seemed burdened by no emotion more visceral than the desire to be a proper hostess.

With no great urgency she moved toward the stepson whose twin brother had just been killed, and gave him a fleeting hug and a cool kiss on the cheek. "It's good that you've come," she said. "The funeral's tomorrow morning."

She said hello to Artisan. To Pru, she said, "I'm sorry. Have we met?"

"Not exactly. Pru Cunningham. I'm a colleague of Paul's."

The two women shook hands, and then, the niceties exhausted, Vivian Widmore finally, belatedly, seemed a little flustered. But why? Because Zander had come home? Because he'd come home with two detectives? Because the heir who stood between her and a very large fortune had come from half a world away and shown up in her sunroom, very much alive?

"Well," she said, with a quick laugh that didn't quite connect with anything. "We have a lot to talk about. May I offer you some coffee? Breakfast?"

There was much to talk about, yes; but the conversation, freighted with suspicion and ambivalence and the recurring realization that Cliff was really dead, did not come easily at all.

There seemed to be evasions on all sides. Of his sojourn in Australia, Zander would say nothing more than that he'd been pursuing a business opportunity. He didn't mention Cuba. He didn't mention the Helios Foundation. Whatever mission he was on, he didn't feel the need to share it with his stepmom.

Vivian was no more forthcoming. Seeming intent on keeping the conversation away from herself, away from the emotions she knew she should be feeling, she talked in conventional wifely terms about her concerns for her husband. He was taking this hard. It had aged him in a day. She was worried about his heart. The arrhythmias had been more frequent lately. Even before this happened, he'd been scheduled for another EKG. Bypass surgery seemed likely. This extra stress was frightening.

Pru said, "A tragedy like this—it must be tough on you as well."

"Of course, of course," said Vivian, and glanced out at the Sound.

Paul Artisan, meanwhile, itched to ask the hard, crass questions that could hardly be uttered in such genteel surroundings. What was the deal between Arthur Widmore and his third, much younger wife? Was there a prenup? Did she get the house if he died? Would she have enough money to maintain the society trappings, to host the benefits and stay on the charity boards? Would there be enough to hold the interest of her lover? Or would it all come down to Zander?

Through the miasma of things that couldn't be spoken, the surviving twin said softly to his stepmother, "You never really liked Cliff, did you?"

The tone was matter-of-fact, not accusing, just the sort of air-clearing that death invites; but still, the naked honesty of the question seemed to rattle Vivian. She gave her beautiful hair a shake and searched for tactful words.

Before she found them, Arthur Widmore came slowly padding into the room.

He was wearing slippers with the backs crushed down, and silk pajamas with a tartan bathrobe over them. His silver hair had not been brushed; it stood in tufts and clumps along his yellowish skull. He moved with the small and shuffling steps of a person no longer certain of his bones, and when he saw his son he hesitated and sucked in breath, as if doubting his eyes and fearing for his battered sanity.

Zander did not remember rising from his chair but suddenly he was on his feet and sweeping toward his father.

The old man said, "Alexander!" And in the next heartbeat he had thrown his arms around his son. He squeezed his shoulders, stroked his back, lay his face against his firstborn's chest and started to weep. The weeping started quietly, a soft purring *hiss* like the prelude to a tidal wave; then the surge flooded in, a lifetime's worth of restraint was swept away, and the urbane and dignified Arthur Widmore trembled like a child and mewled like an infant and gave himself over completely to the twin emotions of grief and love.

His knees grew weak and Zander held him up. Suddenly the parent, the comfort-giver, he purred to his father, "It's okay, Dad. I'm home. I'm home now. It's okay."

Through a gap in his weeping, the old man said, "You were so right, Alexander. I needed to tell you you were right."

"*Shh.* Right, wrong, doesn't matter."

Still clinging to his arms, his father said, "It does matter. This money, this fortune—it's a curse. It's brought nothing but misery. Your mother's death. Shannon. My own wasted life. Now this. Cliff gone—for what? Some fancy watches? Some silver? So stupid! Such a waste! . . ."

Zander felt his father's legs going still more slack; his irises were open all the way, giving his eyes the glowing, depthless look of black sapphires. "You all right, Dad?"

"Fine. Fine. Maybe just a little dizzy."

"Let's sit you down, okay?"

He helped the old man into a chair, then rearranged his rag-doll legs for him and straightened out the tormented lapels of his robe. Arthur Widmore found a handkerchief, wiped his eyes, and blew his nose. Only then did he seem to notice there were other people in the room.

He blinked through stubborn tears at Pru and somehow found his stately manners. "Please excuse me," he said. "I'm Arthur Widmore. I'm not usually such a spectacle."

"Pru Cunningham," she said. "And I thought it was a beautiful spectacle."

In answer to the compliment he blew his nose. Then he recognized Paul Artisan.

A thin smile crossed his lips, and with all the heartiness he could muster, he said to the detective, "Well done, sir! You found Alexander. You brought him home. Not that I doubted you would. Not for a moment. Clifford assured me you were just the right man for the job."

37

After a while, father and son went off to talk alone. The room felt hollow and false when they had left.

Vivian Widmore said, "The two of you have made my husband very happy. We really can't thank you enough."

Paul Artisan understood that the expression of gratitude was in fact a hint that they should leave. But he had the nagging feeling that he hadn't gotten what he had come for. He felt no certainty; he didn't trust his read on Zander's stepmother; he wasn't happy leaving Zander unprotected. He shared a glance with Pru. Her eyes confirmed that maybe it was time to push. He said, "Mrs. Widmore—"

She cocked her head and something creepily and automatically flirtatious came into her voice. "When you visited before, you used to call me Vivian."

"Okay. Vivian. The funeral. We'd like to be there. When and where is it, please?"

"Ten a.m. Peaceful Glen in Manhasset. There's a family plot. It's nice that you want to pay your respects to Cliff."

"It's not about Cliff," said Artisan. "It's about Zander. Someone's out to kill him."

Vivian Widmore's face showed absolutely nothing except perhaps a mild confusion. "I don't think I understand you."

Pru said, "Down in Australia, Mrs. Widmore, an attempt was made on his life. A serious attempt by hired professionals. And Cliff's death—we don't believe that simple robbery was the motive."

The stepmother swallowed. She uncrossed and recrossed her ankles, then straightened the crease in her elegant slacks.

Artisan leaned forward with his elbows on his knees. "We think someone wants your husband's heirs to die before he does. What do you think, Vivian?"

He was hoping for a major flinch, a wince, a grimace. He didn't get one. Vivian just blinked off toward the Sound then stared down at the carpet. Her voice was steady when at last she said, "I just can't imagine that. I think you're very wrong."

The two detectives shared a glance, then got up from their chairs.

Paul Artisan said, "I hope we are. I really do."

Pru said, "We'll see you at the funeral."

Mary called a taxi for them.

On the ride into the City, Artisan said, "So what do you think?"

Pru said, "I think she's a hell of an actress. I think she's the kind of woman who totally gives me the creeps. And I have a tough time believing she's wrapped up in this."

Artisan said, "Why not?" With a hint of needling, he added, "Women make bad killers?"

"Women make perfectly good killers, thank you very much. But killers need to be desperate. I just don't think she's desperate enough."

"Maybe not desperate for the dough. But there are different kinds of desperation, right? Vivian's desperate for men's attention."

"I noticed," said Pru. "But that makes women fools and victims, not criminals."

Paul Artisan pondered that a moment. Then he said, "There's something that we're overlooking. Those pictures you took of her and Mr. Thursday. Cliff had her by the short hairs. He goes to his father, maybe the old man divorces her. Bye-bye inheritance, bye-bye charity galas."

Pru said, "We don't know that Cliff ever used those pictures."

"And we don't know that he didn't. But they certainly would have upped the desperation quotient."

There was a pause. Pru nibbled thoughtfully on an index finger. Artisan let his head roll back against the taxi seat.

Then he went on. "You know what? I'm completely toasted, and I don't know if I'm making any sense at all. But we both knew Cliff. If he had an edge, he'd use it. I just think the blackmail thing has to figure in somehow."

He punctuated the thought with an ecstatic yawn.

It was late morning now. Traffic was light and the ride into town was almost pleasant, the skyline seeming to swivel with each bend in the road. As they neared the Midtown Tunnel, Artisan said, "My place or yours?"

"Me for mine, you for yours," she said.

He put on a rather theatrical pout.

She said, "I'm going to do laundry and sleep until I can't stand it anymore. I suggest you do the same."

The taxi pulled up to her brownstone near Gramercy Park.

He said, "Look, this laundry thing, this sleeping separately— I'm sure it's the grown-up thing to do and all. But just one question before you go. Have you lost your interest in making love with me?"

She kissed him on the cheek. "Actually," she said, "I'm dying to make love with you. But there'll be time for that, okay?"

"Promise?"

"Promise."

"I'll pick you up at eight thirty tomorrow."

"Make it eight fifteen," she said. "It's bad luck to be late for a funeral."

38

The next morning was sticky and still. The sky was white and sodden. It was to be a day of itches and fevers and yearning for the far-off release of an evening thunderstorm.

Pru was waiting on the sidewalk when Paul Artisan pulled up in his ancient Volvo. She was wearing a black skirt and a linen jacket that was loose enough to accommodate a shoulder holster. Getting into the car, she kissed him and asked how he had slept.

"Like the dead."

She could not hold in a little shudder. "Don't say that. Please. I slept twelve hours and woke up really nervous. That never happens. You worried, Paul?"

Heading toward the Tunnel, he turned to her and bit his lip. "Yeah. Very." He paused, then added, "I don't do this kind of work."

They were quiet for a long time. Then, as the oil tanks and billboards of Queens were slipping past, Pru said, "What we were talking about yesterday? The blackmail angle? I've been thinking about it."

"So have I."

"I think there's just one thing that Cliff would have wanted from Vivian."

"We agree on that," said Artisan.

"And it's something she couldn't possibly manage on her own."

"We agree again."

"It makes me very curious to know who Mr. Thursday really is."

To that, Paul Artisan only nodded. He was having trouble speaking, as if he had no breath, no life, to spare. His chest was tight. His jaw was set. His diaphragm had locked down into a shallow arch between his lungs and belly. If this was fear, it was also readiness, a primal narrowing of focus on the cusp of crisis. His gun was resting against his ribs.

As they do in life, even in death the rich control the choicest real estate.

Peaceful Glen was a beautiful small cemetery perched on a knoll above the Sound. Framed by stately iron fences, it boasted magnificent cypresses shaped like candle flames but dark as the grave itself. Narrow roadways wound like country lanes past perfect lawns and pompous mausoleums like something out of Rome; family plots that held the bones and hair of generations of the North Shore gentry were discreetly marked by borders of privet and ivy.

Placards placed along the road guided guests to the Widmore interment.

Paul and Pru were among the earlier arrivals. He parked the dinged-up Volvo in a line of Benzes and Jaguars, limousines and Town Cars. Then, on reluctant feet—as feet always are in a cemetery—they strolled through springy grass to the grave site.

The Widmore family plot was tasteful and austere. No tombs, no wasted ornament. But it occupied high ground with an uncluttered view, testament enough to the family's prominence and

tenure. A dozen granite headstones were laid out in a firm geometry. Dead husbands took their rest at the side of dead wives.
Dead children were arrayed at the feet of dead parents. On a
slight rise in the ground, the headstone of Bernard Bryce Widmore, the founder of the dynasty, stood at right angles to the others, as if presiding over a family banquet.

Off in a corner, a new grave was ready to receive Cliff Widmore. It was covered with a grass-green rug to spare the visitors
the distressing sight of the dank and seeping earth with its beetles
and its worms.

Pru had taken Artisan's arm, and they milled in respectful
silence among the other guests. A few looked vaguely familiar
from his visits to the Widmore Building. Most he didn't recognize. People from the real-estate business, the construction industry, probably; people from the country club; people who had to
show their faces.

At length the hearse pulled up. Like a black goose with a troop
of goslings, it trailed a snaking line of Cadillacs and Lincolns driven
by liveried chauffeurs who dutifully transported the grieving family, the minister, the closest mourners. The vehicles parked; people
emerged. There was a brief delay as the hearse was opened, the
mahogany casket slid into position on its rollers. Then Cliff Widmore's remains were shouldered by the pallbearers.

One of them was Zander. He was wearing an appropriate dark
suit, and Paul Artisan realized that it must be Cliff's. Strange to be
wearing a dead man's suit to his own funeral, carrying his body
while shod in his shoes. Bareheaded now, the surviving brother
revealed extremely short brown hair, hardly longer than a crew cut,
which made him look younger than his years. People who'd known
Cliff stared at his twin as though they were looking at a ghost, an
illusion of mist and shadow that had somehow put on flesh.

Behind the coffin walked the minister, dressed in a robe of purple and white.

And behind him labored Arthur Widmore, supported by his wife. The old man's skin was white and papery, his lips and eyelids a liverish color; there was a gap between the collar of his shirt and his shrunken stringy neck. Vivian Widmore wore a simple black dress and a small hat with a veil that seemed unnecessary, a second mask for her already unrevealing face.

At the grave, the green rug was swept away, the casket placed onto the thick straps that would lower it down into oblivion. The mourners formed an open horseshoe as the minister began to speak. Paul and Pru squeezed each other's hands, then parted. Pru slipped toward the perimeter of the group, where she could look in all directions. Paul sidled as close as he could get to Zander Widmore.

The minister greeted family and friends, said a brief opening prayer, then moved on to his homily, a lesson he had drawn from Cliff's brief life and early passing. His topic was destiny.

Every mortal being, he said, had a unique and worthwhile destiny—worthwhile because it was ordained by God. We might imagine that our destiny was in our hands, but it was not. We might flatter ourselves that we were moving with strength and conviction in the direction of our destiny, but that was not for us to know. Were we striding toward our fate, or simply marking our allotted time as our fate was hurtling toward us? In God's all-seeing view, those two dynamics were the same. Our meeting with destiny was inevitable. Peace lay in accepting that, in putting aside our flawed and limited human judgments, and understanding that even apparently senseless tragedy had meaning and an awful beauty because it came from God.

The religious people nodded their approval. The doubters

went on doubting. And a late-arriving Town Car, charcoal gray with tinted windows, pulled slowly up along the crowded lane.

Pru turned discreetly away from the grave site to track its lumbering progress.

There was nothing to mark this dark car as a threat; it looked like so many of the others, a car for dignified funerals. But now it slowed, then stopped just where it faced the open horseshoe of the guests. The driver's window slid silently open. Pru saw a profile that she thought she'd seen before. A hand came up and she shattered the decorum of the moment with a wrenching shout to Paul.

Artisan could not be sure which he heard first, the yelling of his name or the crack and whine of the exploding gun. Knifing through the line of mourners, he launched himself against Zander Widmore, catching him just above the waist in a jarring, flying tackle. The surviving twin tumbled to the ground, his hands dangling over the abyss of his brother's waiting grave, his face close enough to his brother's coffin to smell its recent varnish, the dead man's suit he was wearing now stained with fresh-turned earth and bits of broken grass.

Paul Artisan, weirdly detached from his body, lay beside the person he'd just saved and realized with appalling calm that he'd been shot. As if it had happened long ago and not just a heartbeat before, he remembered a pinch and slam in his left shoulder, the sudden thick and salty feel of trickling blood.

Pru had dropped to the ground, and braced, and started shooting.

Her first bullet took out the windshield, and as the Town Car screeched and tried to pull away, she blew a hole in a front tire. The car lurched crazily and left the narrow pavement, skidding on damp grass, dodging headstones, spitting wild bullets as it rocked and fishtailed. As it careened past her, she had a clear shot through the driver's window and she thought she grazed the shooter's neck. The car zagged and lunged and ran into a cypress tree.

Artisan was on his feet by now, his 9 mm freed from its blood-stained holster. Using gravestones for cover, he traversed toward the immobile car, its engine still impotently roaring. His gun trained on the driver's seat, he shouted for the occupant to throw away his weapon and come out with his hands held high.

The shooter didn't budge.

Pru slunk off to a better vantage and shot out his back windshield.

Someone in the funeral party had thought to call the cops. Distant sirens could be heard through the stagnant air, which smelled now of gunpowder and burnt rubber.

Finally, without fanfare, a gun was tossed from the window of the ruined Town Car. The battered door fell open, and Vivian Widmore's Thursday lover came out. If he'd ever been grade-A gigolo material, he wasn't anymore. He was bleeding from a deep gash in his forehead where it had collided with the steering wheel. He was bleeding from his neck, where Pru had just missed severing his jugular. His lips were trembling; his eyes held the last glimmer of a defiance which had lost its menace and now seemed only foolish; his posture was lumpy and defeated.

Zander Widmore had come forward to confront the man who'd tried to kill him. In a tone between rage and complete bewilderment, he said, "Who the hell are you?"

It was unlucky to come late to a funeral, and the would-be killer didn't have time to answer. A shot rang out. A purple splotch burst forth where the dead man's heart had been, and he collapsed backward, slumped against the floorboard of his car.

Vivian Widmore dropped a small gun onto the cemetery turf.

"My first husband," she said. "Thank God I'm finally done with him."

39

A week later, Argos the blind and diabetic chocolate Lab was blundering happily through the tangled undergrowth of Riverside Park.

Behind him, trying to trace the secret logic of the dog's scent-driven path, wandered Manny Weissman, and Paul Artisan, whose arm was in a sling, and Pru Cunningham, who was already becoming a steady presence in the ritual of the evening stroll. August had become September. The flip of the calendar had carried with it northwest breezes, and there was a hint of autumn in the air, a hint both refreshing and melancholy.

Manny Weissman said to Paul, "So, you got to visit with your murderess friend?"

"I did," said the detective. "The guards at the Nassau County jail are pretty sympathetic. Half of them probably have crushes on her. And I actually think Vivian was glad to see me, glad to talk things through, clear the air. But I didn't get what I had gone for."

"Which was—?" said Manny.

"I really hoped it might be possible to keep Zander and old man Widmore from knowing that it was Cliff who wanted Zander killed. It makes no difference now, and it would have been a mercy to spare them that."

Pru said, "I remember how relieved Zander seemed during that little time we thought it wasn't Cliff at all. And with old Mr. Widmore just recovering from his surgery . . ."

"The problem is," said Artisan, "that's her whole defense: that she was being blackmailed. Double-blackmailed, really."

The dog, for reasons of its own, took a wide detour around a certain shrub. Its human companions followed along.

Manny said, "Double?"

Paul said, "Cliff was threatening to expose her affair. And Mr. Thursday—who was really her first husband, Monty Alban, but who now went by the name of Sexton—"

Pru waved her hands in Paul's face. "Wait a second. This is getting a little too complicated for me."

"Okay, okay," said Artisan. "I'll back up a step. Vivian's first husband was a crooked cement contractor with ties to the Mob. Not a made guy, but connected. Sometime back in the nineties, he screwed the wrong people on a certain deal, and he was slated to be whacked. He disappeared one day, and the assumption—even Vivian's assumption—was that he was dead. You with me so far?"

Pru and Manny nodded. Argos scratched with more enthusiasm than strength at a patch of dirt that fascinated him.

"Except he wasn't dead," Paul Artisan went on. "He managed to slip out of the country, managed to take most of his money with him. So he hides out in Costa Rica, spends a couple mil on nice hotels and plastic surgery and phony documents, and after a while he's a different person. Sexton. Seven years pass, and Alban is declared legally dead. Meanwhile, three things happen. Sexton goes broke. His supposed widow gets married to a really rich old man. And the people who want to whack him are no longer in a position to do so, as they've been whacked themselves. So Sexton comes back to New York and gets in touch with Vivian."

Manny Weissman scratched his neck. "But Vivian has a wonderful new life, a husband who dotes on her. Why does she see him?"

With some vehemence, Pru said, "Of *course* she'd see him."

Her certainty caught Paul Artisan short. As he'd gotten closer to Pru and come to care more about her, her woman's take on things both impressed and unsettled him. Women saw and felt things differently; that's just how it was. This was both intoxicating and terrifying.

"After all those years?" she went on. "The curiosity? The memories? She'd *have* to see him. Very likely she was still in love with him."

Artisan said, "She was. Even though he was a really lousy guy."

"What's that got to do with it?" said Pru. "Women choose lousy guys over good guys all the time. You see it every day. Maybe it's that crazy, futile rescuer thing. Maybe it's self-destructive, maybe there's some weird masochistic thing that makes it sexy. But look, if there wasn't something really powerful between the two of them, why would she have shot him?"

"I asked her that," said Artisan. "She said she shot him because she finally realized, way too late, that things had gotten totally out of control. She was trying desperately to hold onto her lover—she was blind to everything else. The idea of killing had never seemed quite real to her. Suddenly, with bullets flying, she understood. And she understood her own part in it, her own responsibility. She killed the lover just to make the horror stop."

There was a pause. With some difficulty, Manny Weissman bent down to grab a stick; he gave the dog a whiff of it, then tossed it a few feet away. Then he said, "Excuse me if I'm being dense, but I still don't see what the second blackmail is."

"Call it emotional blackmail," said Paul Artisan. "Look, Vivian was mad for Sexton, but Sexton was in it for the money. Apparently he made no bones about it. If Vivian stopped slipping him funds, he'd leave her. So she was totally stuck. If she didn't play ball with Cliff, he'd blow the whistle and the old man would divorce her. If the old man cut her off, the first husband would dump her. She'd be close to sixty, suddenly alone, and poor."

Manny said, "But if the boyfriend had a new face and a new name, how did Cliff know who he was or that he was someone who could do the killing for him? And why was he willing to do the murders?"

"First question first," said Artisan. "Cliff *didn't* know who the boyfriend was. Not at first. Cliff being Cliff, he just wanted to have some power over the stepmother. But when he confronted Vivian with the pictures, she told him about Alban/Sexton."

Manny said, "Why would she do that?"

Artisan gave a short dark laugh. "You know," he said, "in spite of everything, I like Vivian."

"Because she flirts with you," Pru put in.

The detective let that pass. "She's a passionate person, a slave to her emotions. I guess she thought she could appeal to *Cliff*'s emotions. Fat chance, right? Like he would understand that getting back in the sack with her own first husband, her first great love, didn't really count as an affair. Anyway, it backfired. The plot thickened with Zander, and Cliff realized he had just the guy to do the dirty work, a guy with all the right connections."

Pru said, "But Sexton, being in it for the money, had an agenda of his own."

"Exactly," said Artisan. "Sexton wouldn't have agreed to do a murder just to keep his gigolo's stipend. He realized that if *both* twins died, then Vivian would inherit the whole enchilada and he could marry into a major fortune. So his plan was to whack Zander first, then kill Cliff at his leisure. The wild card was old man

Widmore's heart condition, which kept on getting worse. He could drop dead any day, and if he died first, everything was ruined. So Sexton went into hurry-up mode and staged a phony burglary to make sure Cliff predeceased his father."

They had almost reached the river now. In the softening light, the tops of its small ripples turned pink and the shallow troughs were inky black.

Manny said, "But what was Zander up to in the first place? What was he doing that was such a threat to Cliff?"

Paul Artisan relished the question, and he didn't answer right away. He said, "Well, that's what the whole thing turns on, isn't it? That's what I've been trying to get at from day one."

"So what is it?" insisted Pru.

"Anybody want to guess?"

"Come on!" she said. "Don't be a bloody tit about it!"

But Artisan was having way too good a time. He'd had a long talk with Zander just the day before. The talk took place in a hospital waiting room, just outside the OR where Arthur Widmore was undergoing double-bypass surgery. There were nervous hours to fill. The proximity of death made human secrets seem trivial and pointless. Zander had finally opened up and explained his strange journey from Peconiquot to Cuba to Southern California to Australia.

Artisan said, "I'll give you a hint. What he was up to was probably the most unthinkable, outré, unimaginable thing a person from that kind of background could possibly do."

Manny Weissman pursed his lips in contemplation. Pru looked ready to slug him.

Finally he said, "He was planning to give away the family fortune."

A moment passed while that sank in.

Incredulously, Pru said, "*All* of it?"

"As much of it as he could possibly get his hands on," said Paul Artisan. "The big argument he had with his father? The one right after Shannon's death and right before he took off? That's what it was about."

Pru said, "And Shannon's death—"

"Was almost certainly a suicide," said Paul. "At least that's what Zander thinks. He says they spent a lot of time together in her final months—just as friends. It drove him nuts that Cliff couldn't see how desperately unhappy she was. He was too busy with business, deals, money. When she killed herself, that was the last straw for him."

The old dog, unseeing but undaunted, sniffed his way along the riverfront, the humans who adored him following behind.

Manny Weissman said, "So the big fight with his father—"

"It happened over dinner," Artisan explained. "In the same small dining room we ate in when I first visited the Widmores. Zander said it was totally clear to him that this fucking fortune had never done anything but breed misery and tragedy, and he was laying plans to give his part of it away as soon as possible. The father was shocked and horrified, of course. He took the position that there was a moral obligation to maintain the fortune, that it was a duty owed to the forebears who had worked and scraped to put it together."

"Which is actually a pretty interesting argument," said Manny Weissman.

"Maybe," said Artisan. "But it didn't wash with Zander. He brought it down to specifics. It got pretty personal and heated. He talked about the death of his own mother. Why had it happened? Because she was driving home drunk from the country club. And she was driving home drunk because her husband was behaving shamefully. And he was behaving shamefully because he hated the life that he'd been bullied into living by his own father, by the need to shepherd this goddamn fortune. Everyone was trapped; unhappiness was piled on unhappiness. He, Zander, had had enough of it. He was breaking the cycle. His mind was made up."

Pru said, "And Cliff and Vivian were in on this . . . discussion?"

"They were there," said Paul. "They listened. And Cliff apparently realized that if Zander followed through on his plan, he was screwed."

"Because of the primogeniture thing?" said the old professor.

Paul Artisan shook his head. "Sorry, Manny. You were wrong on that one. One of the few times, I admit. Arthur Widmore is eccentric and archaic, but crazy or unfair he's not. His plan had always been to divide things equally between his sons, with an adequate but relatively modest share for Vivian. But even if Zander took away just his half, Cliff was basically ruined."

"I'm not sure I follow that," said Pru.

"For Cliff," said Paul, "it was never about the money. Or not exactly. He was always going to be a mega-millionaire, whatever Zander did. But Zander had the power—how can I put this?—to undo the myth that Cliff had built up for himself. The CEO. The chairman-to-be. The torch-bearer. He'd sacrificed everything—even his wife—to that myth. He couldn't bear to have it taken away."

Manny said, "But why would—?"

"The Widmore Corporation has other shareholders," Artisan explained. If Zander sold his interest, the family would no longer have a majority stake. Cliff would serve at the pleasure of the board, and it turns out the board was extremely divided. Cliff had only one real ally—a guy named Mittelwerk, from a company called the Hanso Group. The other board members thought Mittelwerk was dangerous—ambitious and brilliantly two-faced, a man acting out an agenda all his own. They would have voted in new management . . . and Cliff, after all his striving and manipulation, would have ended up as one more rich guy with time on his hands and nothing to do."

Pru ran her hand along the river railing. "The sad part," she said, "is that, if Zander freed himself from the curse of the family fortune, he might have freed Cliff as well."

Manny said, "And maybe the prospect of that freedom is exactly what Cliff couldn't tolerate. He'd have to find a whole new way of being in the world."

The sun was nearing the tops of the Palisades. The windows of Riverside Drive were turning into orange mirrors.

Paul Artisan said, "Well, anyway, Zander started working on his plans to get rid of the money, and Cliff and Sexton started working on their plans to get rid of Zander."

Manny said, "The guy on Peconiquot, the guy with the funny name—how did he figure in?"

"Moth," said Artisan. "Zander gave him a power of attorney so he could start liquidating assets for him while he was traveling. Unfortunately, he used family lawyers to draw up the document, and Cliff found out about it. He sicked Sexton onto Moth, to kill him before he could start funneling the money to Cuba."

Pru said, "And the mystery man in Havana?"

"Turns out," said Artisan, "he's the head of Cuba's biggest medical foundation."

Sounding almost disappointed, Manny Weissman said, "Not a gun-runner? Not a counterrevolutionary?"

"Completely legit," the detective said. "He wouldn't talk to me because he had plenty of reasons to be cautious with *yanquis* asking questions. But you see, Cuba has health coverage for everyone, but no money to buy medicines. So half of Zander's money, eighty million bucks or so, was going to go into a big endowment for that.

The mystery man—Chavez is his name—was going to run it. It was one of Zander's two pet projects."

Pru said, "But the fellow who brought you to Havana—?"

"Crunch," said Artisan. "I'm guessing here, okay? But I think Sexton had me tailed in Key West, hoping that I'd lead him to Zander. When I didn't, maybe it seemed neater just to get rid of me. I think some idiot hit man imagined I was still on Crunch's boat."

Argos turned up from the river, back into the park. Blind though he was, he seemed to know that it was almost sunset, and that once the sun was down he would go home and be given not one but two dog biscuits.

Manny Weissman said, "And Zander's *other* pet project?"

"That was the Australia thing," said Artisan. "He was planning to buy some islands on the Barrier Reef, and to establish pearl farms that indigenous people would run. He'd build houses and cisterns, and fund the project until it started paying for itself, and then it would be a little self-sustaining paradise."

Pru said, "Hold on. If half the money went to Cuba and half went to Australia, what about the nudist camp in California?"

"That was not a charity project," Paul said. "In fact, I think Zander got more from the Helios Foundation than he could possibly give back. The man who runs it—Elio—it turns out I completely underestimated him. I thought he was a bit of a phony if not a downright fraud. But in fact he was Zander's closest confidant and mentor. He understood Zander's . . . torment—I don't think that's too strong a word. He believed that Zander was unhappy because he'd been stuck for so long between wanting to be bad and wanting to be good."

"Ah," said Manny. "Sort of in his own private purgatory."

Paul said, "You could say that. Or stuck in the middle of an uncompleted cycle."

The other man said, "Uh-oh, now you're sounding awfully California."

"I know, I know. But cut me a little slack. I'm trying to explain. Anyway, Elio believed that gaining wealth, gaining the world, was half the cycle; the other half was letting go of it again. As long as Zander kept that fortune, he was like a person bloated with a painfully deep breath that he couldn't let out. Getting rid of the money would be the exhale, the release, that would complete the cycle."

Pru said, "Call me cynical. It sounds like Elio wanted the dough."

"He wouldn't take a nickel," said Paul Artisan. "He wanted his advice to be disinterested. He just wanted Zander to understand that being good would also make him happy."

"Ah," said Manny Weissman, "just like in the *Confessions of Saint Augustine*. You've read that one, haven't you, Paul?"

"Well, uh, no."

"Same story," said his old professor. "Young Augustine is a bad kid. Steals fruit from people's orchards. Gets drunk on pilfered wine. Fights and fornicates at every opportunity. But it's exactly those experiences that set the stage for his redemption. You see? He's got the longest road to travel from bad to good. His journey is the most significant because it's also the most difficult."

"Manny," said Paul, "you're sounding sort of California."

The older man let that slide.

Pru said, "Speaking of confessions, I think you owe me one, Paul."

"Excuse me?"

"All your literary quotes?" she said. "*King Lear? Trent's Last Case?* Those smart-sounding references that made me fall for you? I think you stole them all from Manny."

They were nearly back up to street level now. The ancient Labrador, suddenly impatient, chased himself in circles while his human friends caught up.

Paul Artisan fumbled for words. His old professor let him squirm a moment, then decided to help him out. "He didn't steal them," he said. "He *learned* them. It's called education."

Pru looked unpersuaded but took Paul Artisan's hand. "And Zander," she said. "What will he do now that the fortune's off his back?"

"For now," said Artisan, "he'll stay with his father. At least until the old man's out of danger. Then I think he'll move down to Key West."

"Key West?" said Manny.

"He had a girlfriend down there," Artisan explained. "Wonderful woman. Yoga teacher. Seems they're crazy for each other, but the money got in the way. He thinks they might do better now."

They reached the gateway to the park, the same stone entrance they used every day. The dog paused on the sidewalk, as he'd learned to do a lifetime ago. Paul and Pru and Manny faced off toward the west. The sun slipped down behind the Palisades; the temperature dropped by a degree or two; and Manny Weissman slipped into his cardigan.